Anastasia Kirke is a middle-grade and teen fiction writer.

She lived a significant portion of her life in a distant mountain valley between cloud-wreathed peaks, where she graduated from a school that is not nearly as cool as Hogwarts (though at times it came close).

Her current travels have brought her to an island where the hot is too hot and the cold is too cold and there's nowhere inbetween.

A Literary Omnivore, she is a fan all things bookish and strange. Her favorite things include: cats, tea, classical music of the Romantic Era, and that feeling you get when a story gives you goosebumps.

To find out more about things she's working on, follow her at:

https://anastasiakirke.com/

or at Dying Arts Press at:

https://dyingartspress.com/

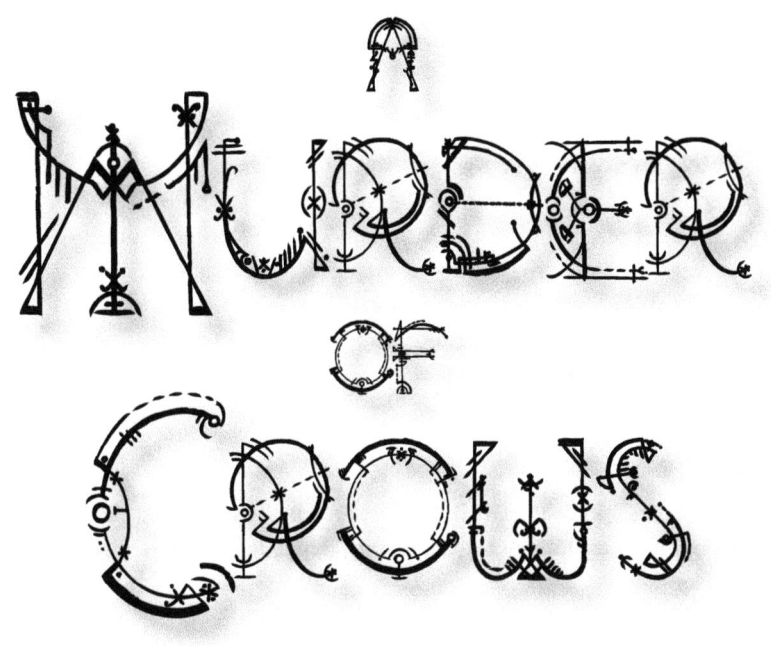

A Murder of Crows

A. Kirke

Copyright © 2018 by A. Kirke

All rights reserved. No part of this book may be reproduced in any form or by any electronic or mechanical means, including information storage and retrieval systems, without permission in writing from the publisher, except by reviewers, who may quote brief passages in a review.

ISBN 978-1-9164536-1-6

The events and characters in this book are fictitious. Any similarity to real persons, living or dead, is coincidental and not intended by the author.

Editing by Keleigh Jade Carter
Cover and internal images by Steffe Warrington
Book design by Keleigh Jade Carter

First Printing August 2018

Published by Dying Arts Press, London

https://dyingartspress.com/

*For Mom,
who read it first.*

A Most Dismal Prospect

The worst part was not being allowed to scream.

If I'd had it my way, everyone from the hunchbacked pallbearers, to the long-faced priest, to the undertaker with his black hat and long coat would have gotten a scream in the face, just so they'd know exactly how I felt about the whole affair. Unfortunately, the proper bearing for funerals is non-negotiable: you are to shed tears (but not *bawl*), be respectful (but not *dour*), and stand up straight and tall throughout the long-winded preaching (all without being too *stiff*). Considering that, screaming is not generally considered appropriate, even when you think it should be.

Even when it's a better option than breaking things.

Even when it's your dad who's died.

The undertaker had brought him into the house the previous evening, all readied for the Resting. So, while Mother and William dressed upstairs, I sneaked down to our black-curtained parlour to spend one last morning with my father.

The first thing I noticed were the Deathmarks. It was the first time I'd actually seen Deathmarks, but they weren't difficult to recognize. Lines and circles covered Dad's face and hands in a dizzying pattern of ash, drawn on his skin by the undertaker to make sure his spirit didn't end up haunting our attic, to protect all of us from stray magic, and to keep Dad intact for the Resting. The sight of them made my skin crawl. The Marks weren't anything like magicians' spells, but they still held power. And more than anything else, the Marks were a certain sign that the mourning drapes, the coffin, the silence left behind in his absence – all of it was real. He was gone. And there was nothing any of us could do about it.

I didn't even notice when William came downstairs – our creaky old steps never made so much as a single complaint for him: my brother was too small and sneaky. I only noticed when he stepped up next to me, lifting himself onto tiptoes to see into the casket. With a sigh, he fell back onto his heels and said:

'It doesn't look right, Abby.'

I gave him a look – *the* look, if you know what I mean. 'Of course it doesn't,' I said. 'He's dead.'

Still, I turned back to Dad, lying there in the middle of our parlour, and I had to admit that William was right: despite the arrangements (and even ignoring the Deathmarks) there was something off about it – something that didn't quite make sense. Dad's hands lay folded across his chest: he looked more like a doll or some sort of waxwork than my father. Even sleeping, Dad was never so still.

Yet, somehow, we'd mistaken it for sleep at first. The morning he died had been traitorously bright and blue and beautiful, and waking late, I wondered why Dad wasn't already up. He was usually up before the rest of us – examining plants in his study, or tending to the overgrown patch of yard out back that he insisted on calling the garden. But the house lay silent: he was nowhere to be found, and so at last, I knocked on his half-open door to find him pale and still and sleeping – or so I thought.

It wasn't until Mother came by with a kiss to wake him that we knew.

The doctor was called, and the coroner, and a pair of pale-faced lawyers came by to talk to Mother about 'necessary considerations' – which I guess is what lawyers call all the paperwork they need to do when someone dies. All the while, I sat with William in our parlour, going over my Defences and helping him with his smoke bombs and watching the bustle of strangers pass through our house. And all the while, I wondered, *how could any of this be real?*

But finally, at the end of the day, after the coroner had satisfied himself with his poking and probing and Mother had talked to a priest about the funeral arrangements (she had needed to sell her favourite pearl earrings to pay for all of it), after the sun had set and the house had darkened, after even William had gone upstairs, I was left in our empty parlour to stare at the dying fire and wonder about a different question, the most obvious question, the one question that no one else seemed bothered about asking:

How did he die?

At least the Resting service gave Dad a chance to answer that question himself. At the Resting, Dad's spirit would rise – 'like light,' Mother had told us – and Dad would be able to talk to us just once more before passing *on*. It was small comfort. After that, Dad would truly be gone – wiped away with the black ash on his forehead.

But it would still be a couple hours before then, and right now, William was fidgeting next to me, rocking onto his toes to look into the coffin once more. And then – before I could think to stop him, he reached in with one hand–

I kicked him in the shin.

'Ow!'

'What do you think you're doing?'

He glared at me sideways. 'I was just removing his glasses!'

'Oh.'

He removed the wire-rimmed spectacles from where they'd been set on our father's nose, and folded them up, tucking them into the pocket of Dad's jacket instead. 'There,' said William. 'Now it doesn't look so strange. He could be sleeping, if—'

'If we didn't already know he was dead,' I finished for him.

There was a knock at the door, and William stepped back from the coffin, hands disappearing into his pockets as Mother appeared at the top of the stair. She was wearing a veil of black lace to hide her face, which, as far as I can tell, is either supposed to make you feel less ashamed of crying your eyes out or make it easier for other people to ignore the fact that you're crying your eyes out – not that Mother had let anyone catch her crying at all. Her red hair was pinned neatly under her hat, and as she caught sight of us at the casket, she tsked – though with the mourning veil, I couldn't tell whether it was at William's untucked shirt or my hair, which, unlike hers, was escaping its pins to stick up in all directions.

She descended the stair to open the door. The undertaker and his pallbearers trooped into the house, exchanging a few short words with Mother. In less than a minute, Dad was closed into his casket, and the pallbearers carried him out of the house to the waiting carriage.

The world outside was withering and grey. We followed the black horses through our tiny town, the November wind tugging at our skirts and trousers and coats and doing nothing to improve my hair. Before too long, we were standing at the gate to the cemetery, engraved Wardmarks looming over us.

Like my father's ashen Deathmarks, the cemetery Wardmarks traced an unreadable pattern of intertwined lines and shapes along the stones of the cemetery wall, meant to keep people from trespassing and disturbing the dead. Their power prickled against my skin even before we entered. Anyone crossing the Graveward without a good reason was certain to be caught – quickly, if they were lucky. If not, a night trapped in a Graveward had been known to drive people mad.

In any case, I'd never stepped foot in this cemetery before, as no one in our family had ever been buried in it – until now. Yet, even with the undertaker driving Dad's coffin under the gate ahead of us, I wasn't taking any chances – I twisted my silver ring in my fingers, Dad's words on the Spiritual Defences echoing in my mind:

The First Defence is always with you, but this ring will help you remember it.

Immediately, warmth coiled through all my limbs, making the rainy air and the cold wind less harsh, as if I were feeling them through another layer of skin. If I did it right, the Defence would make my spirit a little dimmer, a little less obvious, blocking magicians from reading my mind and letting me avoid any unwanted attention from people or spells… or Wards.

Still, I needn't have bothered. As we passed beneath the stone arch of the gate, the eerie prickling of the Graveward washed over me in a wave of goose bumps – like a twinge of magic. But it wasn't magic of course, and within another moment, we were on the other side, the Ward's power fading with a sigh. We weren't trespassing, it had decided.

No, we were burying my father. It was yet another sign that this was all real.

The carriage pulled up next to a freshly dug grave. The priest was already waiting, and Mother ushered us to the other side, pressing bouquets of white flowers into our hands. The pallbearers pulled out the casket, the priest pulled out his Book, and the service began.

'Today,' wheezed the priest in a voice as old and cracked as his Book, 'We mourn the passing of Lewis Crowe. He was a beloved husband and father and his death is truly a loss...'

The flowers grew heavy in my hands. As far as I knew, the priest in front of us had never met Father. How could he possibly know how much we'd lost?

'I am the resurrection and the life, saith the Lord. He that believeth in me, though he were dead, yet shall he live...'

He might as well have been speaking ancient Aegyptian for all I could understand. But I had to get through it for Dad's Resting. That was all that mattered: the last chance I would ever have to speak to him, to say goodbye properly... if only the priest would get his sermon over with.

Finally, he set aside his Book. 'While the body rests in the earth, the spirit rests in heaven,' he said, pulling open the casket lid once more. I clutched the flowers. This was it. 'Let the shackles of this world be unbound.' He poured holy water onto Dad's forehead and hands. The ashen Marks melted away into nothingness. For a moment, the world held its breath.

Nothing.

I waited for something, *anything*, but there was no sign of Dad's spirit rising from his body, no prickle of magic or Marks, no light. Nothing but a choked silence, and the sickening clutch of disappointment in my chest.

I threw down the flowers and walked away.

The priest whispered harshly at the undertaker, and I knew, even without looking, that Mother's eyes were following me as I stalked away, but I didn't care. I didn't stop, didn't look back – not until I'd reached the other side of the graveyard, hidden beyond one of the mausoleums.

Still, I wasn't alone. A man stood at the gate with a cane at his side, wearing a black suit and a frown that seemed severe even by graveyard standards. As I slowed to a stop next to a granite headstone *(Maeve Finche, beloved wife and mother, 1823-1862)*, the man nodded at me and tipped his hat. I could've sworn I'd never seen the man before – he didn't look like any of the people in town, and my parents had never been too keen on visitors or friends, so it was unlikely that he knew them. As much as I tried to place him, he didn't fit anywhere in my memory, yet…

There was something about him – about the way he stood, the way he moved, the fact that he'd tipped his hat at me – that held a threat of recognition.

He slipped into the cemetery, stepping through the boundary of the Graveward without even the smallest flinch of discomfort. He had to lean heavily on his cane as he crossed the cemetery, but he barely looked down: if he'd come to visit someone, he didn't waste time looking for them among the graves. I marked his halting walk across the grounds, and just as he was about to turn the corner of the mausoleum, I made to follow him–

He shot a glare over his shoulder, and our eyes met, his severe frown as clear a warning as any. I froze. He shook his head, once – a small gesture, almost invisible – and the next moment, he'd continued on, to disappear among the stones.

I was left standing with Maeve Finche's femurs somewhere below my feet, wondering if there was any point in trying to find out what was going on with Dad's service.

Before I could convince myself that there was, William wandered over, picking his way carefully around the graves to avoid stepping on the dead. With a huff, I sank down into the grass sprouting above Maeve's skull, and waited for my brother to join me.

'Mum's in a fit,' said William. 'The priest went to fetch an Inquisitor.'

'Well, they have to report the missing spirit, don't they?' I said, trying to keep my voice light. But the truth was that Inquisitors were bad news. The Inquisitorial Order was the humourless group of men and women who made sure that everyone was suitably afraid of magic, which was supposed to prevent us from trying to hire magicians to Curse our enemies, or from studying to become magicians so we could Curse our enemies ourselves. Of course, if any of the Inquisitors' scare tactics actually worked, they'd all have been out of a job, because really, their main purpose was to hunt down magicians and make a big show of burning them alive – or hanging them, though burnings tended to be more popular.

In their endless quest to stamp out magic, the Inquisitors were naturally interested in any spiritual anomalies, which apparently included botched Resting services.

'The priest insisted,' said William. 'I bet they'll pin it on the undertaker and arrest him for magic. I mean, who else could they blame?'

Part of me felt sorry for the undertaker. If the Inquisitors did decide to blame him for a stolen spirit, there'd be very little he could do besides burn for it. But I hadn't gotten to Rest my dad, and there was another part of me that wanted *someone* to burn for that. 'Would serve him right,' I said.

William frowned. 'What if Dad just managed to pass on without their help?' he said.

'He's still gone.'

'So you don't think there's a heaven?' asked William.

'No.'

'No eternal life?'

'He's quite dead.'

'So you think the spirit just... disappears, after everything?'

I gave him another look – his second one this morning. 'I didn't say that.'

He went silent for a minute, the way he does when he's trying to sort out a math problem in his head. And then:

'What's it like to be dead then, I wonder?'

And because that was a question with no easy answer, I said: 'Don't ask stupid questions,' and held out my hand so that he'd help me up from the grass.

We wandered back toward Dad's grave as a light drizzle began to fall, to find Mother talking to an Inquisitor. His silver-trimmed cloak flapped in the breeze.

'They're quick,' said William.

Too quick, I thought. I went to join Mother next to the grave.

'...in any case,' the Inquisitor was saying, 'we would like to ask you some questions to get to the bottom of this regrettable incident. First things first: did your husband have any enemies, Mrs. Crowe?'

'Enemies, Sir Inquisitor?' echoed Mother, her face pinching into a frown. 'Surely you aren't suggesting–'

'Murderers often find it useful to cover their steps with magic,' said the Inquisitor with a shrug.

Mother's voice was chilly as she informed the Inquisitor that, no, Dad didn't have enemies, which was the single truest thing I'd heard today. There was absolutely no reason why *anyone* would've wanted to hurt Dad, much less kill him. He'd always kept to himself, more interested in plants and flowers than making trouble. The very thought of Dad having enemies was absurd, at best. And yet–

And yet, he'd dropped dead one night for no reason. There was no explanation for it that made sense.

A blotch of shadow shifted at the other side of the graveyard, and I looked away from the Inquisitor to find the stranger from the gate standing there, hat pulled low over his face, watching. He leaned against one of the gravestones and lit a pipe while the Inquisitor continued to ask questions:

'Is it possible that he ran afoul of someone in town?'

'Any neighbours who might have had a grudge?'

'Could Lewis have been involved in any sort of magic himself?'

'Sir Inquisitor,' said Mother sharply. 'I don't know what you're hoping to discover. I've already told you what everyone already knows, and if you honestly believe–'

'My apologies, Mrs. Crowe,' said the Inquisitor. He shifted, suddenly uncomfortable. Mother had a way of doing that to people. 'I suppose that this must be a difficult situation for everyone involved, so I want to assure you, once more, that we will do our utmost to uncover the culprit.' He coughed. 'If there's nothing else, I think I'm done here–'

'But you haven't told us when we'll be able to Rest him,' I said before the Inquisitor could make his easy exit. 'You're going to find out who took his spirit, and you're going to get it back, right? That's what you're supposed to do.'

For the first time, the Inquisitor set his eyes on me. I refused to look away, scowling right back at him until he shook his head. 'Unfortunately,' he said, 'in cases like these, it's rare that a spirit is stolen intact. I'm sorry to say that, whether lost by accident or foul play, it's unlikely we will be able to recover Mr. Crowe's spirit.' He gave one last nod to Mother, before walking away into the drizzle.

Mother let him. She wasn't watching the Inquisitor; she was staring at the other side of the graveyard, where the stranger had been smoking while the Inquisitor talked. I looked to see if he'd seen her–

But the stranger was already gone.

We were alone.

By the time we returned home, the drizzle had turned into a proper rain, fat drops of water plopping heavily against the cobbles. Mother hurried us inside and locked the door against the storm.

The house lay cold and empty, its ragged edges showing. Dad's favourite tattered armchair sagged, fraying, next to the dead fireplace, and the warped windows were dull and dark behind the black mourning curtains. While Mother and William removed their coats and shoes, I ran my fingers over the Wardmarks that Dad had carved into the frame of our doorway, meant to keep out harm. He'd put them together himself, without asking the local Warder, and I'd always assumed he knew what he was doing – that the Wards worked.

Apparently not.

William drifted upstairs to his room, and Mother wasn't far behind. I followed suit, and all three of us closed our doors, tired of dealing with the world. We hadn't even gotten a chance to say goodbye, and now Inquisitors were asking if Dad had been involved in magic. I hadn't thought it was possible for the day to get any worse than it already was, but there you have it. I sat watching the darkness rise outside my window. The sun had fully set when there came a knock at the front door.

I rose from my half-sleeping stupor and poked my head into the hallway. William was doing the same at the door next to mine. He raised his eyebrows in a question, which I answered with a shrug before we both crept to the banister of the stair, to see what was happening below. William crept too far down, and I had to pull him back, but he batted my hand away.

Eventually, we settled for crouching side-by-side at the top of the stair, just far enough down that we could see most of the parlour.

Mother was peering through the peephole. A moment later, she pulled open the door for whoever it was that had knocked. The visitor stepped into the house, and I had to choke down a gasp.

It was the dark-haired gentleman who had tipped his hat to me in the cemetery.

'Who's that?' whispered William.

The man removed his hat, and the memory hit me like a wave of *déjà vu*. This was the man who had come to our house that night, six years ago, on William's fifth birthday, not long after my brother had suffered his first fit. The man had stepped into our house in just the same quiet way he did now, but by the end of the night, he and Dad had gotten into a raging row, and the one thing I remembered was Dad yelling at the man to leave our house and never return. The man had. And that, I thought, had been the end of it.

'It's our uncle,' I explained to my brother. 'Edward. Dad's brother.' I leaned further down the steps to peer at the scene below. Mother stood with her arms crossed while Uncle Edward hovered by the doorway, leaning on his cane, his eyes passing over the house as if cataloguing everything.

What was *he* doing here?

'I came as soon as I heard,' said Uncle Edward finally.

'I figured you'd show up sooner or later.'

'Maris, you know that I am fully invested in what happens to all of you. Whatever Lewis' attitude about it may have been, that has always been my stance. Still–'

'I worry, Edward.'

'About the Court?'

Mother's voice was soft. 'About the children. About William. Especially given–'

'I know,' said Uncle Edward. Mother turned away, drifting to the other side of the parlour, and Uncle Edward followed her. I couldn't go much further down the steps, but their voices were clear in the silent house.

'Perhaps you should come to Ravenscourt for a bit – just a few weeks,' said Uncle Edward. 'I can contact people, and we can figure out the next move.'

I looked at William, who frowned back. The man couldn't possibly be serious. Dad had kicked him out of our house with an order never to return. Surely he didn't think...

'Perhaps we should,' said Mother softly.

Silence rose up again. I couldn't fathom what was going through her head.

'Shall we say that you will visit by the end of the month?' said Uncle Edward.

Mother sighed. 'The end of the month it is.'

Uncle Edward made quick steps back toward the door. 'I look forward to seeing you then,' he said, and with a short bow, he replaced his hat and let himself out. 'Farewell, Maris.'

'Farewell,' whispered Mother.

The door clicked closed, and Mother turned the lock and latched the chain. Her eyes moved to the top of the stairs, where she found us staring. If she were surprised, it didn't show.

'I think we'll be going on a little trip soon,' she said, her voice oddly light. 'Won't that be fun?'

RAVENSCOURT MANOR

Time is an odd thing. In the days leading up to a funeral, time can drag so slowly that you doubt it's moving at all, and then, suddenly, there's no time to even breathe. It starts passing so dizzyingly fast – a flying frenzy of packing and planning and repacking and cleaning and yelling at your little brother because he *won't stop touching your stuff*, and more packing, until before you know it, your entire house is stuffed into storage boxes or wrapped under sheets, and all the rooms have been stripped bare. Within a week, our entire tiny house had been clipped, cleared, and cleaned, and we were leaving. Mother piled our scant suitcases on the stoop of the house ('nothing more than you need,' she'd said. 'It's not as if we won't be coming back, after all'), and after cutting off the gas lamps, she locked the door, and that was that.

A buggy brought us to the station. We settled into our compartment, and while Mother paged through her worn copy of *Wuthering Heights* and William amused himself swiping matches from the snack trolley every time it passed, I watched the grey mountains of Caledonia sink outside our windows, turning into the moors and rolling hills of Anglica. Towns raced by in blurs of colour, and clouds grew thick overhead, a storm gathering as we sped towards a place I had never heard of in my life.

'What's it like?' I asked, at last. 'Ravenscourt?'

Mother paused her reading, looking up to meet my eyes. 'It's where your father grew up. It's where we met.'

I blinked at that. Before this moment, I'd never heard either of my parents talk about where they'd met or how they'd grown up – which was strange, even though I hadn't realized that it was strange until now. Mother looked peaceful, almost nostalgic, fingering the metal locket that she was wearing under the collar of her travelling jacket as she thought back. 'It's built in the middle of a forest called the Blackwood,' she continued. 'Some of the trees are older than humanity itself. I remember, we used to walk by the lake in summer...' She sighed. 'And the house is something else altogether. I think you'll like it. Your father certainly did.'

'If he liked it so much,' I said, turning back to the window, 'then why did he leave?'

Mother pursed her lips but said nothing, and our compartment fell back into silence.

By the time the train pulled into the station at Eboracum, the sky was dark with storm clouds, though the storm hadn't broken yet. Mother hurried us through the station, its roof built like the nave of a great glass cathedral, all steel and smoke-stained glass arcing above us. William kept getting distracted – and of course it was up to me to make sure he didn't get tripped over while ducking down to tie his shoe, or get caught swiping sweets from the overcrowded candy stalls, or get lost because he'd stopped to watch one of the street magicians floating balls and fruit and candles in mid-air next to the ticket stalls.

It wasn't *really* magic of course, which was why the man wasn't worried about Inquisitors. The tricks were all thread and distraction and sleight of hand. Magic might be useful for a great many things, most of them fairly evil, but floating apples was not one of them.

The way Dad had always explained it was this: the real world was really two worlds. There was the world of *things* – of apples and oranges and wooden balls and lit candles – and that world was ruled by the laws of physics, which were simple and immutable and easily reasoned out if you knew what to watch for.

But then, there was another world – the world of *ideas*. And *that* was where you had to watch out for magic. The reason magicians were so dangerous wasn't because they could create flame or shoot lightning from their fingers, but because they had studied how to control *minds*. A skilled magician could trap a person in an Illusion of their worst fears or drive them mad with a Curse – but if he wanted to create so much as a spark in the world of things, he would've had to use phosphorus and gunpowder, just like the rest of us.

Maybe it would've been better if magic weren't invisible. If it left bruises or burns, you'd be able to see the danger and avoid it. But thoughts are trickier things, and that's why the Inquisitors insisted that we needed them to protect us.

The 'magician' made a show of turning his floating apple into an explosion of colourful sparks, and the gathered crowd clapped. A trio of passing Inquisitors didn't even spare him a glance.

'Think he'd let me borrow a firework?' asked William before I managed to drag him away.

Uncle Edward's coach (apparently, he was rich enough to have his own coach, coachman included) was waiting for us outside the station. After the coachman had loaded both us and our luggage into the carriage, there was yet another hour of sitting in silence while the world passed us by, dark, bare-fingered trees scraping the carriage windows as the rain broke over us, the horses' hooves and our wheels clattering over the rough roads. William started to shiver, and I gave him my scarf to keep out the chill.

Finally, the rutted roads gave way to a cobbled drive, and in the distance, light flickered from the window of a high tower. The trees grew thicker, and a brass fence loomed out of the half-dark. As we passed under the gate that marked the boundary of the manor grounds, an icy chill ran under my skin, cold enough to make my bones rattle. I looked out to see the gate passing over us, strange shapes twisted into the wrought metal.

A Ward.

I twisted the ring on my finger, focusing my First Defence until my teeth stopped chattering, but the feeling refused to fade. Whatever Ward we had just passed through, it was even stronger than the Graveward at the cemetery, and it didn't quite like the idea of us being there.

Why ever would Uncle Edward need a Ward like that?

Dark things flitted in the murk outside – but when I leaned forward to see what they were, there was nothing: just the rain and the leafless trees passing beyond the window, and my breath leaving a cloud of fog on the glass, until Ravenscourt House came into view.

Blurred through the windows and the rain, the house was a great big jumble of rough walls and dark windows and tiled roofs, the gables and towers all mixed up and twisted together to form a puzzle of black stone. The windows lay empty behind iron bars, without a single glimmer of fire or lamp light, except for the high tower. I wouldn't have been surprised if someone had told me it was abandoned – it wasn't the sort of place that invited people to live in it.

And yet...

And yet, those empty windows gave me the creeping sense that someone – or *something* – was waiting behind them, watching.

The carriage rolled to a stop, and the driver hopped down to open the door, holding out a hand and an umbrella for Mother, both of which she took without hesitation. I leapt down without his help (earning a tsk from Mother) to take a proper look at the great double doors of the house's main entrance. They lay wide open, revealing a dark, empty space that managed to be the complete opposite of welcoming. The rain pounded on the stones around us, and Mother drew me and William next to her, sheltering all of us under the umbrella as she ushered us through those doors and into the darkness beyond.

It took a moment for my eyes to adjust to the gloom. The entrance hall was smaller than I'd expected, though also taller: a square space with a ceiling so high that it lay hidden in darkness, the walls lined with cobwebby statues and dull portraits, and in every corner, some marble face or painted portrait was frowning about something. In front of us, a pair of grand staircases arced upward to the first floor. While Mother shook the rain out of her coat, William tugged on my arm, pointing to the doors behind us, which had begun to move. As I watched, the doors swung shut, gears and levers ticking and grinding, the light and the wind and the rain of the world outside disappearing with one final click –

'Clockwork,' I whispered, but William's fingers continued to clutch my sleeve. I didn't push him away.

'Ah, Maris!' rang a voice from the top of the stairs. I looked up to see Uncle Edward making his way down the stairs, trailed by a lopsided couple in black. The man was tall, with a long, severe face while the woman was short and round and dumpy – servants, I realized with a twinge of something like annoyance. Of course Uncle Edward would have servants. Mother had never had so much as a cleaning lady to help her with the housework, but Uncle Edward had apparently inherited all the things that Dad hadn't: coaches and manors and Warded gates and even the help.

He shuffled down the last few steps into the hall, and took Mother's hand in his own. 'It is so good to see you here,' he said. 'How was your trip?'

'Exhausting,' answered Mother, handing her gloves off to the manservant and dismissing him with a wave. He took them with a bow and turned to busy himself with the luggage while the other servant lingered at the bottom of the steps. 'But overall, quite a pleasant journey, even if long,' continued Mother. 'I just wish this had all been under better circumstances.'

'Of course.' Uncle Edward stepped back, his gaze shifting from Mother to land on me and my brother. There was something intense and searching in the way he looked at us, something quietly discomforting – I'd seen the same look on Dad's face far too often: it was the look of a scientist who'd just discovered some fascinating new specimen.

'William and Abigail, I take it?' he said at last. He held out his hand, waiting for my brother to shake it. 'You have grown a bit since I last saw you, young William.'

My brother simply stared at the offered handshake, before looking back up to our uncle, his hands refusing to let go of my jacket. 'I don't remember ever seeing you,' he said simply.

Mother shot him a glare, but Uncle Edward gave a short laugh and let his hand drop. 'It was quite a while ago,' he said. 'Five or six years, now, I think. You must be thirteen by now?'

'Eleven,' said William shortly.

'And have you been taking all your medicines?'

William looked to Mother for some sign, and she gave a short, exasperated nod. My brother refused to look up as he answered: 'Yes, I have.'

Uncle Edward considered him for a moment, as if he wanted to ask more, but at last, he nodded. 'Good boy,' he said. Though he didn't go so far as to pat my brother on the head, he might as well have. He turned his focus to me. 'And you, Abigail, my dear? How are we?'

His attention made me suddenly, keenly aware of the cold water still seeping from my coat, of the wind howling outside the closed door and the rain pounding against the stone walls. I was already twisting my ring without realizing it, and my heart was pounding, though I didn't know why. I didn't trust myself to answer. Instead, I took several deep breaths, coiling them into the bottom of my lungs: the Second Defence.

The Second Defence is self-control, and you must master your breath to maintain it.

Slowly, the panic faded, like the tide going out, and I looked up to meet my uncle's eyes. 'I am quite well, sir, thank you,' I answered evenly.

He tilted his head, and I refused to let my gaze drop, breathing in my defences to keep me steady. Finally, he shook his head and laughed, turning back to Mother and talking to her again – as if we'd never existed.

'I do think it has been far too long since you have visited, Maris. Perhaps a tour is in order?'

'Of course,' said Mother, though her hand moved to clasp my shoulder.

Uncle Edward didn't miss it. 'No need to worry about a thing,' he said, gesturing to the servants still hovering close by. 'My Housekeeper, Mrs. Thompson, will settle them into their rooms. And Galen will take care of the luggage, of course.'

Mother's eyes flicked to William. 'You're certain that–'

'They can come to no harm within these walls. That much I can assure you.'

At last she seemed convinced. When Uncle Edward offered his hand, she took it, following him into the shadows of the house. I almost called out for her to stay – but she was already gone, and William and I were left staring at the sour-faced Housekeeper.

The Housekeeper seemed just as pleased as we were. She was pale and bulging, with heavily-lidded eyes, a wide mouth, and very little neck, which rather made her look like the unfortunate result of a misguided prince kissing a toad and turning it into a Housekeeper. As soon as Mother and Uncle Edward had disappeared into the house, she stalked toward a door on the other side of the hall and pulled it open. A dust-dark hallway lay beyond – I'd met closets that looked more inviting.

'Well?' said the Housekeeper, her voice a low, rasping croak. 'Are you coming or not?'

William and I exchanged a look. My first instinct was to turn around, get back in the carriage, and catch the first train back to Caledonia, but that, unfortunately, did not seem like an option. So, with a deep breath, I made my way to the door, William still clinging to my coat. The Housekeeper nearly shoved us through, before slamming the door behind us, and pushing past to take the lead.

The house was a dizzying labyrinth of tight corridors and high-ceilinged galleries, and hall after hall after hall of locked doors. As the housekeeper led us down passages and up stairs and through windowless rooms, the keys at her belt jangling with every step, I tried to keep track of our route, counting rooms and paces and turns, but it was impossible. Past a set of double doors, we turned down a side hall, and at last, the Housekeeper unhooked the keys from her belt, unlocking the door to a small, dreary parlour.

A cloud of dust rose into the air as we entered, and William tried to wave it away – but before I could do much more than glance at the room (all I noticed was that the walls were painted a most disagreeable shade of grey), the Housekeeper spun us both to face her.

'These are your rooms,' she said shortly. 'The main bedroom is through the door on your left, while the second door on the right leads to the other. The maid will bring you dinner in an hour. I hope you're not picky.'

William coughed.

'Now, before you get too *comfortable*,' continued the Housekeeper, 'there are some rules you are expected to obey during your stay here. First of all, locked doors are locked for a reason. You are well advised to keep your snotty little noses where they belong.'

Fair enough, I thought.

'Secondly, though the woods and gardens are free for you to explore, you may not leave the grounds without an adult or express permission. And of course, if you are not back inside before nightfall, the doors will be locked, and you will not be allowed admittance,' her face broke into a cruel grin. 'The grounds are rather... unpleasant at night.'

I looked to William, who raised his eyebrows. Neither of us wanted to know what sort of unpleasant she meant.

'Finally,' said the Housekeeper. 'Remember that you are here by the goodwill and charity of Doctor Crowe. If he asks you to do something, you are to do it immediately and without question. Is that clear?' When neither William nor I responded, the Housekeeper gave a little sniff. 'Of course,' she said, 'if you wish to be *obstinate*, there will be punishments.'

'What sort of punishments, ma'am?' asked William.

But the Housekeeper didn't answer. Instead, she gave us one last heavy-lidded scowl and stepped back into the hall. 'Welcome to Ravenscourt,' she said, before slamming the door on us.

Her exit raised another cloud of dust, which set William coughing while I pulled off my boots, shook the water out of my coat, and took a moment to look at the room properly. My first impression hadn't been wrong: a crumbly fire smouldered in the fireplace, a vase of wilting flowers drooped on the mantle. The warped shadow of iron bars darkened the windows, and the couch and the cushioned chairs had become a feast for moths. I'd never seen a more disagreeable room in my life – up to and including the sitting room of our neighbour, Mrs. Evans, who owned a dozen smelly cats.

Dad would have had choice things to say about all of it. Perhaps he would've tried to identify the mould growing on the walls: *P. Creeperserus* or something like that – or made jokes about the paintings and the strange statues. The Housekeeper would've found it impossible to be so sour to him: he would've laughed it away, or perhaps even charmed a smile out of her. And Uncle Edward–

I wondered what he would've said to Uncle Edward. After all, they were brothers: they'd grown up here together, once. But now I'd never know what they would've said to each other, because of course, the only reason we were here at all was because Dad was gone–

He was gone.

It still didn't feel completely real. Half of me still expected him to walk through the door with a smile and a laugh, saying it had all been a marvellous joke. Part of me even wanted to believe he was here – just waiting behind one of those locked doors.

But of course, that couldn't be true. He'd left all of this behind long, long ago, and he'd never wanted to think about it again. How Mother could have ever thought of bringing us here, to this unfamiliar house among strangers, I still couldn't fathom.

'I hope we won't be staying very long,' said William.

'I guess we'll have to wait and see.'

Dinner was a sorry plate of cold meat and soggy potatoes, and Mother had tucked a note under one of the forks to let us know that her room was 'just down the hall' though she'd conveniently left out exactly which way and exactly which hall. Afterward, I busied myself unpacking our suitcases, and William tried, with little success, to coax the fire back to life – but with our suitcases being so small, the entire thing didn't take very long, and so I tucked myself into the lumpy sheets of my lumpy bed for lack of anything better to do. The day had made me tired, but I still couldn't sink into sleep. So I took deep breaths and tried running my defences, Dad's words echoing in my head:

The First Defence is always with you, but this ring will help you remember it.

The Second Defence is self-control, and you must master your breath to maintain it.

The Third Defence is your heart and your sanctuary. Know how to find it and you will never be deceived for long.

I twisted my ring and counted my breaths and coiled the warmth of those defences into my chest, but no matter how I tried, I couldn't find my way back to my sanctuary: the Third Defence wouldn't work.

The rain pounded against the windows and the wind howled over the stones and I could hear the hallways creaking. Without my sanctuary, there was no escape from the strange, discomforting darkness of this unfamiliar room, and my mind couldn't stop questioning what it meant, that the Third Defence wouldn't work. Was I simply tired – or did it have something to do with the Ward? Or with Dad? Still, I must've slept a bit because I dreamed about a woman with ice for eyes and a pale face and somewhere a boy was screaming. But then I opened my eyes, and there was a face hovering above me: white and flickering with a strange, orange glow.

I screamed, and then hit it with my pillow.

'Ow! Abby!' exclaimed William as he tumbled to the floor, the room plunging into complete black.

My heart was hammering. I glared at my brother – or at least, toward him, as best I could figure, in the darkness. 'What do you think you're *doing?*'

'I couldn't sleep,' said William, rustling in his pockets for another match. It hissed as he lit it, summoning a sphere of warm, yellow light.

'Yes, well, *I* was sleeping, if you didn't notice!'

William frowned. 'I just – I think there's something in the attic,' he said, his voice small. 'Maybe we should check on Mum? I mean, just in case – ow!' He shook out the match as it nipped at his fingers.

'Just in case?' I said while my brother fumbled with the matches. 'She's an *adult.* She can take care of herself. Besides, I'd be more worried about *letting your sister sleep*, if I were you.'

Another hiss, the match flared. William frowned at me. 'But–'

'But nothing!' I said, pulling the blankets over my head. 'I was sleeping, and you should be too!'

And with a sigh, he shook out the match and shuffled out of the room.

But now, I was fully awake, and finding my way back to sleep was worse than impossible. The howling and the creaking and the dripping refused to fade. And William's worried question gnawed at me as well: *just in case.*

Just in case *what?*

What was a very unpleasant thing to think about.

'You want to go check on Mum?' I asked him as I stomped back out into the sitting room. Luckily there were more than enough candles scattered around the fireplace where he'd been trying to sculpt them. I swiped one up and held it out for him to light. 'Let's go then.'

We poked our heads into the hall, looking for any sign of which way to head, but there was none, so we settled for picking a direction at random and trying every door we came to.

Most of them were locked.

The few that weren't led only to empty rooms. There was one done all in blue (and cobwebs), and another done all in red (with more cobwebs), and one wide hall with a beautiful grand piano forgotten in the corner, which scattered sharps to the air as William ran his fingers over the keys.

'Shhhhhh!'

There was one dark corridor that seemed to go on and on into oblivion, and another wide hall lined all with windows, which showed nothing of outside but a thrashing sea of treetops. A set of towering doors led to a grand library, lightning flickering through the far windows to reveal shelves upon shelves of books. But among all those corridors and all those doors, there was still no sign of Mother.

We came to a gallery lined with portraits – all the former masters of Ravenscourt Manor scowled down on us from the left, while on the right hung their Lady Crowes. Atreus and Rosemarie, James and Elsabeth, Grahame and Lily Isabella – sixteen pairs of portraits stood guard over the hall until at the very end of the row, where the most recent Master should have sat, there was only an empty space, and across from it:

'Ariel Raban-Black,' I read from the nameplate. A woman with ice-blue eyes smiled down at us, her black hair pulled back from a delicate, bone-pale face.

A chill ran through the hall, and the candle went out.

I reached for William in the darkness, and his hand found mine. Every noise in the house sounded a thousand times louder – the drafts creeping through cracked windows, the drip and drizzle of water outside, the soft patter of footsteps–

Footsteps?

The warm glow of a lamp appeared at the other end of the hall, and I pulled William behind me, stepping forward toward whoever it was. The corridor flooded with light–

And there she was.

Mother paused at the end of the hall, raising the lamp to look at us properly, and I had to raise an arm to shield my eyes against the light. For a moment, all three of us stood frozen, as if caught in the middle of a crime. But then Mother tsked, and she stalked toward us, adjusting the collar of her travelling coat.

'What are you doing, wandering the halls?' she said. 'At this hour! Why, you should both be in bed!'

'We were worried,' I said. 'We couldn't sleep.'

'We think there's something in the attic,' added William.

'*William* thinks there's something in the attic,' I clarified.

Mother tsked again. 'Come now, there's no use for all that. Let's get you back to your rooms, and no more wandering!'

She ushered us through the corridors, back down the gallery and past the dark hall, the light of her lamp throwing everything into sharp relief. 'Are they taking good care of you?' she asked as she led us past the library doors.

William stifled a snort, while I shook my head. 'Not really.'

'Well, that's not at all–'

A scream sounded from above – a sudden, piercing shriek, silenced as soon as it was heard. I looked at William, whose face had gone ash-white, before both of us looked to Mother.

She was looking upward, but her eyes quickly flicked back to the floor. And then she was urging us forward again, down one of the side corridors near the library. 'I shall have to have a word with the housekeeper,' she said, as if there'd been no interruption at all. 'I daresay they haven't had to accommodate guests for a long time, but that's hardly an acceptable excuse…'

William and I exchanged a look that said all we wanted to say to each other. We had all heard that scream – so why was Mother pretending she hadn't?

'This is my room,' said Mother, unlocking a door near the end of the hall. 'Now just let me–'

'We can get back to our room ourselves,' I offered. 'It's not far from here.'

Mother hesitated, her eyes darting to the hallway stretching behind us, and back to me. But then she bent down with a swift kiss for each of us. 'Mind that you go directly back,' she said before stepping into her room, though she watched us make our way back down the hall before finally closing the door.

'You heard that scream, right?' said William as we turned into the next corridor. 'I didn't just imagine it?'

'I heard it,' I said. 'Though Mum didn't seem to pay it much mind.'

'And you don't think that's strange?'

Of course it was strange. Even stranger was the fact that Mother had been wandering the halls at all – and still in her travelling clothes, no less. What reason could she have to still be up? Had she been up and about all this time?

What had she been doing?

'I'm not going to be able to sleep,' said William when we reached our rooms. He made no move to open the door.

'What do you want to do then?' I asked.

In the end, we decided to go back to the library, slipping through the halls with the quiet purpose of a quest. The monstrous doors opened easily, despite their height, and we found ourselves among the books, the ghostly light of dawn just beginning to tint the windows blue. The library was so tall, so wide, that the corners were still cloaked in darkness. And all the walls of that entire space were lined with books: three full stories of them, with a maze of shelves below.

I didn't know where to start. But before either of us could so much as take a single step toward any of the shelves, the doors slammed closed behind us.

I turned, only to find myself face to face with the old Housekeeper.

WARDS AND WARNINGS

The housekeeper grabbed us both by our collars before I could even blink, pulling us away from the books and back out the door. She proceeded to drag us through the dusty halls back to our rooms, muttering under her breath the entire time. Whatever else I might say about Mrs. Thompson, the fact remains that she had a truly respectable vocabulary of swears, and a lot more strength in her short, wrinkly arms than you'd expect.

'Up and poking into everything already, and it not barely dawn!' she screeched, as she shoved us into our sitting room and finally released us from her claws. 'Perhaps we were not completely clear on the rules: you are not to be out of your beds past ten o'clock and you are certainly not to be wandering about the house at all hours of the night!' Conveniently enough, she left out the part where she definitely had not mentioned those rules before. 'Mind you, if I do catch you at it again – ' she slashed one of her gnarled fingers across her throat.

Of course, that part, she *had* mentioned before, though I rather hoped throat-slashing wasn't one of her usual punishments. 'Since you're up, you might as well get dressed,' she croaked. 'You'll be having lunch with

Doctor Crowe today, and it's in your best interests to be presentable.'

And with that, she left, slamming the door behind her.

'Taking good care of us, aren't they?' said William.

At one point, one of the maids slipped in to put breakfast on the table, and at another point, William had finished off the entire plate, assuming I wasn't hungry because I could barely keep my eyes open. I practiced my defences and let myself drift, while William took up his candle-making experiments where he'd left off. And then, of course, at some other, third point, the Housekeeper barged in again, and since we hadn't even begun to get dressed, she continued yelling at us as if she hadn't paused, and let me tell you, lacing up the bodice of a mourning dress is no easy task when there's a toad-faced Housekeeper yelling at you for not being able to tie knots behind your back instead of just tying the knots for you.

Finally, we were ready. I finished lacing up my shoes, and William pulled on his jacket. The Housekeeper ushered us once more through the dusty house and we came, at last, to the Dining Hall, a huge, draughty space that was smaller than the library (but only just). There was only one table in that Dining Hall – a single, heavy, wooden table, long enough for a dozen chairs to be lined up on either side – and Uncle Edward was sitting at the head of it, already waiting. He stood as we stepped through the doors, beckoning us to sit:

'Come, come! Don't be shy.'

There were four places set, but Mother was nowhere to be seen – and so we sat down in awkward silence and began to eat. Eventually, Uncle Edward spoke:

'I hope your stay has not been too unpleasant thus far?'

There was nothing honest we could say to that without offending him. William took a keen interest in his green beans, picking at the bits of bacon that had been stirred into the sauce, leaving me to make an attempt at being diplomatic, if I dared.

'Well–'

'Mrs. Thompson tells me that you have been getting well acquainted with the house – a most fascinating structure, is it not? Even I must admit to knowing little of its full extent.' He didn't wait for us to comment before pressing on. 'But perhaps a little history. You see, the first Master of Ravenscourt was Sir Atreus Crowe, who was granted the lands of the Manor in 1485, after the Battle of Bosworth. He began construction on the house the following year. However, the work was set with ill luck from the start. Less than two months in, several workers were trapped by a collapsed wall. Their bodies were never recovered. Some time later, the head architect was struck down by plague. But still the work continued, until in 1487, two of Sir Atreus' children disappeared.'

Here he paused, taking a long drink from his water glass, as if washing down his words. 'No one was quite sure what happened to them,' he continued, setting down the glass. 'Some believed they had wandered into the Blackwood, others that they were buried in rubble from the construction, their bones turned to mortar. It was not until the house was completed that their fate came to be known.' He set down his silverware. 'For you see, Sir Atreus, upon completion of the house, decided to throw a celebratory dinner. In this very room, he and his guests gathered, sitting around this very table. The appetizers were brought out, then the soups, and finally the main dish. It was said to have been a magnificent feast, and only Sir Atreus refused to partake. But finally, near the end of the main course, he gave in to the urging of his wife and uncovered his plate – and what do you think he found there?'

My stomach had started to churn. There were very few pleasant endings to a story like that.

'Er... a roast pheasant?' guessed William.

Uncle Edward shook his head, and gave a small, mirthless laugh. 'Heads,' he said, as if it were a punch line. 'Human heads. Those of his eldest son and his only daughter.'

William put down his silverware, and I didn't blame him. The plate of roast beef and greens in front of me turned suddenly horrific, bits of bacon like cooked skin. Could you make bacon out of humans? I sincerely hoped I would never actually need to know the answer to that question.

'Did they ever find out why?' I asked.

Uncle Edward shrugged. 'Perhaps someone wanted revenge on Sir Atreus, or perhaps it was the work of a jealous and troubled younger sibling.' He took another sip of water and met my eyes.' Or perhaps the children merely ended up in the wrong place at the wrong time. In any case, it serves to remind us that even the most innocent curiosities can be deadly. Perhaps it is better not to venture into uncharted territories, lest you run into things best left alone.'

At that moment, the door to the Dining Hall creaked open, and Mother poked her head into the hall. I couldn't help the sigh of relief that escaped me as Uncle Edward stood to greet her, pulling out the chair next to him for her to sit.

'I do apologize for my tardiness,' she said as she took her seat. 'Now, what are we eating?'

Our first three days at the Manor, the rain did not stop. Wind and sleet and water battered against the windows while the sky churned with storm, and every night, the echo of ghastly wails sounded from somewhere above, just weak and eerie enough for me to wonder if they had come from the wind or my imagination, or if they were the same as the scream that we'd heard the first night. There was no escape from the cobweb-curtained corridors of the house, and we had nothing to do but lose ourselves in the library, or when that grew tiresome, to attempt explorations of the other wings, though that was almost impossible without provoking the Housekeeper ('that old toad,' as William started calling her). And with every exploration, I couldn't help but hear Uncle Edward's story echoing in the back of my mind, as if he'd meant it as a sort of warning.

Still, we never ran into him – or Mother, for that matter. Whatever the adults did all day, we saw them only during the shifty silences of lunch and dinner. And so, when the rain finally did let up and the sun decided to cast a few damp rays of light into the Dining Hall, it was all I could do to stop myself from jumping up right then and there and running outside with William in tow. No, we had to wait until the adults had laid down their silverware and then politely ask to be excused. Only when we'd done that, and the adults gave us their permission, could we jump up and run.

Manners.

In any case, our explorations had not been in vain. We'd found several doors leading outside, though most of them opened into courtyards and walled gardens, and there was one just downstairs from our room that let you out near the servants' quarters, with nothing but the stables in front of you. But there was one door at the end of the hall lined all with windows – a stained glass door that had been locked and bolted tight, and *that* was the door I wanted to open, as I was sure it led down to the back lawn and the woods beyond.

When we got there, light was shining through the stained glass. I had brought an extra hair pin in case William needed to pick the lock – but I needn't have bothered. A note had been tucked behind the door handle, a square of cream-colored card with a message in green ink:

> Dear esteemed guests, Miss Abigail and young Mister William,
>
> you are cordially invited to the Rose Garden for a moment of reminiscence in honour of your late father.
>
> with deepest sympathies,
>
> *Anastasia LaNoir*
>
> (The door is unlocked, I think you'll find.)

I couldn't even begin to read the signature at the bottom, except for an overlarge B and a looping L with far too many lines and curves. William squinted at the note himself for a minute before shrugging and trying the door handle.

It was, in fact, unlocked. We pulled open the door and stepped into a place bathed in daylight, the air fresh and warm – too warm for late November. William looked up, blinking, and I looked up too, at the cage of glass and rusting metal arcing above us, and then down at the iron stair twisting away below, leading into a teeming jungle of plants. Trapped birds chattered among the leaves and vines and the air was full of the thick, damp smell of growing things. The door, it turned out, didn't lead outside at all, but rather to a greenhouse – the largest greenhouse I'd ever seen: big enough to hold the tiny patch of yard behind our old house (which Dad always insisted on calling the garden) several times over. Perhaps it was even big enough to fit the old house itself.

'Oh lovely,' said William flatly. 'Plants.'

'Don't be that way,' I said, pulling him down the stairs and into the jungle. There were drooping clusters of kingsfoil and blooming mandrakes, and dark, rusty bloodmoss, all of which I pointed out to William, while he pointedly ignored me. But there was no sign of roses, or of the stranger who had invited us there. It wasn't long before William started complaining about the stuffy air and the stuffy light and the stuffy plants, and so, at last, we found the door that led outside, and with it, another note:

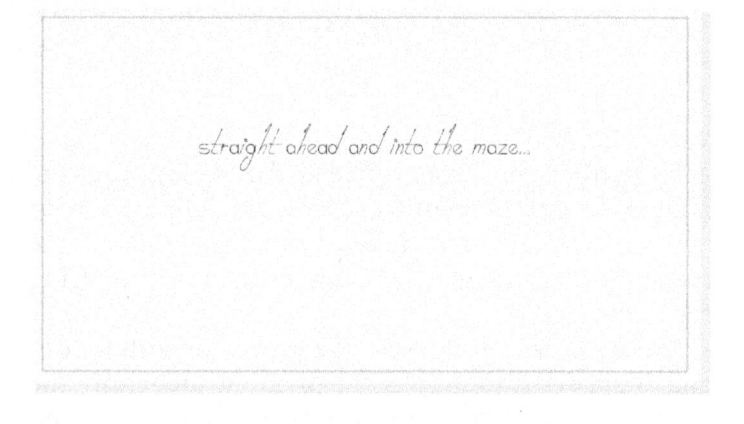

> *straight ahead and into the maze...*

I stuck the note into my sock, and together, William and I ventured out into the manor. The outdoor gardens lay withered and dull under the tattered clouds. In the distance, the dark tree line of the Blackwood marked the edge of a grey sky. Our path cut through a forest of bushes sculpted in the shape of giant chessmen, before ending at the trellised arch that marked the entrance to the Rose Garden. Naturally, our mysterious host had left a third card perched among the thorny branches.

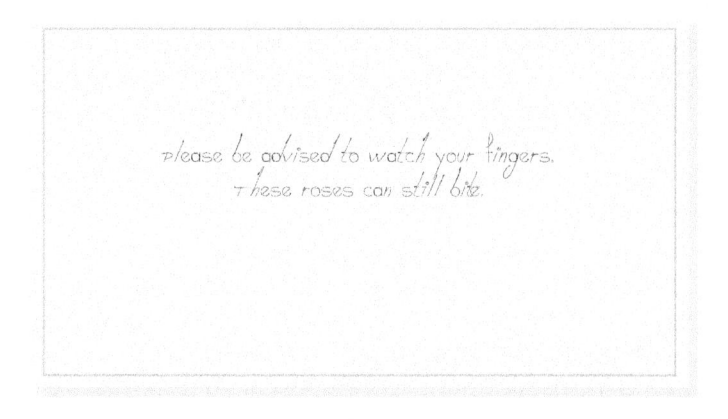

> *Please be advised to watch your fingers.*
> *These roses can still bite.*

William raised his eyebrows at that one. Whoever our host was, I was starting to doubt that they were particularly sane – which was, perhaps, all the more reason to find out exactly who they were. I took William's hand, and we stepped into the rose garden. The path twisted and turned and it took only a few minutes before we were completely lost within the maze, the thorny hedges rising, unbroken, on all sides, and the dead leaves rattling in the wind, and our feet squelching over brown, fallen petals, as we looked in all directions for an escape – but there was no escape, just more hedges, and more thorns, and more dead leaves, and somewhere, very close by, the snip, snip, snip of scissors clipping trimmings from the hedge.

I paused, and William looked at me. He'd heard it too. And without exchanging a single word about it, we started running toward the sound. But it shifted and softened and echoed, and it was no use trying to tell where it was coming from, really, because every single time we thought we were close, the path turned away. At last, after hours, we found ourselves at a dead end, with the snip of the scissors, or the clippers, or whatever they were, very close by. We could even hear the soft whisper of the rose branches as they fell at the feet of whoever was trimming them. They were just on the other side of the hedge – the bushes trembled a little, and I could hear them humming – but the only path was behind us. There was no other way to get through the foot or two of rose hedges between us and the gardener.

Except, of course, by going through the hedge.

When you do something unfathomably silly or stupid – or rather, when you're about to do something unfathomably silly or stupid – it's often in your best interest to think about it for another moment to stop yourself from doing it. The important exception to this is when that silly or stupid thing you're about to do has got to be done anyway. In that case, it's best not to think about it at all, and rather to just step forward, thrust your hands into the hedge full of sharp, bloodthirsty thorns, and push your way through to the other side.

It only took a few difficult steps – less than ten seconds, really – though the thorns were everywhere, scraping my face and hands and dress. I stumbled into the corridor on the other side, nearly toppling into the woman who was standing there tending to the bushes. The snip of the hedge clippers fell silent, and she looked over, her eyes hidden in shadow beneath her wide-brimmed hat and her flyaway hair, and even though her lips were quirked in amusement, I could tell she wasn't particularly surprised.

And then William tumbled through the hedge after me, and of course he *did* trip into the gardener, crashing into her skirts before falling backward into the dirt with a muffled 'ow!'

'Sorry!' he spluttered. I had never been prouder.

Before I could step forward, the gardener bent down, to grasp William's arm in her long, dark fingers and pull him standing. 'Well now,' she said once he was on his feet, still holding him steady by his arm. Her voice was laughing, even if she wasn't. 'What do we have here? Are you a sort of insect?'

William stared at the gardener, though if she found it rude, she didn't show it. 'Do we look like insects?'

The gardener let go of him at last and dusted a bit of dirt from his sleeve. 'No,' she said, 'I don't suppose you have the legs for it. Shame, really. Aphids are easily dealt with, but humans? Now there's a real pest.'

I guess we'd found our host, though I was starting to wonder whether that was a good thing. She turned back to her rose bushes and bent down, as if to sniff the flowers – except that all the roses were already dead. 'So, Miss Abigail and Young Mister William,' she said as she took up her clippers once more. 'How are you enjoying your stay in the house?'

I didn't even begin to answer before she'd cut me off:

'I find it rather too draughty for my tastes,' she said. 'Too much dust and cobwebby stuff and you can never be sure about the shades.'

'Shades,' echoed William. He'd started looking at the gardener as if she might be slightly dangerous, and I didn't blame him.

'You mean unrested spirits?' I said. 'You can't be serious. Surely we would've noticed.'

The gardener pursed her lips. 'How do you figure that?'

'Well, you can't *live* in a place with shades,' I said, which was true. 'They'd drain all the spirit out of you, and then you'd be dead yourself, with nothing left of you but your own shade.'

'There are ghosts and shades in any place this old, Miss Abigail,' said the gardener. She picked a withered rose from the hedge and tossed it mindlessly over her shoulder. 'Oh, certainly, not the kind that screech and wander about as they wish and feed on living spirits all the time. But in a place like this – well... shades and ghosts tend to like dusty old houses and overgrown manors and all the forgotten corners of the world. Or didn't Lewis teach you anything?'

At the mention of Dad's name, my fingers went automatically to the ring on my thumb. 'You knew our father,' I said, trying to keep my voice even.

'Yes, I knew him,' said the gardener, punctuating her words with snips from her hedge clippers. 'And look, there it is, talking about him in the past tense. Never thought I'd live to see the day... I was very sorry to hear of his – how shall we say? – *unfortunate demise*.' She let the hedge clippers fall still, lowering her head and tracing a circle in the dirt with her shoe. Quiet settled over us. 'Tell me, then: how did it happen?'

I glanced at William, who shrugged back. 'Well,' I said, 'we don't know, really, you see. We just woke up and–'

'And he was gone,' finished William for me.

The gardener went suddenly still, her foot poised in front of her. 'You mean–?'

'We weren't able to rest him or anything,' I said.

The gardener turned to look at us, and finally, she pulled back her hat so we could see her eyes – golden eyes, quick, sharp, and piercing as a cat's, as if they could see through anything. Those eyes ran over me, and then over my brother, and perhaps they saw something in us under the thorn scratches and grime, because the gardener put down her tools altogether and focused on us fully for the first time. 'So then tell me now: what do you make of that?'

What did we make of it? What sort of question was that? What were we supposed to 'make of' it? I looked to William, only to find that he was focused fully on the gardener.

'The Inquisitor was asking about enemies,' he said. 'He seemed to think it meant Dad was murdered.'

'Only it couldn't have been,' I said, before the gardener could get the wrong idea. 'It simply couldn't–'

'And why not?' asked the gardener softly. She was staring straight at me now, those golden eyes watching, and her once-quirked lips had bent into a half frown.

'Well, Dad didn't have enemies,' I said, though as much as I believed that, as much as I said it, I was starting to wonder: how could I be sure of that? How could I be sure of anything when Dad had just suddenly dropped dead one night, and when he had never mentioned a single thing about Ravenscourt before, had never talked about why he'd left, or how he and Mother had ended up in a tiny town on the north tip of Caledonia? How could I be sure of anything at all?

The gardener's face went suddenly grim. 'Did they never tell you?' she asked.

'Tell us?' I asked at the same time that William said, 'What?'

'What happened when your father left? How he was disowned?'

'Disowned?' The word felt like a punch in the chest.

'So they didn't tell you,' said the gardener, half to herself. She shook her head, and when she spoke again, I got the feeling that she'd forgotten we were there. 'To think that he wouldn't have told them! You'd assume, considering everything... Irresponsible! Irresponsible as always – but no, it's not my place. Best not get involved.' And with that, she packed up her trowel, her clippers, and her gloves, picked up her basket, and began to walk away.

'Wait!' I called, running after her.

She didn't even turn. She was humming to herself, actually *humming* as she rounded a corner with the express purpose of leaving us completely in the dark. And she was quick about it too – I had to run to catch up with her, trying to get her to stop. 'You can't just ask all of that and then walk off!'

She kept walking.

'It's not fair!'

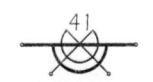

She didn't even look.

William was hurrying behind me, but rather than helping, he kept looking at me like he wanted us to leave. Before the gardener could round another corner and get away entirely, I darted in front of her to block her way.

'Tell us what you know!'

Finally, she paused, and under the shadow of her hat, her lips curled into a smile. 'Determined, are we?'

'We ought to know, if it had something to do with Dad's death,' I answered.

'Very well then. I'll tell you what I can tell you, but not here, and not now. These roses have ears and they're all terrible gossips. Besides, they'll be looking for you for dinner–'

And just as she said it, the manor bells rang out for six, and somewhere, far away, the Housekeeper's voice called our names.

'Well, if you're not going to tell us now, then when?'

The gardener looked toward the sky, at the scattered clouds and sinking sun. 'Tomorrow...' she said, savouring the word. 'Tomorrow, we can talk. Meet me at the entrance to the maze an hour before noon.'

'I guess we'll see you tomorrow then, Miss... er...' She hadn't even told us her name, I realized, though she knew ours well enough.

'Beatrice, child,' she said. 'Beatrice LeNoir.' And with a tip of her hat, she disappeared into the hedges.

Of course she'd left without showing us the way out, and we couldn't even backtrack, not unless we wanted to step through another hedge. The Housekeeper's voice sounded from beyond the high hedges:

'Where are you, you useless brats!'

William pointed up, to where the very tip of Ravenscourt's highest tower just managed to peek above the roses, and using that as a landmark, and the Old Toad's voice as a guide, we began trying to find our way out of the maze. It was like playing a game of

Marco Polo: every time we came to a crossroads, or a turn where we couldn't see the tower, we stopped, and listened, and sure enough:

'I *know* you came out here, you worthless–'

At last, we stumbled out of the maze, right at the entrance where she'd been yelling the whole time. 'Where were you?' she demanded, grabbing us by the arms, before noticing the scratches left by the thorns. 'And what have you done to your clothes!'

'We got lost in the maze, ma'am,' which of course was perfectly honest.

'Well, that maze has made you nearly twenty minutes late for dinner,' said the Housekeeper, and her face curdled into a smile. I doubted that a smile from the Housekeeper could mean anything good. 'And seeing as how it would take at least another hour to make you even half-way presentable, I rather think that going to bed without supper would be a good–'

A soft cough sounded from the path.

We all turned to where Mother had appeared on the path, prim and proper as ever, though for once, her pointed frown wasn't directed at me or William, which was a relief. She glared directly at the Housekeeper, who let us go immediately, and bobbed her head at Mother – just low enough to avoid being completely disrespectful.

'Mrs. Thompson,' said Mother.

'Please, Mrs. Crowe. Ellen will suffice.'

'Ellen, then,' said Mother, giving the Housekeeper the small, tight smile that she usually reserved for beggars and door-to-door salesmen. 'Edward told me he had entrusted the care of my children to your capable hands. I'm sorry we haven't had the chance to speak before now. Have they been much trouble?'

'Nothing worse than I've had to handle before,' croaked the Housekeeper shortly.

'Good,' said Mother. Her voice had taken on a dangerous tone that I knew well. It was the tone she'd used when the catechism teacher had told her I was looking up Curses to use on the other girls – though really, all I'd been trying to do was find an Illusion or Charm to make them not quite so horrifically annoying. It was the same tone she'd used when she'd caught Dad sneaking carnivorous plants into the house, or when William–

Well, William probably thought it was her normal voice.

'Because I would hate to tell Edward his trust was ill-founded,' continued Mother. 'In any case, I'd rather their punishments were discussed with me, rather than handed out at whim.'

The Housekeeper's face had gone positively sour. 'Of course, Mrs. Crowe,' she said, bowing her head, though she still couldn't hide the malice in her lidded eyes.

'Now,' said Mother. 'I'll see them to dinner – I rather think you have things to clean and organize tonight?' And without waiting for a response, she turned back toward the house, waving for us to follow. The Housekeeper couldn't do anything but glare as we walked away. I had to fight the urge to stick my tongue out at her.

But then we were inside, and when Mother closed the door behind us, her lips were still pressed into that tight frown. 'Would you care to explain to me what you were doing that you managed to do *that* to your clothes? Never mind the fact that the Housekeeper had to drag you in for dinner!'

'We were just exploring,' I said. Surely she could've understood that? 'We've been trapped in this stuffy old house for nearly a week!'

'We got lost in the rose maze,' added William.

It didn't help. 'I guess it doesn't really matter,' said Mother with a sigh. 'But Abigail, William, *dears*, there are rules here. You're *guests*. I can't have you running wild the way you have been–'

'We weren't running *wild*–' I said, as William protested, 'We weren't *breaking* any rules–' but Mother held up her hand.

'I don't want to hear it,' she said. 'If you insist on spurning your uncle's orders, there really won't be anything I can do about it. This is his house after all.' She sighed again, and looked up at the ceiling, as if searching for guidance. 'I rather think a lack of dinner would actually be a good lesson. So just... just go to your rooms. And try not to get into any more trouble? Please?'

I couldn't imagine how she could be serious about the whole thing, but she was, and she completely ignored any further arguments. And so, there was nothing for us to do but go back to our rooms, Mother peering after us, as if to make sure we didn't set the house on fire right then and there just to spite her.

'She's one to talk,' said William sullenly when we'd finally left her behind.

And there was really nothing I could say to that. Lunch had been ages ago, and an unpleasant feeling had settled into my stomach – though it had very little to do with hunger. 'That gardener,' I said at last, 'Beatrice... what do you think she meant about Father being disowned?'

William paused, frowning in thought. 'Well, it would make sense, wouldn't it?' he said.

'What do you mean?'

'I mean, the fact that Dad never talked about Uncle Edward – and also that we never knew about all *this*–' he gestured to the whole wide house: the cobwebbed ceiling and faded carpets and peeling, ancient walls, and the great doors of the library standing closed in front of us. 'I feel like we should've known,' he said. 'But you know what is interesting? She said something about places like this attracting ghosts. Do you think that's true?'

I couldn't tell what he was thinking. 'I don't know, why?'

'I just... well, there's an entire section in the library about Wards and Restings and magic and stuff, and I was wondering... if Dad's spirit wasn't rested... well, then...'

'What could've happened to it?' I said, voicing the question that I hadn't dared to ask since the Resting. The library doors with their carvings of intertwined trees and mysterious words glared down at us. 'I don't think it would hurt to try to find out. And since we've got nothing else to do tonight...'

William grinned. 'I was hoping you'd say that.'

THE GARDENER'S TALE

Proper books about magic were a rare thing to find, seeing as, strictly speaking, everything in them was 'utterly profane', as the Inquisitors liked to call anything that the Church Fathers shook their heads about. Of course, that didn't stop people from writing such books, selling them, reading or buying them. Even Dad had kept one or two dusty tomes on Wards and Cursebreaking tucked away on the bottom shelf of his bookcase. It was lucky that the Inquisitors had never set eyes on *those*.

There was only one book about magic that I'd ever actually been *allowed* to look at, and that was the official *Spiritual Protection Handbook* that every catechism student received from their Dame Inquisitor when they began their Sunday lessons. My Dame Inquisitor had been a dusty-haired old lady who seemed to take particular joy in describing the horrors magicians could inflict with Curses – controlling your every thought and action, so that it was almost like you didn't have a spirit of your own anymore. And when she wasn't doing that, she would insist that we memorize rhymes from the *Handbook* to ward away any temptations we might have had of trying out magic for ourselves.

Illusion, Curse, Command, and Charm
Keep me far from magic's harm,
Or if I am to temptation led,
Let noose be tied or fire my bed...

Needless to say, Dad hadn't been particularly pleased to hear me chanting *that* after one afternoon lesson. So, even though he couldn't keep me away from the catechism classes without some excuse ('What do you think people would say, Lewis, if she didn't show?' Mother always asked), he made sure to teach me proper defences – ones that would actually work against magicians and their Curses – and he was always there after every catechism class to explain all the things the Dame Inquisitor avoided explaining. And that would've been good enough, if William hadn't started suffering his fits.

The first one happened while we were in worship. It was a warm, cloudy Sunday. As usual, the mass was dragging on forever, and Mother was getting annoyed at us fidgeting, and I had nothing to look forward to after but an hour of catechism with the Dame Inquisitor and the other village girls, all of whom were horrendously dull and irritating.

But as the service ended and people started shuffling out of the pews, William went still and staring. He wasn't even five years old yet, and he was *never* still, and I remember feeling as if someone had stuck their fist into my chest, squeezing out all the air. For one choking moment, the world stood frozen–

And then people were screaming as William fell. His head made a terrible cracking sound as it hit the wooden pew. Mother pulled me into the aisle, as my brother began thrashing, his eyes wide and rolling and tinged with blood.

Dad scooped William up into his arms, trying to hold him still and failing. He strode down the aisle and out of the church, ignoring the questions that followed, leaving me and Mother to deal with what everyone else would say. The problem was, my brother never got better, not completely. He could go a few weeks, maybe even a month or two without the slightest hint of being sick, but the fits always came back eventually. Mother started keeping us at home as much as possible, but it wasn't long before the rest of the town started talking – about illnesses, or Curses, or sheer bad luck.

It was just a couple days after that first fit, on the evening of William's fifth birthday, when I woke up to a knock at the door. And by the end of that night, Dad had kicked Uncle Edward out of our house, with an order never to return.

Yet here we were, in Ravenscourt's grand library, surrounded by more books on magic than I ever thought I'd see in a lifetime.

I didn't realize I'd fallen asleep until William slammed his book on the table – a good bit closer to my head than could be considered polite.

'Nothing!' he exclaimed.

I'd fallen asleep on page 24 of *Grimm's Complete Novice Guide to Cursebreaking*. Apparently, it had been a particularly comfortable page, because light was already slanting through the library windows. I only hoped that the introductory text of 'Chapter 2: Whatever You Do, Don't Panic' hadn't ended up on my cheek.

'Did you actually drool on that?' asked William, when he finally noticed that he'd woken me up.

'Shut it,' was the only valid response. It was definitely morning – and not just sunrise. But William's shirt wasn't even ruffled, and he was still picking through books. 'Did you sleep at all?' I asked him.

'No,' he said. 'I've been trying to find *anything* about what happens to lost spirits, and there's *nothing*. Absolutely nothing! You'd think with a section this big...'

He'd been awake for hours then. And his face had gone pale – even if he didn't feel exhausted, he looked it. 'William, you shouldn't–'

'Don't do the worried older sister thing,' he said. 'I'm fine. At least I didn't pass out and *drool*–'

'Shut it!'

'Good morning anyway,' he said. 'We should probably head back to the room if we want breakfast – or lunch.'

'Lunch? What time is it?'

'Almost noon.'

That was enough to get me going. 'We were supposed to meet Beatrice at the maze!' I said, stacking the books into a hasty pile and dragging him out the door before he could protest.

We were lucky that the halls were still mostly empty, though William was definitely dragging his feet about the whole thing. 'What are you expecting her to tell us, exactly?' he asked as we hurried toward the greenhouse door.

'Well, she seemed to know things.'

'*Seemed* being the important word here. Didn't you get the feeling that she was a little... batty?'

Truthfully, I *had* gotten that feeling, but William didn't need to know that. 'Don't you want to know what happened to Dad?'

'You look like Mum when you frown like that,' said William. 'And of course I do, but do you honestly–'

I shushed him as one of the maids came around the corner, frowning at us as she walked past. There was no reason to keep arguing – the quicker we got to Beatrice, the better. Through the upper halls and the greenhouse door, out into the back lawn. Within a few minutes, we were at the entrance to the maze, Beatrice waiting for us with her wide straw hat, and no sign of her gardening tools whatsoever.

'I almost thought I'd have to give you up as a loss,' she said.

'Well, we're here,' I answered.

Beatrice smiled, her eyes full of laughter, as if I'd made a joke. 'Come on then. We've got a bit of a walk ahead of us, and a great deal to discuss.'

'These woods once stretched without break from Yorktown all the way to the coastal cliffs, and north, over the moors and hills,' said Beatrice as she led us through the Blackwood. 'Of course, they're thinner now, broken by farms, roads, houses, what have you. And of course, your ancestor, Sir Atreus built the house somewhere in the middle of it. But back in the day, these trees stood tall and close all the way to the River Tees.'

A bird's wings flapped through the air above. It was easy enough to imagine these woods when they were ancient and dark – Beatrice seemed to be leading us through the thickest part of it anyway. Looking up, you couldn't see more than a few small patches of sky through the twisted branches of the trees, and their wide black trunks stood like military guardians on either side of the path.

''Course, in ancient days, it was Fey territory,' continued Beatrice. 'The Court claimed sovereignty over everything, and anyone venturing out into these parts was lucky to be seen again.'

I couldn't help but laugh at that. 'Fey? You mean like the Raven King, who lives trapped on the other side of the mirror? Those are children's stories – Dad used to tell us the one about Red-Cloaked Maggie so we wouldn't talk to strangers.'

'Children's stories... is that what he told you?' I must've offended her, because she fell silent, and refused to say anything until we came to the edge of a still lake, pebbles shining, icy and wet, on the shore. 'Does that look like a children's story?' she asked, gesturing to the water, an island just visible through the fog.

William and I exchanged a look.

'It looks like a *lake*,' said William, so that I wouldn't have to.

But Beatrice shook her head. 'Giants used to roam these woods. And I mean the real kind, taller than the trees. That's one of them, lying in the middle there.'

I was starting to regret my decision to talk to the gardener.

Still, there was no graceful way to leave. Beatrice led us down another path to an almost perfect circle of trees, a pair of tall aspens, smooth and white and skeletal, standing in the middle, their bony branches twined into an arch, as if marking some kind of gate. 'The entrance to the High Road, mark it well,' was all Beatrice said before dragging us further into the wood.

The forest opened up once more, and we found ourselves in a bright, green clearing with tiny purple wildflowers poking out from the grass. At the other edge of the field, a small stream trickled past, and a cottage stood next to it: a tiny, boxy house that was exactly the sort of forest cottage you'd expect to find in one of those children's stories the gardener was so keen on. And though Beatrice didn't particularly seem the kind of person to cook us into stew, if Fey stories were supposed to teach you anything, it's that you never could tell about witches.

'Home sweet home,' said Beatrice, pushing open the door.

The room on the other side was warm, with a glowing fireplace and bundles of herbs and flowers poking out of every nook and cranny. In one corner, a broomstick stood bristles-up next to a cauldron full of books, and in the other corner, a door stood half-hidden behind a curtain. William barged in to plop down at the table in the middle of the room, but as I stepped inside, a prickle of strange warmth tickled my spine, and sure enough, while Beatrice closed the heavy door behind us to keep out the cold, I turned to find the gardener's Wards engraved over the door frame. There were two lines twisted into spiralling curves on either side, and in the middle, a coin of amber had been set in the wood like a precious jewel, carved with a crescent and a dot. It had to be one of the simplest Wards I'd ever seen, and yet, the power of it continued to poke at me, searching for reasons to keep me out.

The gardener noticed my staring, and she stepped up next to me. 'It serves me well enough,' she said. 'Though I think, for today, we could use a little more privacy.' And with that, she pulled a piece of white chalk from some pocket and started tracing Wardmarks on the door and the windows.

I'd never seen a person draw Wardmarks the way an undertaker drew Deathmarks – as far as I'd ever known, Wards were supposed to be permanent: carved into stone or wood, or twisted into metal. But as Beatrice worked, filling the walls with circles and crescents and wandering lines, I could feel the Wards growing stronger, wrapping the cabin in a blanket of silence and secrecy.

'Well enough then. We shouldn't be disturbed,' she said as she finished, slipping the chalk back into her pocket.

William had been watching her work as well, gears ticking in his head as usual. 'Where'd you learn magic, then?' he asked.

'William!' I hissed in warning. It was probably not the best idea to insult our host, and she was obviously not a magician, but some sort of Warder–

'What?' said William, rolling his eyes. 'It's all the same – Wards, spells, whatever. I mean, isn't it?'

He was looking at the gardener for support this time, and to my surprise, she didn't look at all offended. It was dangerous enough being a Warder or Undertaker. Making even the smallest mistake while working with Marks was a sure way to attract the attention of Inquisitors. But Beatrice didn't mind – or didn't care. She shook off the question and turned to the fire, coaxing new flames from the coals.

'Well, for what it's worth,' she said, 'part of my job requires maintaining the Ravenscourt Wards, which makes me a Warder, which is all quite official and legal as far as anyone's concerned. Now, as for what difference that makes from a magician, I'm sure you could ask an Inquisitor to give you a better explanation than I can.'

'So it *is* all the same,' insisted William. Silently, I wished that my brother would one day learn to take a hint.

'They all work on the same level, if that's what you mean,' said Beatrice, half speaking to the now-roaring fire. 'For all that Wards and Deathmarks provide protection, they do affect all that flimsy, flickery, immaterial stuff that makes up our minds – or our spirits, if you prefer – in much the same way that a magician might, if he cast a Command or Illusion–'

'Or a Curse,' I said.

Beatrice paused at that and blinked at me. 'Or a Curse,' she confirmed.

But that still didn't quite make sense. 'But Wards aren't at all like spells,' I said. 'They're protections *against* spells. Spells control people, protections don't–'

'A Graveward can have effects every bit as unpleasant as a Curse, believe me,' said Beatrice. 'But that doesn't make being a magician any less illegal, and I rather like not having to worry about Inquisitors, if that's all the same to you.' And with a great deal of clunks and thumps and clangs, she started pulling out vegetables, pots, and pans, making it clear that we'd reached the end of that conversation.

'I'm afraid I'm a bit lacking for gourmet food at the moment,' she said, as she started preparing the vegetables. 'But vegetable soup will have to do! I daresay you haven't had breakfast?'

It was true: I was starving. But the gardener's distractions were starting to irritate me. 'You said you'd tell us about Dad,' I said.

The gardener went silent, dumping chopped parsnips into the pot over the fire. 'I did, didn't I?'

'You *said*–'

'I'm well aware of what I said, Miss Abigail. But if your parents kept this information from you, then it's likely there was a reason for that. And I want to know whether or not you're completely certain that you want to hear it – from me, no less, and not your mother.'

William was giving me his 'I told you so' glare, but I ignored it. I hadn't come all this way for vegetable soup and a lecture. 'Miss LeNoir–'

'Beatrice, child.'

'Beatrice. We have to know – if Dad's death might've had something to do with it, we *have* to. And if Mother didn't want us to know, then that's all the more reason to find it out ourselves.'

Beatrice looked me over one last time, as if measuring me for fitting. Finally, she nodded. 'I did tell you I would, after all. But you might as well settle down, because it's not a story to be told on an empty stomach.' And she returned to the soup, humming a little to herself as she did.

I joined William at the table and set my head down, watching the gardener's dark hands peel potatoes. My stomach rumbled, and I realized that we hadn't just missed breakfast – between sleeping in the library and both Mother and the Housekeeper's annoyances with us, the last meal we'd eaten was yesterday's lunch.

Hunger was exhausting.

'Don't drift off on me now,' said Beatrice the very moment I was about to do just that. 'Did neither of you get any sleep last night?'

I looked at William, and William set his head down on the table himself. 'Not really,' I said for the both of us.

'I see,' said Beatrice. 'The screams keep you up?'

That question woke me up quick enough. 'What do you know about those?'

'More than I'd like to. But I can only tell you the same things you might learn from others. Started some time after your grandmother died. Always at night, some nights worse than others. Tends to drive people away.'

'But you don't know what they are?'

Beatrice opened her mouth to answer – but the words didn't come. Perhaps she changed her mind, because she shook her head and turned back to the soup, and instead of giving us any answers about those strange screams that I was now sure I'd heard every single night, she said:

'You have to learn to ask the right questions.' She wouldn't say anything more until the soup was done.

To be fair, the soup was delicious, especially after a night without dinner and a morning walking all through the Blackwood without breakfast. I ate more of it than I probably should have, but at least I stopped well before William. Still, it wasn't until we were finished and full that Beatrice finally began to explain anything at all. She set out a pot of tea and a plate of biscuits, and at last, she started talking.

'I hadn't known before you told me that Lewis' spirit had been lost,' she said, getting down to business. 'But if that's what happened (and I must admit, I am only mildly surprised that it is), then it bodes nothing well, I'm afraid, because–'

'Couldn't his spirit just've wandered off?' interrupted William, and I had to fight down the urge to kick him under the table. 'I was actually wondering if he hadn't ended up *here*. I mean, you did say ghosts were attracted to places like this.'

But Beatrice shook her head. 'Ghosts and shades tend to haunt one of two places: the place where they died, or the place where they felt most alive. Sometimes those are the same place – more often than you'd expect, actually…'

Considering what she'd already said about Ravenscourt's shades, then that meant… 'Wait, but then how many people have died here?'

'More than I can tell you,' said Beatrice pointedly. 'But your father wasn't one of them, and so unless he felt unreasonably fond of the Rose Garden, we must conclude that he isn't here. No – the most likely explanation for the absence of Lewis' spirit is that someone didn't want him rested, because someone didn't want him to say anything about how he had died.'

'But *who*–?'

'Your father never told you why he left,' said Beatrice. She sank into her chair, as if the thought of what she was about to say were weighing her down. 'And I can't say I blame him. You know so little about your family. I'm sure that's the way Lewis would've wanted it, but now he's gone, even though we thought him far from harm, and you are here, despite everything. But we must begin at the beginning to get to the end. And it begins with your grandfather, Grahame – and Lily.'

So that's where she began, her tale long and rambling and sometimes nonsensical, as if she wanted to tell us a great many more things, but couldn't quite find the words. Still, the simplest facts of the story were clear. In short, our grandfather, Grahame Crowe, had never been a pleasant man – in fact, to hear Beatrice tell it, Grahame made Uncle Edward look downright friendly by comparison. Our grandfather drank, he yelled, he brawled, and by the time he was twenty-six, Grahame Crowe had made more personal enemies than most people make in a lifetime. Unfortunately for him, this made him one of Yorkshire's *least* eligible bachelors, which would've been bad news for us Crowes, seeing as how the whole family estate went to him.

And then came Lily.

No one was quite sure from where. There were rumours of course: some said that she was disgraced nobility, or that Grahame must've put her under a Curse – after all, no sane woman would've settled for him. Others claimed she was a member of the Fey, sent to lay spells on the town and reclaim it for the Court.

'But there's no such *thing* as Fey.'

'I'm just telling you how other people talk about it, child. Now hush up and listen.'

Wherever she came from, Grahame made her his wife, and soon they had two sons. Edward and Lewis grew up terrified of their father, who was cruel and violent as ever, and suspicious to the point of paranoia. And as they grew, the boys began to fight back. More often than not, it was Edward who started the arguments, leaving his older brother to take sides, and his mother to smooth things over after.

'And then,' said Beatrice, 'one night, about fifteen years ago, there was a fight.' I leaned forward to grasp every word: the gardener's voice had gone soft, and our tea lay forgotten on the table. 'I mean, there were always fights those days – between your uncle and your grandfather, arguing over the finances or his studies or whatnot. I've never liked chemistry – do you?'

She waited for us to shake our heads before continuing.

'But that night... that night was bitter cold. It was deep into December, you see, and this fight was worse than any that had come before. Things had been building up. Something terrible had happened – something far worse than a disagreement over tuition or classes. Your uncle and your grandfather stood ready to kill each other, and it was everything your father could do to stop them from it. But before either of them could land a blow – well... Lily died.' Beatrice shook her head.

'They say she just collapsed at the table. They couldn't save her. The undertaker was called, but it didn't take long for them to realize that Lily's spirit would never be rested, because she was already gone.'

'Just like Dad...' I breathed.

Beatrice nodded. 'Anyway, your father didn't stay around long after that. He fled with your mother. And... well, the rest of that, you know better than me.'

The cabin fell quiet, and for a full minute, I sat waiting for the gardener to say more. There was no way that was the whole story – there was too much she hadn't explained, too much that didn't make sense. It was as if she'd set out a puzzle with half the pieces missing. But she'd already decided she was done; she took a sip of her cold tea in silence, and it was up to me to ask:

'But... why did he leave?'

Beatrice avoided looking at me. She stood and wandered toward the window, lost in thought. 'There is much that you would know, and unfortunately, I cannot tell you most of it,' she said. 'Terrible things have happened here – in that house, in these woods. The trees whisper about them at night. I need help. I can't fix all of it, not by myself.'

William was frowning in confusion, and I couldn't say I blamed him. 'You want us to help you fix things?' I said.

Beatrice nodded.

'But... *how?*'

Beatrice turned suddenly toward the door, and I did too – something had twinged in the back of my mind, like a warning, as if someone had reached forward and pulled my hair, telling me to *watch out!* William looked up at us, he was about to ask us what had happened, what was wrong, but he didn't have the chance, because all at once, there was a knock on the door.

The Wards, I realized. Someone had come to the cabin, and the Wards had warned us.

'Come in!' said Beatrice from her place at the window.

The door burst open, and a chill breeze whirled throughout the room. Uncle Edward's butler stepped inside, ducking his head so as not to slam it on the lintel.

'Ah, Galen!' said Beatrice, cheerfully. You could never have told that she'd been discussing our grandmother's death just moments before. She gestured to the table, smiling. 'Would you like a cup of tea?'

The Butler, however, did not smile. 'I have come to collect the children,' he said.

'I guess I have kept them rather late.' Beatrice glanced out the window once more, where the light was already dimming, and everything was turning gold from sunset. I hadn't even realized we'd been an hour in the woods and cabin, much less four or five. The afternoon had passed.

'Indeed,' said the Butler, cracking his knuckles.

'Ahem, yes, well, I guess you should be going, you two. Wouldn't want to keep your uncle waiting.' Beatrice gave us a wink and a smile – the least reassuring wink and smile I'd ever encountered in my life – and ushered us out the door along with the Butler. 'It was lovely talking with you, Abigail, William!' she called as the Butler led us away. 'Do feel free to come by any time!'

She was soon swept away beyond the trees, as the Butler led us quickly down the forest path, pausing every few minutes to make sure we weren't lagging. The silence was smothering. With Beatrice, the wood had teemed with stories and strangeness, but with the Butler's stiff pace and the setting sun's blood-coloured light and the long, threatening shadows of the trees, the wood felt suddenly unsafe, every bird call and scurrying sound a threat. It wasn't until the gardener's cottage was left well behind us that the Butler finally spoke.

'Your uncle,' he said, 'was most dismayed that you did not make an appearance at lunch. I believe that Ellen was very clear about the rules, was she not.'

If he'd meant it as a question, it didn't sound like it. In fact, nothing we'd heard him say so far had any tone at all – his glares said more than his words did, and I got the feeling that he would prefer to glower and crack his knuckles rather than speak any day. In any case, he didn't seem to actually want any answer from us, because he continued: 'You are not to be out after nightfall. If your uncle had not sent me to fetch you, it is likely that unfavourable outcomes would have ensued. We are cutting it very close as it is.' Again, voice like an icy lake. Whatever unfavourable outcomes *would have ensued*, they didn't seem to matter much to him.

The screech of a wounded animal cut through the trees. William's hand was suddenly in mine.

The Butler glared behind him again, and for the first time, his voice wasn't toneless: there was a distinct hint of danger in it. 'Since you are new here – and guests – you will not be punished this time. However, from now on, you should know that you will either dine with your family when required, or not at all. When we reach the house, you will proceed straight to your rooms. You will not have dinner.'

I don't know which part worried me more: the fact that a second night without dinner was not considered a punishment, or the fact that this meant the only food we'd had in the past day was Beatrice's parsnip soup. My stomach was already starting to grumble, and I was tempted to devote the evening to breaking into the kitchens.

But that wasn't to be, because the worst part of the entire day was already waiting for us at the greenhouse doors. As soon as the Housekeeper spotted us coming out of the woods, she stalked forward and wasted no time dragging us back into the house.

'So,' she said, her croaking voice low and sinister. 'Now we think that Mummy's got our backs and the mean old housekeeper won't be allowed to do anything worth complaining about?' She jerked us through a door, ignoring William's 'ow!' as his arm hit the frame. 'So now we think we're free to run around and do as we please and listen to that gardener *witch*?'

I had to clench my teeth to stop myself from saying anything. We were in enough trouble.

'I wouldn't be able to get away with leaving even a single scratch on that pretty little face of yours,' she said, 'and more's the pity. But fortunately for both of us, there are *other* ways to make you cooperate. So don't go poking your noses into things you aren't involved in. It didn't end well for your father, and if I have any say in the matter, it won't end well for you either!'

'What would you know about our father?' The words were out of my mouth before I could stop myself.

'More than I care to!' spat the Housekeeper. 'He was a disobedient brat, and he came to the end he deserved–'

That was *enough*. The Housekeeper continued to wrench at my arm, but I'd stopped in the middle of the hall, and there was no way she was going to get me to move. 'You take that back.'

The Housekeeper rounded on me, but she was welcome to scowl all she liked. 'You watch your mouth, you ungrateful little–'

I pulled my arm from the Housekeeper's grip. 'I said *you take that back.*'

'Think your father's some kind of martyr here, do you? Well you might as well hear it from me now, whatever else your *mother*,' she spat the word like a curse, 'decides to threaten me with. Your lying, murdering rat of a father wasn't welcome here after what he did, and none of us were sorry to see him go, traitorous ba–'

'You dare insult my father like that!'

But the Housekeeper's face had twisted into a nasty grin. She wasn't just insulting us; she was *gloating* about it. 'Oh dear little girl,' she said, 'you'll hear it from others sooner or later. Did you really think your father just up and left simply to be with your shrew mother?' She laughed, bitterly, and her gnarled fingers clenched around my throat as she pushed me back against the wall. 'Your grandfather disowned him, and not a moment too soon. Not when he'd murdered his own mother!'

There was a moment that seemed to stretch forever, while the old toad's accusation hung darkly in the air. She stood, pinning me to the wall, but I was stuck on her words, trying to understand them, trying to make them make sense. No matter how I went over them, they didn't fit together correctly. They didn't fit together at all.

'You're *lying*,' was all I could say.

The Housekeeper laughed before finally letting me go. And without even giving us the satisfaction of an argument, she jerked us down the hall to our sitting room, shoved us inside, and shut the door behind herself as she left.

Even after the dust had settled and the Housekeeper's footsteps had faded down the hall, I could still feel her claws at my neck. William shook my shoulder.

'Are you alright, Abby?'

He took my arm, and he set me down on the couch, my hands still trembling from the encounter. There was so much Dad had never told us – so much that had seemed unimportant while he was here. But now, he was gone, and we hadn't even been able to bid a proper goodbye, and worst of all he would *never* be able to tell us the truth, to explain away the accusations, to warn us of the dangers. Because if the Housekeeper's lies proved anything, it was that when Dad left Ravenscourt, he must have had more than a good reason.

'We can't let her think she's gotten to us,' I said.

William sat down next to me. 'So what are we going to do, then?' he said.

The fire was burning to the coals and the room was growing cold. We were trapped in strange, unfriendly territory, with no way out. There was only one thing to do, really. 'We're going to find out why Dad left. We're going to find out what killed him. We're going to figure out what happened to him–'

William finished the thought for me: 'And we'll prove that old toad wrong when we do.'

Hide and Co Seek

'This is hopeless,' said William.

We were in our sitting room one morning not even a week after hearing Beatrice's tale. Finding the evidence we needed to prove Dad innocent was turning out to be harder than we'd expected, and it wasn't as if we'd been lazy about it. Over the past few days, we'd explored as much of the second floor as we could, scouring every desk and shelf and looking for hidden doors and panels by knocking on walls. With the help of my hairpins, William had opened every locked door we could find, and just the day before, we'd uncovered a stair off the dark hall that led to the upper stories of the house. The problem was that before we could so much as step foot on those stairs, the Housekeeper had caught us and dragged us back to our rooms.

'Locked doors are locked for a *reason!*' she'd yelled.

We'd found precious little else. Most of the locked doors simply led to abandoned rooms, filled with nothing but old, faded carpets and mouldering mothballs. The last night had been restless and full of scattered shrieks, and so now we were sitting by our fireplace, trying to see if we could pull anything else from the gardener's story.

V

'So, according to her,' said William, 'Uncle Edward and our grandfather got into a really bad fight.'

'And by the end of it, our grandmother was dead, and Dad had fled.'

William shook his head. 'That's strange too – Lily's death.'

'You mean the fact they couldn't rest her,' I said. That point had been bothering me too, ever since Beatrice mentioned it. Both our grandmother and Dad had died under mysterious circumstances, their spirits gone before anyone could give them a proper resting. In Dad's case, the Inquisitors had been quick to ask about murder. Even Beatrice had said that spirits didn't disappear without a reason and that it was likely someone had stolen it because they didn't want Dad's spirit to talk.

Except, that's where it got tricky, because of course a murderer wouldn't want their victim telling everyone exactly who killed them. But as far as we knew, there was no reason for anyone to want to kill Dad. Unless... What if there was something *else* that Dad might have had to tell? Something about why he'd fled, for instance? 'What do you think our grandfather and Uncle Edward were arguing about?' I asked aloud.

William shrugged. 'You could always ask Uncle Edward.'

I gave him his first look of the day. 'You're not serious.'

'Of course not! He'd probably decide you were being cheeky and serve you for dinner.'

I sank back down on the couch. 'I think we need to do more investigating. There *has* to be something–'

Footsteps sounded in the hall. It was time for breakfast, and the last thing we needed was to be caught talking about how to open locked doors. I shut my mouth just as the door flew open.

But it wasn't the maid with a plate of eggs and bacon, not this morning. Instead, the Housekeeper stalked into our room, yelled at us to get dressed, and dragged us to the dining hall, to sit with Mother, Uncle Edward, and two visitors: Mr. Silas Carver and his pale daughter.

Mr. Carver was a paunchy old man with a large, shiny forehead and a rat's tail of thin blond hair gathered at the nape of his neck. His pale suit had patches on the elbows, and he made a constant habit of cleaning the small, round spectacles that he wore perched on his nose. Uncle Edward introduced him to us as the town's mortician, though he really needn't have bothered, because within a few minutes, Mr. Carver started talking about his work, and within a few more, it became obvious that he was very fond of it, and before they'd even brought out the eggs, he began explaining – at great length and in even greater detail – the various processes involved in embalming dead people.

'Contrary to popular belief, the Deathmarks are done last,' he told us. 'The spirit of the deceased is usually secured in a significant item while the body itself is being preserved.' He shovelled eggs onto his plate, and then into his mouth, and if he saw how Mother's face blanched, he didn't seem to care.

The maid laid a platter of bacon in front of me, but I pushed it aside, all my focus on Mr. Carver. Perhaps he could answer a few pressing questions. 'What if there isn't a spirit?' I asked, ignoring the *tsk* I knew I would get from Mother, and carefully avoiding Uncle Edward's suspicious glare.

Mr. Carver chewed his eggs thoughtfully, before scrubbing an invisible smudge from his glasses with his napkin. 'It takes powerful magic to completely sever a newly dead spirit from its body or deathbed,' he answered finally. 'In most cases, when a spirit can't be found, the undertaker should notify the Inquisitors at once.'

'So only a magician would be able to–'

Mother set down her silverware. 'Abigail, stop pestering the man.'

But Mr. Carver wasn't at all pestered. In fact, he seemed flattered by the interest. 'Other than a trained and certified mortician,' he said to my unfinished question, 'only a magician with solid knowledge of the necromantic arts would have the ability to capture and contain a severed spirit, it's true. But of course, a magician's reasons for doing so would hardly be considered... wholesome.'

'What do you mean?'

'You understand, of course, that an undertaker severs a spirit only in order to rest it?' said Mr. Carver with a bland smile. 'You see, without a mortician's skill and a completed resting, the spirits of our loved ones might linger – turning into shades or worse. The resting allows the spirit to pass on and prevents any magician from taking control of it to serve their own ends.'

'That's... very interesting, Mr. Carver,' said Mother weakly.

He turned his smile on her, before stuffing a piece of toast into his mouth. But that still left some very important questions, not the least of which was:

'What would a magician want with a severed spirit?'

The table went still, Mother frowning at me as William and the mortician's daughter looked down at their plates. Uncle Edward chewed a mouthful of bacon, and when, at last, he swallowed it, he was the first to break the silence. 'A most fascinating question,' he said. I didn't need to look at him to know that he was staring at me. 'Perhaps you could enlighten us, Silas?'

Mother had gone death-pale.

'Simply out of pure conjecture,' began Mr. Carver, 'There are a few things I could think of.' He removed his glasses, scrubbed them, and held them up to the light, as if looking for the answers in his lenses. 'The most obvious would be, of course, merely to prevent a spirit from being rested – and perhaps, at the resting, from speaking out against the magician. In that case, the magician would want to find a way to completely destroy the spiritual remains. Otherwise, the spirit would decay into a shade. Other than that... well, Curses often require a spiritual sacrifice – controlling a victim's actions without direct intervention by a magician himself requires more power than simpler Commands. And of course, the magician may simply wish to keep the spirit around–'

There was a clatter as Mother dropped her fork. She recovered herself with a whispered 'pardon,' but her hands continued to tremble as she picked up her silverware and rearranged the food on her plate.

Mr. Carver seemed to realize, suddenly, that he'd upset her. He coughed a little and replaced his glasses. 'But that is all conjecture, and hardly cheerful. What was I talking about? Oh, yes. Preparing the body. So, after the spirit is secured, all the vital fluids must be flushed out.' He took a long, loud slurp of his tea. 'And then they must be replaced with formaldehyde, which is done intravenously – through the veins.'

Mother very politely excused herself.

The mortician's daughter, Samantha Carver, was hardly better. With her flat, blond hair and watery green eyes, she looked like the sort of distressed damsel that a romance novelist would call 'limpid,' which is really just a fancy way of saying empty-headed as air. It didn't help matters that she spoke in a high-pitched drone that seemed to come out entirely through her nose.

'Do stay a moment!' she said, cornering us in the hall just after breakfast. 'I'm afraid we didn't get much chance to talk at the table, Abby – you don't mind if I call you Abby, do you?'

Of course I minded, and I'm sure the fact that I minded was obvious by the way I winced, but if Samantha Carver noticed, she certainly didn't show it. Instead, she took my arm as if we were dear old friends, and began leading me down the hallway, William trailing after us for lack of other options. 'It is so wonderful to finally meet you two,' she said as we walked, her nasally voice gushing out of her in a stream of words without any pauses for full stops or general punctuation. 'To think you've been here nearly two weeks and we haven't met before this, why it's simply unbelievable I mean certainly I heard about your father, I was very sorry to hear about it, and I know you must be going through a rough time but believe me—'

I was cringing. Samantha was exactly the sort of snotty girl that I'd gone through pains to avoid in my catechism classes – the kind that would've fawned over the Dame Inquisitor and leapt at any chance to demonstrate how 'nice' she was. But even if she'd been perfectly pleasant, she would *still* have been an annoying problem, because there was no way we were going to be able to break into any upper rooms or open any locked doors or uncover any clues about Dad's exile if she insisted on tailing us everywhere.

'But come,' Samantha said. 'There must be something to do here besides listen to me, why don't we go outside, it is such wonderful weather or perhaps a game?'

At that, I perked up. A game? Perhaps there was a way to get rid of her after all. 'A game would be lovely!' I said, forcing myself to smile at her. 'And of course, in a house such as this one, we must play Hide and Seek.'

'But of course! What a lovely—'

'But,' I said, to keep her from letting out another stream of non-stop words, 'I'm no good at seeking, so surely you wouldn't mind being It? Just for the first round.'

Thankfully, she didn't complain. And so, she covered her eyes, and William and I spun her around, and as she started to count backward from one hundred–

'One *hundred*?' she asked. 'Are you sure?'

'Yes, it's got to be one hundred.'

–I grabbed William's hand, and we made our getaway, racing away from Samantha and through the halls, barrelling toward the dark hall and the locked door that led to the upper floors of the house.

With the first days of December, the house had grown even colder and greyer, and the halls lay nearly empty. There wasn't a large staff to begin with, and you couldn't blame the maids for wanting to stay in the oven-warmed kitchens, instead of venturing through the drab, winding corridors with their chill drafts. Still, I didn't dare slow down until we'd left Samantha far behind, her counting silenced by the sheer size of the house.

'Shouldn't we be looking for places to hide?' asked William.

'We're not playing Hide and Seek,' I told him.

William's face lit up as he realized what I meant. 'Oooooh.'

A few turns brought us to the long dark hall with its locked doors, and I handed one of my hairpins to William, keeping a lookout for any sign of the Housekeeper while he picked the lock. The halls stayed empty and quiet, though somewhere further into the house, a sad melody drifted up to us from an untuned piano – I wondered if perhaps it was Mother plucking those notes from the keys. It wasn't as if she had much else to do these days.

William managed to open the door, and we hurried up the stairs. The music faded as we climbed, and at last, we reached a landing, stepping out into a wide hallway. The hall was lined with tapestries, dozens of them, all of them with strange, faded images, each one hanging in one of the shallow alcoves that lined the walls all the way down the hall. There was nowhere to go but forward, the strange images glaring down at us–

Voices sounded at the other end of the hall.

'It's Uncle Edward!' hissed William, just in time for us to duck sideways into one of the alcoves. The voices grew louder as Uncle Edward and Mr. Carver turned down the corridor toward us, their footsteps echoing while they continued their discussion.

'It can't be correct–' Uncle Edward was saying. 'If there'd been any hint of this sort of thing before–'

I pulled William as far back from the hall as we could go, hoping against hope that the men would miss us. We weren't supposed to be here – the rules were very clear about that – and I didn't want to know what punishment they'd give us for breaking through one of the doors. Still, the alcove was far too shallow, even though I was pressing myself as far back as I could manage against the tapestry, leaning into the wall behind it–

Except there was no wall.

We went tumbling backward. I had to bite down a curse as we stumbled through the hidden doorway, tumbling into the space on the other side, just as the men came to a stop right in front of the alcove where we'd been hiding not a moment before.

'You see, of course, what I mean,' said Uncle Edward. A sliver of a gap between the edge of the tapestry and the wall gave us just the barest view of them. 'I haven't been able to test it properly yet, but if this preliminary reaction is any indication–'

'I wouldn't expect a single bad reaction to be completely indicative,' replied Mr. Carver, removing his glasses and wiping them with a worn handkerchief. 'It may take some time for any effects to show – the boy is, after all, a rather unique specimen.'

'But if we're treating the symptoms and not the disease–' the men continued down the hall, and I couldn't help but breathe in relief as their voices faded.

The question now, of course, was where we had ended up. I could count on William to have his matches with him, and in a flash, he held one of their tiny flames in his fingers. We stood in a corridor running behind the tapestries in the main hall – apparently each and every one of them had been hiding an empty doorway – and at the very end, a rickety, wooden stairway spiralled upward, into–

'Ouch!' exclaimed William as the match singed his fingers. 'Da–'

'Don't curse.'

'Sorry.'

'It doesn't matter much anyway,' I said. 'We can feel our way up the stairs. There's no need to risk burning the thing down – it looks quite beat up as it is. Take my hand, if you like.'

So, hand in hand, we crept forward, past the empty doorways and their worn tapestries, and up the old staircase. I had to reach out blindly, running my hand along the rough, peeling walls, up the splintering banister. The stairs groaned with every step we took, and every few steps, the damp clutch of cobwebs against my face made me shudder, but at last, we were at the top: there was no handrail left. Instead, I found a cold, metal doorknob.

The door creaked as I opened it. We were standing at the end of a short, murky hall perched on the fourth floor of the house. Gas lamps, dusty and translucent as ghosts, stood guard along the walls. There was no light in the corridor except for a bit of musty sunlight, drifting in through a single window at the other end of the hall, curtained with ribbons of webbing and dust. Beyond, the Blackwood trees were swaying. It took a moment for my eyes to adjust.

There were only two doors on this hall: the one on the right was firmly closed, while the other one, on the left, swung on its hinges. I pushed that one completely open and stepped into the room beyond.

I paused, unable to go a step further. The room had been a bedroom once: in the centre of the floor, a broken mahogany frame held up a bare mattress. To the left, a three-legged (formerly four-legged) desk leaned against the wall like a drunk, and the carpeted floor was covered in dead leaves. The smell of old soil lay thick in the air.

William came to a stop next to me. 'It looks just like Dad's study,' he breathed.

The signs were everywhere: there were the planters on the windowsills, the books stacked messily (and sideways) on the bookshelves, the dry vines that covered the walls like scraps of wallpaper. I drifted into the room. The crippled desk was covered in a thick layer dust, and I ran my fingers over the surface, revealing the shine underneath. Dad had left behind a few small treasures. A beautifully painted globe spun slowly in mid-air, hovering over its magnetic base. Light scattered through the cracked lens of a magnifying glass, its hinged arm starting to rust. There was a photograph as well – Mother peering out of the frame, her face young and strange and warped by water, but Mother all the same.

A tiny bundle of flowers gathered dust next to the picture, their dry, papery petals nearly crumbling under their own weight. Touch-me-nots: Dad had always kept a pot of them blooming somewhere in the house.

I remembered when he first introduced me to those flowers, showing how they would bloom at the lightest touch of a person's fingers. 'Everything has a mind of its own, its own spirit,' he'd said. 'Everything that's alive, anyway, and then some.'

That day, he'd given me his ring and taught me the First Defence, explaining how important it was to be able to shield your mind from others who would try to control it.

'The First Defence is always with you,' he'd said. 'No mind, however weak, is defenceless. But knowing how to *use* that defence, how to consciously protect yourself, makes it that much harder for anyone to turn your own thoughts against you. This ring will help you with that.'

It was just a plain silver ring, small enough for Dad to wear on his pinkie, but too big for every one of my fingers except my right thumb. Still, by focusing on it, I could channel my thoughts and clear my mind, making it easy to find that single thread of spirit to protect me.

Or, at least, *easier* – that first day, it hadn't been much more than a tiny wisp, knotted at the top of my skull. Still, I'd managed to untangle it, and Dad had been delighted: I'd won a kiss on the forehead for the effort.

'Promise me you won't tell anyone, Abigail. Not even Mum,' he'd said, handing me the blooming touch-me-nots.

I'd kept that promise.

'Abby,' said William, drawing me back to the dusty room in Ravenscourt's upper stories. 'Abby, look.'

He was kneeling next to the fireplace, and he pulled a cracked leather book out of the cold ashes. He held it out to me, the pages burned by fire, the cover caked with soot. I eased the cover open. The first page held Dad's handwriting:

Lewis Crowe's personal property
DO NOT TOUCH
(That means you, Edward)

It was a diary – Dad's diary, the entries anything but regular, sometimes with months or even years passing between the date of one page and the next. Near the end, a faded photograph had been tucked into the pages – a woman, her black hair stark against her pale, haughty face. The back of the photograph told me it was Lily Crowe, our grandmother.

She'd been beautiful, though her wide eyes held something dark in them and she most definitely wasn't smiling. I held the book closer to my face to try to make out the words:

> ...just recently returned from Tara speaks to their enduring ties with the Court. Mother, of course, only complains that we should have nothing to do with them: her prejudices are rather ingrained for someone who openly defied the Queen. I'd almost think she was jealous of Mrs. Astor – and not without reason...

The names meant nothing to me, though I wondered what Dad meant by 'the Court.' For some reason, those words sent a shiver up my spine, the same way they had when Beatrice had mentioned them in the woods, summoning up stories about the Fey. But I was being silly – of course Father hadn't meant the Fey Court – that was nonsense. I flipped forward to see what Dad's last entry had been–

But someone had ripped out the pages. There was only a ragged gap where Dad would've written about his last days at Ravenscourt – nothing at all left, except for the top of a single torn page, clinging precariously to the back cover:

> ...Edward's fool stubbornness may soon turn dangerous – and not just for...

And that was it. Without the rest of the pages, it was impossible to know what Dad had meant – stubbornness about what? Dangerous for who? Only one thing was clear: he'd been afraid for Uncle Edward–

Or, perhaps... *because* of him?

A thought had started gnawing at the back of my mind: a thought that I realized I must have been thinking without even knowing it, without wanting to know it. Seven years ago, Dad had kicked Uncle Edward out of our home with an order never to return. And Uncle Edward had respected that order, he hadn't stepped foot in our house again – not until the day of Dad's funeral. But why did he come back now? How had he known? And what if his return hadn't just been a show of brotherly concern?

What if he'd had something to do with Dad's death?

'A-Abby?' gasped William.

I looked up. My brother's face had gone pale, and he was shivering, and immediately, I began calculating: how many weeks had it been? How long since he'd last–

His eyes rolled back into his head, and he collapsed in a heap on the floor.

'William!'

I had to dodge his kicking feet as I rushed to his side, cradling his head to prevent him from slamming it into the floor. You couldn't hold down a person in a fit – Dad's warnings had always been clear: get him away from the wall, away from the furniture, away from anything that could injure him. Remove his tie, loosen the collar of his shirt. Other than that, you couldn't do anything – that was the worst part. There was nothing to do but wait it out.

So I did it: collar, tie, all of it. And I waited. One minute, two. And all the while, William continued to thrash, completely insensible, his eyes rolling. How long had it been now? Four minutes? Five? None of his fits had ever lasted more than a minute or two – and yet...

The fit wasn't calming. If anything, it was only getting worse.

The urge to hold him down – to try to shake him back into consciousness – was overwhelming, but I knew it could only injure him: there was nothing I could do – *nothing*. His fists were flailing, the convulsions growing even more violent. And then–

The room began to tremble.

William's feet were slamming against the floorboards, and that could've explained the way the floor shook – but then the window began to rattle, and even the walls began to shake. Books and pictures and planters shuddered on their shelves. This must've been what it was like to witness an earthquake: everything shaking uncontrollably, the world threatening, with every moment, to fall into complete chaos, the floor ready to crumble–

But how could that be? Why here? Why *now*?

A flowerpot jittered toward the edge of its shelf, and I lunged forward to shield William from the shards as the pot smashed to pieces on the floor. I pulled him into the middle of the room, but there was no escaping – everything was shifting, shaking, shattering. I tried to hold him steady, tried to protect him against it all–

The next moment, I was crashing into the bookcase. Something had thrown me backward – some impossible force. I pushed myself up from the floor, dazed. Another pot crashed next to me. Splinters cut across my cheek. I tasted blood.

Before I could even attempt to stand, strong hands had grabbed me under my arms, and someone was lifting me to my feet.

I couldn't see William.

'He is being taken care of,' said the Butler as he pulled me up. I must've called William's name out loud.

Behind the Butler, in the middle of the room, Uncle Edward and Mr. Carver were bending over my brother. Mother was there too, clinging to the door frame, holding herself up against those impossible tremors.

Uncle Edward drew a long needle from some pocket. I had to look away as he sank the point into William's neck. At once, my brother fell quiet, and at the same moment, the room was still, the tremors and the fit vanishing at the same instant, leaving behind only a breathless silence. They'd been connected somehow, my brother's fit and the quake.

But that was impossible. Whatever had happened – earthquake, explosion, a dozen other things I couldn't imagine – there was no way for it to have anything to do with William. Not even magic was capable of such things, and yet–

William lay dreadfully still.

'What did you *do*?' I realized I was screaming. I struggled against the Butler. Part of me wanted to punch Uncle Edward, punch him, kick him, shake answers out of him, though I wasn't sure he had them. But the Butler didn't let me budge.

Mother was staring. 'Edward?'

'He is quite fine,' said Uncle Edward. 'Just a little sedative to relax the muscles and calm the seizure.'

But I was still shaking.

'Should we take him to his room?' said Mother.

'I do not believe that would be best,' answered Uncle Edward. 'Better that we set him up in my office, where we can keep an eye on his condition.

Mother hesitated. 'You won't–'

'We will take very good care of him. I think the best we can do for now is observation – there are a few medicines that may be of use. But Maris, you should distract yourself. There is nothing you can do for him at the moment. We must be patient.'

Mother released a heavy breath, then nodded.

'Silas,' said Uncle Edward, turning to Mr. Carver. 'Please see to it that Maris is taken care of. Galen and I will treat the boy.' His eyes shifted to me. 'I also want to talk to Abigail for a bit, to see what events led up to this incident.'

Mr. Carver wasted no time ushering Mother out the door. She didn't look back, and I was left to face Uncle Edward and his Butler, while William still lay unconscious on the floor.

'You can let her go, Galen.'

At last, the Butler loosened his grip, and I was able to get to William. I suddenly saw how small and vulnerable he really was, even as Uncle Edward helped me roll him over onto his side, so that he wouldn't risk choking. And when Uncle Edward stood once more, I stayed kneeling at my brother's side, brushing dirt from his jacket.

'So,' began Uncle Edward quietly. 'We presume we are above the rules of this house?'

I refused to look up at him. 'We just wanted to explore,' I said. 'We didn't think we were doing anything wrong.'

'And it turned out well, did it?'

At that, I clenched my fists. William's fit had nothing to do with any of the rules we were or weren't breaking, but I didn't think Uncle Edward would let me say that.

'The rules that have been laid down for you are in place for your own protection. If you defy – if you circumvent them – I cannot guarantee your safety, nor that of your brother. If only one of the staff had known where you two were, we would have found you sooner and perhaps prevented...' He shook his head. 'But the mistake has been made. As for you, you are to stay in the rooms of the East Wing, unless accompanied by your mother, the Housekeeper, or myself–'

'But–'

He held up his hand. 'You are not to leave the East Wing without an escort, that is all there is to it. After an incident such as this, I have half a mind to confine you to your room indefinitely...'

I swallowed my protests. He could probably do much worse than demand I spend quality time with the Housekeeper. But that still left one issue: 'And William?'

'What about him?'

'Wh– what will you do to him?'

Uncle Edward paused at that, frowning at me in confusion. And then, impossibly, he laughed. It wasn't a happy sort of laugh – it was cold and mirthless and full of disbelief. 'Abigail, my dear, I must wonder what you think of me? Rest assured, William will be well taken care of. We will observe him, do what we can for him, and allow him to rest. With any luck, he should be returned to your care within a few days.'

'But that wasn't just any fit. It's never been that bad before–' And it had never rattled so much as a teacup, much less caused an entire house to tremble, though I stopped myself before saying any of that. The idea that William's fit could've caused those tremors was more than impossible: it defied every single law of reality that I could think of.

'Which is why we must take every precaution in caring for him,' said Uncle Edward. 'I'm sure your brother's illness has been a source of concern for you, but believe me when I say I will do everything in my power to aid his recovery.'

'Do you even know what he has?'

Uncle Edward tilted his head, considering me, eyes narrowed in thought. 'A rare form of epilepsy,' he said at last. 'Incredibly rare, but perhaps not beyond my abilities to fix.' My glare told him all he needed to know about what I thought of that. He sighed. 'Abigail, I had hoped my distance over the past few years would not prevent you from seeing me as family. You must believe me when I say that I want only to help you, your brother, and your mother in this difficult time. Your father, after all, was my brother, and though we were–'

'Do you know why he left?'

The question brought him to a stop. 'Excuse me?'

'It's just, he never mentioned this place to us. Ever.' I was ready to get answers, if he insisted on saying he wanted to help. 'Apparently he wanted to forget it. And I want to know why. What exactly happened to–'

He didn't let me finish. At once, he turned to the Butler. 'Galen, please escort Abigail to her room. I will be in the laboratory.'

I managed to shake my head at my uncle one last time, before the Butler grabbed my arm again. He steered me out of the room, even as Uncle Edward turned back to William. And then we were in the hallway. The Butler shut the door, and there was nothing left to do but let him lead me away.

'THE GROUNDS ARE RATHER UNPLEASANT AT NIGHT'

Uncle Edward's punishment – his order that I wasn't to go anywhere without the Housekeeper to babysit me – turned out to be completely unnecessary, because with William gone, there was really no reason at all to go anywhere further than our sitting room. In fact, I spent most of the days after William's fit leafing through novels in my room, turning my bedroom lock whenever I heard the maids coming in to leave breakfast on the sitting room table, and ignoring the Housekeeper when she yelled at me to come down for meals. At first they tried to starve me out, but after three days of no lunch and no dinner, Mother must've taken pity on me. The next day's breakfast was bigger than usual, and soon followed by a plate of sandwiches for lunch.

Still, I barely picked at it. With William gone, I just didn't have the appetite. Whatever else Uncle Edward decided, the real punishment was the fact that they'd taken William away. There were very few times that we'd ever been separated for more than a few hours. Even when William first started having his fits, Dad had always allowed me to stay by his side as he recovered.

But now, Uncle Edward had spirited him off somewhere, and worse than that, they refused to tell me a single thing.

Another day passed, and still no news. When breakfast arrived the next morning, I let it go cold. If they weren't going to let me know what was going on with my brother, then I would just have to go and find out myself.

I had only just stepped out the door when Mother caught me. She'd been waiting for me – how long, I couldn't guess.

'Abigail,' she said. 'It's good to see you up and about. We were getting wor–'

'Where is he? Can I see him?'

Mother sighed, and she reached out to brush a stray curl of hair out of my face. I shook it back into place, ignoring her frown. 'We're all worried about William, dear, but your uncle is taking very good care of him. You just have to trust that it'll work out,' she said. 'We should get you out of the house, in any case – get some colour into you. I was thinking of going into the village.'

At any other time, I would've jumped at the possibility of getting as far away from Ravenscourt house as possible – but now? There was no way I was going to leave while William was stuck here somewhere, sick. I shook my head, and went to push past her, but she stopped me:

'Now, Abigail–'

'I don't want to go to the village, I just want–'

Mother tsked. 'Don't be so sour. Samantha Carver's here, and she's eager to see you as well.'

'I *definitely* don't want to go anywhere with Samantha Carver.'

'Abigail,' said Mother, her voice taking on a tone that said I was being exasperating.

But I was exasperated too. 'Why won't you let me see William? And what makes you think Uncle Edward's any different from all those other doctors? None of *them* were able to do anything–'

'These things take *time*,' said Mother. 'And I know how difficult this is, but Abigail, you need to trust me. And you ought to trust your uncle – he's doing everything he can–'

'Well I *don't* trust him, and I don't care,' I said, the words tumbling out of me. I couldn't hold them back any longer. 'Dad didn't like him, and I don't have to either – you knew that much when you brought us here. And I don't understand why we're even here! You're the only one who wanted to come. I just want to go *home*.'

It was true. I knew Mother could see as much, but she didn't say a thing. All she did was stand there with that small, tight frown, while I fiddled with my ring, trying to steady my breaths.

'Wash up and get dressed,' she said finally. 'I expect you downstairs by the hour.'

And that was the end of it. There was no use arguing. Mother stared me down, until at last I turned back to the room, shutting the door behind me – slamming it, rather, though I hadn't meant to. And when I took more than an hour to change my clothes, running a brush through my hair over and over in front of the bathroom mirror to avoid facing Mother again, she sent Samantha up to fetch me down anyway.

Uncle Edward's coach took us into the village, the rutted roads making the wheels bounce and rattle, the sunlight drifting down through the Blackwood trees. The window was cool against my forehead, though even that couldn't soothe away my annoyance, especially not with Samantha chattering away at Mother the entire time:

'I'm so glad you'll finally get to see the village, I can't believe this is the first time you've been off the grounds, though I don't blame you, Ravenscourt is very pretty, I much like the gardens in spring but I'm sure they're all withered by now, my brother Isaac is very fond of the roses though he's off at university for the moment, still we're expecting him back within the fortnight–'

At last, we pulled into the main square of the village. The coachman jerked the horses to a stop, and I escaped from the carriage as quickly as I could. In front of us, in the very centre of the square, a clock tower stood stark against the bright sky. It was built of the same stuff as the house: black stone, smooth and bleak. Its long shadow cast the houses at the edge of the square in darkness, its ivory face staring out over the town.

'That's the clock tower,' Samantha informed me, straightening her hair bow.

'I'd noticed.'

Mother paused just long enough to let us know that she would be spending the afternoon with someone called Mrs. Carol, and that the Carols would see her home, which meant that we were free to take the coach home by ourselves whenever we chose – so long, of course, as we were back before nightfall. Which was all very well and good for her, except that it meant she'd brought me all the way here *just* to abandon me to Samantha. The girl didn't waste a second. As soon as Mother turned toward the church, Samantha took my hand and decided to give me a grand tour of Corvick.

'You've already seen the clock tower and over there's the church, don't ever get into an argument with the pastor,' she said, completely oblivious to the fact that I couldn't care less. She pointed out the apothecary, the inn, and the junk shop with the same breathless enthusiasm, as well as the doorsteps of everyone from the Mayor to Mrs. Mews, whom I gathered was the resident cat lady.

Down a tiny side street, we ended up in the tinker's shop, a small, cosy space filled with clocks and ticking and all sorts of strange gadgets. As we stepped inside, a bell rang out to announce our entrance, and a clockwork mouse scurried between our feet, its mechanical paws clicking as it disappeared through the back door.

A moment later, a boy emerged, turning the key in the mouse's back to rewind it. He was tall, but round, with black hair let down to his shoulders and a thick frame that strained against his waistcoat. His eyes were hidden behind a pair of wire-rimmed glasses, but as soon as he spotted Samantha, his face lit up, and he set the mouse back down on the floor, letting it scurry away before waving her over.

Finally she'd found someone else to bother. I was more than happy to leave them to their conversation, and as soon as it became clear that they were suitably distracted with each other, I took the opportunity to make my exit, slipping out the door and back into the street.

I was ready to head back to the square – perhaps even take the carriage back to the house – but it turned out that finding your way through the village wasn't nearly as straightforward as Samantha had made it seem. I followed the alley back toward the main road, but instead of reaching the road, I ended up on a street that twisted and turned down the hill to the lower part of the village before coming to a sudden end. Somehow I'd missed the turn. Doubling back, there was no sign of the tinker's shop, and none of the houses were ones that I'd seen before. There were no signs or numbers that I could see – not that I would've recognized the names if there had been – and it seemed that every street had been designed for the express purpose of keeping people lost.

At the end of it all, I found myself on a lonely back road, a low brass fence wrought with Wardmarks separating me from the cemetery. Beyond the rows of graves, the church stood guard, and I remembered that the church sat almost directly on the town square.

The problem, of course, was the Ward. Cemeteries were sacred ground, and even if I'd fancied a stroll among the dead, the Gravewards were there *specifically* to stop me from abusing the churchyard by using it as a short cut. I didn't much fancy getting caught in them. But there was no end to the road in sight – it continued past the cemetery and into the Blackwood, plunging straight into the forest – and if there were any sort of turn or side road or bend that led back to the village, I certainly couldn't see it. As for turning around, there was no telling how long I could stay lost in that maze of alleyways. As far as I could tell, it had already taken me the better part of an hour to get *here.*

How bad could the Graveward be? Worse than another hour of aimless wandering? Worse than having to walk three or four miles to try and find another road into the village? Worse than getting lost in the Blackwood at night?

Probably. But at that moment, it didn't feel like it, and that meant I'd already made my decision.

Before I could decide to unmake it, I lifted myself over the fence and dropped down into the grass on the other side. Immediately, my breath turned to ice in my chest. I had to close my eyes for a moment, twisting my ring, counting my breaths, and willing the First Defence to warm me against the chill. The air was cold – unnaturally cold, *Graveward* cold – and I found myself wondering if it wasn't already too late to turn back–

But no, the church was right *there* – not even half a minute's walk away. If I held my defences, I could make it. I took another deep breath to tighten the threads of my Second Defence and focused on my ring, the warmth of the First Defence cocooning me head-to-toe, though somehow the chill of the Ward remained. Not quite there, but not quite gone either. Still, that was the best I could do. I set off down the row of graves, following the path to the church.

Whenever I'd heard stories about people caught in Gravewards, I'd always wondered how the trespassers could stay trapped in a cemetery for so long. Of course I knew that the Ward was *meant* to keep you from escaping and also that it was spirit work, close enough to magic to be monitored by the Inquisitors, meaning that, to some extent, it took control of your mind. But I figured that there must be *some* part of you that would be able to resist it – at least for two steps, even if you didn't have any defences.

It turns out that it's impossible to imagine what it's actually like until it happens to you. Two steps into the cemetery, and an icy chill began seeping into my skin. Three, and I was shivering uncontrollably. I twisted my ring and forced myself forward one more step, and then another, before I realized I couldn't turn back: when I looked over my shoulder, the fence had disappeared, leaving only an infinite row of graves – *there was no back*. I could only try to keep breathing and push myself forward. But with every step I took, the air grew colder, the sky darker, every inch was like wading through mud. I was trying my best to keep my eyes focused on the bell tower of the church, but it slipped further and further away, evaporating into a haze of mist and fog, and the world was melting, twisting, collapsing, and worst of all, there were *things* crawling between the graves – things with crooked fingers and too many legs, things with too many eyes, but no faces, things that disappeared as soon as I tried to look at them. I realized there could be worse things than Wards in a graveyard, so many more worse things than a Ward–

After all, this was where we buried the dead. This was where we put spirits to rest. But where did spirits go after their Restings?

The air was choking cold, and every muscle in my body had started to tremble. The church had disappeared, and so had the fence, and I was drifting through a wasteland of endless graves. My body had grown unbearably heavy, impossible to move. If I left it behind, it would be easier – if I could just lift myself out of that heavy, clumsy contraption, I could drift completely free. And it would be easy to do it – so easy...

The bent, whispering creatures in the shadows clustered close – close but always out of sight – as I sank to my knees in the grey, lifeless grass. I couldn't breathe.

Was *this* what it was like to be dead?

I tried to find the colourless sky, but my head was too heavy, I couldn't lift it. And then–

There was something coming toward me across the plain – something brighter and stronger and taller than the shadows, something that made them fall silent and creep back into the darkness. And as that brilliant light came to a stop in front of me, the entire world seemed to exhale. The shadows faded, everything took back its edges, the bells of the church chimed the half hour. The graveyard sat quiet in the hazy afternoon sun, the stones peaceful and still. I gasped for breath, my entire body gulping down air like a thirsty man gulps down water.

'Better?' said the light in front of me.

Except it wasn't a light at all anymore. It was just a girl, maybe a couple years older than me, with black hair cut in a sharp line at her shoulders, wearing a smart grey dress without ruffles or lace. She peered down at me, her dark, upturned eyes showing more curiosity than concern, one eyebrow lifted in a question. She stepped forward and held out her hand.

I took it.

'Now,' said the girl, once she'd helped me back to my feet. Everything was still a little shaky, but she didn't seem to care much about that. 'You'd best tell me what you're doing here, quick, lest I pin you for a grave robber. You weren't trying to gather bodies for golems, were you?'

'I– what?'

'You got caught in the Graveward,' drawled the girl. 'I'm trying to figure out what your excuse is.'

'I was trying to get back to the square,' I managed after a minute. My tongue still felt oddly heavy, even if everything else was mostly back to normal.

'The square?' The girl's eyes went wide in something between confusion and amusement. 'Trespassing a Graveward to use the cemetery as a shortcut? Are you some special kind of daft?'

There wasn't much I could say to that, other than: 'I got lost.'

Everything was still quivering slightly, and the girl shook her head, as if already regretting her decision to save me from the Ward. Slowly, I managed to recover myself. My breathing evened out, and I twisted my ring to steady my defences. A thin breeze whistled among the graves. The girl frowned at my hands for a moment, before catching my eyes once again.

'That's an impressive spell you used,' she said finally. 'Most people are lucky to last half as long – even if they do bring a counter spell with them.'

I blinked at her. 'Spell?'

'That thing you did with your breath and that ring.'

I looked down at my hands, before glaring back up at the girl. 'That wasn't a spell.'

'Sure looked like one,' said the girl with a smirk.

'It was no more magic than Deathmarks or Gravewards.'

'Who says those things *aren't* magic?'

'They're protections *against* magic,' I said. 'Everyone knows that.'

She gave me a pitying look. 'I bet you believe everything an Inquisitor tells you,' she said, laughing as the heat rose to my face. 'Not that it matters at this point, because magician or not, you've just been caught trespassing a Graveward, and *I* have to decide what to do with you. I *could* just leave and let the Ward take care of you itself, but that's never pleasant. Perhaps you'd like me to call an Inquisitor? You can explain your spell that isn't a spell to him.'

'Do I *look* like a magician?'

'I didn't know magicians looked any particular way,' said the girl. 'They might very well look like warty old ladies caught enchanting their cats, or perhaps nobles secretly laying Curses from their closets, but they're just as likely to be little girls trying to cross a Graveward with nothing but a ring to protect them–'

'What does that make *you*, then?' I asked.

The girl sank into an exaggerated curtsy. 'Emily Carol, the pastor's daughter and unofficial Ward-keeper, grave-keeper, and record-keeper of the dead, lucky for you.' She looked me up and down one more time for measure. 'And I think you must be the Crowe girl, if I'm not mistaken.'

'Abigail,' I said before I could stop myself.

'Pleasure to meet you, Abigail Crowe,' said Emily, baring her teeth in the slightest hint of a smile. 'I must admit I've been hoping to run into you, though I never quite expected to be rescuing you from the Graveward.'

That was a surprise. If I'd not-quite-trusted the girl before, I definitely didn't trust her now. 'Why, exactly, did you want to meet me, Miss Keeper-of-the-Dead?'

'Curiosity,' drawled Emily with a shrug. 'You must admit, your family is most… well, most *curious*. I'm sure even *you've* heard the stories by now.'

'And which stories would those be?' I asked, trying to keep my voice light, though it was obvious that I was bristling. Emily moved closer, circling in, preparing to strike:

'Tell me,' she said. 'What's it like to have a *murderer* for a father?'

I refused to let myself flinch at the accusation, setting my jaw and matching Emily's stare with my own. 'I don't know what you're talking about.'

'Really? Because from what I've heard, Lewis Crowe was disowned for murdering his own mother. Murder is a rather fascinating profession, when you think about it–'

'Except my father was a botanist, not a murderer–'

'Who said he couldn't be both?' said Emily, flashing another of her disconcerting smiles. When I refused to give that question the courtesy of an answer, she continued: 'But then, there are some parts of the story that don't *quite* make sense. For example, most people say that your father confessed to the crime – which, considering the circumstances, would have been a very *stupid* thing to do. Absent spirits don't talk.'

'So now he's not just a murderer, but a magician too?'

Emily gave a laugh. 'That *would* explain how you did your spell,' she said.

I'd had enough. I was prepared to walk away right then and there, but just as I made to head back to the church, the girl's next words brought me to a complete halt:

'Of course, from what I've read of your father's diary, it's pretty obvious he didn't actually do it.'

I spun to face her: *'What* did you say?'

'Your father's diary. He didn't do it.'

'How would *you* know what's in my father's diary?'

'Let's just say we have friends with mutual interests. I can show you the pages I have – and you should probably also take a look at your grandmother's grave. I think you would find it… how shall we say? *Enlightening.'*

I refused to answer, but she knew as well as I did that there was no way for me to walk away now. And so, as she started picking her way across the graveyard toward the mausoleum standing on the other side, I followed, still not quite able to shake the feeling that there might be things hiding among the graves.

The mausoleum stood stark and black against the grey sky, the name 'Crowe' carved over the door in tall letters. Apparently our family was important enough to have its members buried in their own private tomb, and Emily was about to introduce me to my dead ancestors. Through the creaking door, we stepped into a dim space, as chilly and musty as you'd expect a tomb to be, the bare stone walls sheltering a stairwell leading into the depths of the crypt. Emily lit a candle from the lamp burning next to the door and led the way down.

The Crowe family crypt was little more than a single, long corridor, but it held countless coffins, most of them set into square hollows in the walls, dozens of names flashing in the candlelight as we made our way down the hall. Every once in a while, the dark doorway of a side chamber would gape open on either side, but Emily walked swiftly past, refusing to pause even long enough for me to catch a glimpse of the rooms beyond – until we came to a stop in front of a doorway marked with a crescent moon.

The hall of the crypt continued on into the darkness in front of us, and our little circle of candlelight had long left behind the stairs we'd come by. Emily ushered me through the door, setting the candle in front of a mirror to light the room. Like every other part of the crypt, the chamber was small and dim – and here too, someone lay buried, but unlike the other coffins in the hall, this one was set in the middle of the room. And it wasn't carved of granite or marble stone, but of blue-tinted glass, frosted to give some measure of privacy to the dead.

Emily had circled to the other side of the glass coffin, and I drifted forward to take a closer look. It wasn't *just* glass, I realized. An intricate inlay of dark, twisted metal traced Marks into the walls of the coffin. And peering down at the casket from above, I could see the face of the woman within: pale, flawless skin, her lips tinged blue, dark hair splayed around her shoulders, as if she'd been drifting underwater before being frozen in the grip of death. I recognized her.

'That's Lily Crowe,' I said.

Emily didn't respond; she'd turned her back to the coffin to run her hands along the far stone wall. A chill ran down my spine. It was definitely my grandmother, no doubt about that. She had the same sharp nose, the same full lips. The face in front of me matched the photograph I'd found in Dad's diary so closely that I wouldn't have been surprised if someone told me it had been taken on the day she died. And she looked as if she'd only died yesterday.

I searched for the plaque that would show her name and death day, and sure enough, there it was, set in the foot of the coffin:

Lily Isabella Raban-Corvinus Crowe
December 27th, 1877

Fifteen years. She'd been dead for fifteen years. *Buried* for fifteen years. And yet…

'Emily?' I said, speaking low to keep my voice from echoing in the hollow chamber. 'This might be a silly question, but… how long is a body supposed to look like that?'

Emily slid a loose stone from the wall, pulled a long, thin *something* from the hollow, and turned to me with her widest, toothiest smile yet. 'Well, ladies and gentlemen, it looks like we have a winner! Because *that*, my dear, magician friend, is the *right question*.' She slipped her prize into some pocket and put the stone back in its place. 'The answer, of course, will be far less disturbing when we're not standing in an ice-cold skeleton closet. So. Back to the land of the living!' And with that, she plucked the candle from its holder and swept out of the room, setting a quick pace back up into the graveyard.

The clouds had thinned, but the sun was low on the horizon as the afternoon faded into evening. The church bells were chiming four o'clock.

'Well, land of the living might not be *completely* accurate,' said Emily as she locked the mausoleum behind us.

The prickling in my skin refused to fade, and I still didn't trust the shadows to stay still. I was just about done with the dead. The sooner I got out of the graveyard, the better. Thankfully, Emily seemed content to wander toward the church.

'Alright, so explain,' I said when we'd nearly reached the steps. 'What did you just show me?'

'The extraordinarily well-preserved corpse of your dead grandmother,' said Emily. 'In fact, some might call it *unnaturally* well-preserved, especially considering that no one ever thought to involve an undertaker.'

I was also just about done with Emily. 'You have five seconds to say something that makes sense–'

'Think about it Abigail. I'm sure you've heard stories about crystal caskets and bodies that don't decay–'

I knew the obvious, impossible explanation she was getting at. 'Fairy tales, you mean.' I shook my head. 'But there's *no such thing* as Fey.'

'You might want to have a good long talk with an Inquisitor about that one too. *If* he lets you ask questions after you explain your not-a-spell,' said Emily.

If I stayed any longer, I was going to end up punching that grin off her face. Luckily, we'd made it to the church.

'So, this has been exceedingly unpleasant,' I said. 'Thank you for rescuing me from the Graveward. I'm leaving.'

'Without your pages?' asked Emily, stopping me in mid-turn.

I sighed. 'Right. The mysterious pages from my father's diary that prove he didn't murder Lily.' Of course I wasn't leaving without my pages. 'Which happen to be... where? Exactly?'

Emily pulled the thing she'd rescued from my grandmother's grave out of her pocket and held it up for me to see: a scroll of papers, held in a neat cylinder with a piece of twine. 'Right here.'

But before I could swipe them out of her hand, an even more annoying voice rang out across the cemetery:

'Abigail! There you are, I was looking for you everywhere but the graveyard honestly why would you even–'

Samantha. Emily and I groaned at the same time, the pages disappearing back into her pocket as she stalked toward the church. Samantha was standing at the doors, the round boy from the tinker's shop fidgeting next to her, head lowered to avoid Emily's eyes. I couldn't tell if he did that with everyone, or if he was afraid that Miss Keeper-of-the-Dead might take it as a challenge. Either way, I didn't blame him for trying to stay away from her bad side. I wasn't even sure she *had* any other side.

Samantha, on the other hand, had no such foresight. 'I see you've met Emily,' she said to me.

'And I see that you've been looking after my brother again,' responded Emily. '*How kind.*'

'Oh no trouble at all,' answered Samantha with all the oblivious cheer of a mouse that's just found the cheese in a mousetrap. 'Oh but I have rather forgotten my manners. Abigail this is Laurie Carol, Laurie this is Abigail.'

Laurie gave a small, furtive bow, looking up for just the briefest moment to meet my eyes before gluing them, once again, to the floor. 'Pleased to make your acquaintance,' he said – just a bit too stiffly. 'I hope my sister has not been discussing anything too… unnerving.'

'Oh, we were simply discussing the murder of Lily Crowe,' said Emily, waving away the question. Laurie seemed to deflate slightly, and Samantha rolled her eyes.

'You're awful, Emily,' said Samantha. 'She doesn't need to hear your morbid theories on why her grandparents died.'

'I also don't need someone to tell me what I do and don't need to hear.'

The words were out of my mouth before I'd even realized I was thinking them, and by then it was too late. For once, Samantha had lost her words. She opened her mouth, closed it again, and looked back and forth between me and Emily. Laurie deflated a little more.

'Well… fine then. I – I guess I'll go,' she said at last. 'I can tell when I'm not wanted.' And she ducked back into the church, fleeing between the pews toward the doors at the other end. Laurie threw Emily a frown before running away after Samantha.

'She can't actually tell, you know,' said Emily when the others had disappeared through the church. 'I mean, she was here for a full five minutes.'

As much as Samantha grated on me, I wasn't sure whether that statement made me feel worse for Samantha or Emily. But there were more important things to consider now, such as *how* the pastor's daughter had managed to get her hands on pages from my dad's diary.

'Unimportant,' said Emily when I asked her. 'What *is* important is what they *say*–' and she whipped out the pages once more, unfurling one from the roll. 'This one for instance: …*if it wasn't bad enough protecting a fugitive*–'

'Let me see that!'

But Emily pulled the pages out of my reach. 'No no no! We see with our eyes, *not* with our hands!'

She couldn't possibly be serious. 'If that's the case, then I suppose I'll go. It was a displeasure to make your acquaintance.' And with a curtsy to Miss Keeper-of-the-Dead, just to be perfectly polite and proper, I started up the stairs to the church.

I hadn't gotten three feet before Emily blocked my path once more, thrusting the pages out in front of her. 'Oh very well then,' she said. 'You're no fun. Go on and take them. They rightfully belong to you now, after all.'

She dropped the pages in my hands, and I stared down at them, noticing all the little details I couldn't see before – my father's handwriting, neat and precise as always, with the little curls over his a's and his short-tailed y's; the uneven edges, dark and crinkled, as if they'd been rescued from fire; a small stain, rust-dark–

Emily was still grinning down at me, and I looked up at her, frowning, trying to figure out exactly which screw happened to have gone loose in her head. 'Uh, thanks?'

The door to the church creaked open once again, and Laurie poked his head through, catching his sister's eyes before looking immediately down again. 'Em, we were supposed to be back by quarter-to. Adeline's asking for us.' He glanced at me, and bowed his head further. 'It was a pleasure to meet you, Miss Crowe. I hope we shall be able to see you again at some future juncture.'

'Of course we *shall*,' said Emily, following her brother to the door. As Laurie ducked back out into the town, Emily paused only to blow a kiss back over her shoulder, before exiting the church behind him.

I was alone. The church was silent and dark, the afternoon sunlight long extinguished from the stained glass windows, but still, I wanted to see exactly what I had ended up with. I unrolled the pages.

The first held only one line:

> I'm done keeping your secrets, Edward.

The second one was longer, a rambling entry dated about a week after the first. It jumped from topic to topic, with only the barest connections from thought to thought, and I soon realized that this was the one Emily had read from:

> ...her but for all of us. If it wasn't bad enough protecting a fugitive of the Court, I dread to think what would happen if the rest of the situation ever came to light. But for now, I will do everything I can to protect them, both my brother and Ariel, however I can.

I stared at the page. *Ariel*. The name plucked at something in the back of my mind, but I couldn't figure out where I'd heard it before, and unfortunately, the rest of the diary entry didn't make much sense at all. The third one was, once again, short, but blotched with water and stains and scribbled as if Dad hadn't trusted himself to write it. I'd seen Dad write letters to the newspaper and scribble notes to stick on Mother's door. I'd seen his writing in ledgers and diaries and receipts, but I had never seen him write like this. The letters on the page barely looked like letters, and in the dim red light of evening, I couldn't even try to read it.

I stuffed the pages into my sock, and stepped out of the church into the main square. It was almost dark, and as Mother had reminded me and Samantha earlier, I wasn't to be out after dark. After all, according to the

Housekeeper, *the grounds were rather unpleasant at night*. It was time to track down Samantha and the coach.

It was only when I'd circled the square twice and asked one of the other coachmen that I realized both Samantha and the coach were long gone. Samantha had left me stranded in the village.

Evening was falling quickly, and as far as I could tell, I had ten minutes at most to make it back to the manor before full nightfall. Of course, it had taken fifteen minutes to get to the village – and that was *with* a carriage, which meant that I would be lucky to make it back to the house in the next half hour. Still, there was nothing else I could do. I had no money for the other drivers, and I didn't trust myself to be able to escape one of them without paying.

So I started walking.

Down the beaten dirt road out of the village, through the mud and muck – the underbrush and brambles of the Blackwood crowded close on either side. Within a few minutes, the lights of the village were hidden beyond the trees, and within a few more, I wasn't so much walking as *wading* through the darkness, hands held out in the hopes that it would prevent me from wandering into the forest.

With every twist and turn, I was sure I was going the wrong way entirely, and all of it was so much worse with the *silence*. There was no sound but the wind in the trees, and *that* sounded eerily like whispering voices. I didn't want to know what they were saying.

At last, after what felt like forever – though it must've only been an hour or so – the sparse lights of the house glittered through the trees. I never thought I'd be so relieved to see the Wardmarked fence, or the high tower, like a beacon in the night. I passed through the gate, the Wards washing over me like a half-remembered dream.

The front door was, of course, locked. I tried the servants' entrance in the East Wing next, but that was *also* locked, and I couldn't even get the greenhouse door to budge an inch, no matter how hard I tried.

Worst of all, I could still hear those whispers, though there were no trees and no wind left to make them. Again, that eerie, creeping feeling of things lurking just out of sight – the dark things from the graveyard, *dead things* – closed around my throat.

'Abigail!'

The call came from above, and I looked up to see a small, pale someone leaning out one of the upper windows.

It was William.

'Abby! Go back to the servants' entrance and I'll get the door for you!'

I needed no more urging. Back to the East Wing it was. But those whispers were growing closer, louder, closing in, even as I reached the servants' door. It was still locked when I got there, and as the whispers sounded just behind me, I turned to face the hissing darkness, squinting into the night to get a proper look at whatever-it-was that was following me.

The night was thick, and there *was* something there – something writhing and *alive* – the air snapping with sudden cold. The same heavy terror that had clung to me in the graveyard returned, and I found myself trembling. I wasn't supposed to be out here, I realized. *No one* was supposed to be out here – there was a reason it wasn't allowed. My breath was steaming. The whispers grew clearer, words hissing in the noise:

Intruderssss? Naughty, naughty...

'Abby!'

I spun, startled, to face the threat. But it was only William, standing framed by the bright light of the servants' quarter, holding the door open for me. He looked past me into the darkness–

But the shadows were gone.

'Abby, hurry up! They're going to catch us.'

We rushed through the kitchen and to the foot of the servants' stair, up, up to the second floor. William pushed open the door to our rooms with a laugh of relief.

'The Toad said they'd make you sleep outside if you didn't get back by nightfall. Didn't think you'd fancy that.'

'William, you are the absolute best. Are you feeling better?'

'Right as rain. I don't know what they did to me but I feel wonder– ' His words died as we stepped fully into the sitting room. Uncle Edward was already there, perched on the moth-bitten couch, the dim orange glow of a pipe throwing light on his face.

'Ah, well. I am truly glad you decided to join us, Abigail,' he said without turning to look at us. 'And I hope that both of you get a good night's rest, because tomorrow, Mrs. Thompson will have some tasks for you.' He stood and made to leave the room. I looked down to avoid his eyes as he pushed past.

The door creaked open and he looked back over his shoulder. 'Good night, dear children. Sweet dreams. And do watch out for the bedbugs.'

A Cry in the Darkness

Just as Uncle Edward had promised, the next day, we weren't woken by the smell of breakfast or by pleasant strains of birdsong, but rather by an overly-cheerful Housekeeper, who barged into both our rooms and dragged us from bed, throwing a couple of grimy work smocks over our heads, and crowing:

'Up, up, up! Rise and shine! *There's work to be done!*'

She wasn't lying. There were rooms to be cleaned and floors to be scrubbed, chimneys to be swept and rugs to be beaten, dishes to be washed and tables to be set, and all of this was just the work that had to be done before lunch. That came and went – and though we didn't have to spend our lunch hour picking awkwardly at a roast while Mother and Uncle Edward discussed the weather, it was rather ruined by the fact that there was nothing to eat but a plate of soggy potatoes, boiled to the point that they'd almost gone to mush. And then we were off again, scrubbing, sweeping, beating, washing, all of it – until, at last, after a sorry dinner of beans and wilted broccoli, the Housekeeper marched us up to our rooms and let us go. I immediately crawled into bed, too worn out to do anything but sleep.

But it was the same thing the next day, and the next, *and the next*, until it seemed that we were doomed to this cycle forever, that the entire rest of our lives would be spent spinning laundry and wiping tables and getting yelled at by the Housekeeper. By the end of the week, William had taken to collapsing on the couch just to save him the ten steps to and from his bed, and I could barely bring myself to change out of my work clothes. By Friday evening, it hardly seemed worth the effort: I went to bed in my smock.

What seemed like a minute later, the Housekeeper was yelling *yet again*.

'Get up! Get up! Get up!'

I stumbled blearily out of sleep and back onto my feet. It was morning again, but only barely; the world outside the windows was all but dark. The Housekeeper yelled at me to straighten my work smock, and to tie my laces properly, and then, as if to make the situation as dire as possible, she told me to get my coat.

'You'll be working in the stables today. We wouldn't want your arms to freeze off on your way there,' she said, without any hint that she was joking. So while William tried his best to make sure the old work boots we'd been given would stay on his feet, I rifled through the wardrobe for my coat, pulling it on and slipping my hands into the pockets–

The pages.

In all the chaos and flurry of the past week, I'd completely forgotten them, but there they were, still bundled into the pocket of my coat, waiting to be read and understood. I gripped them between my fingers, and stepped out the door behind the Housekeeper, determined to find a way of getting away from her, so that I could finally take a proper look.

The Housekeeper led us through the halls and toward the servants' quarters. As we went, I tried my best to catch William's attention without alerting the toad, but he was so exhausted that all my meaningful looks went unnoticed. Finally I resorted to tugging on his coat sleeve to get him to look at me. I pulled the pages halfway out my pocket so that he could see them.

His eyebrows furrowed in confusion. 'What–'

The Housekeeper looked back over her shoulder with a terrible glare, and I had to shove my hands back into my pockets without looking suspicious. It failed spectacularly, of course, and the Housekeeper came to a stop just so that she could stare me down properly. 'Is there a problem?' she asked.

'No ma'am,' I said.

She sniffed, and though she didn't seem completely convinced that I was, in fact, *not* plotting to escape from her in order to look at some pages that I'd found in a graveyard with the help of the Pastor's daughter, she didn't press the matter. We continued down the hall, and William turned to me, his eyebrows knotted into a question:

What are those?

I gave him a meaningful look, and tilted my head toward the doors, lifting my own eyebrows, as if to say:

We need to talk.

William looked toward the Housekeeper, eyes narrowed in calculations, before turning back toward me with a grin. He dug into his own pocket and pulled out something small and dark and round – something with a dull surface and a waxed wick:

A smoke bomb.

I had to choke down a laugh. *Perfect.*

William pulled out a match and struck it against the wall. The Housekeeper froze. But before she could quite manage to turn on us, the fuse was lit. William tossed the smoke bomb into the air.

BANG.

It exploded, spewing clouds of blue-grey smoke. The Housekeeper screamed. And as the hallway disappeared in the billowing haze of sulphur and brimstone, William's hand found mine, and we made our escape.

Down the echoing passageways, up two flights of twisting stairs, past locked doors and grimy windows, the Housekeeper's shrieks followed us as we fled through the house. It was only after a good minute of running and too many twists and turns to count that we were sure we'd left her behind. At last, we stopped to catch our breath, huddled in one of the back stairs down to the second floor. William burst out laughing.

'She screams like an angry duck!'

'Don't be mean,' I said. 'Ducks are majestic, *musical* creatures compared to that!'

'Like a duck being eaten by a drowning cat, then?'

I tried to swallow my laughter, but it came out as a snort instead. 'I don't even care if they give us another week of chores for it; that was absolutely brilliant.'

William beamed with pride. 'I try,' he said. 'So what did you want to show me?'

Unconsciously, I'd been gripping the pages through the entire ordeal, and now, as I pulled my fist out of my pocket, the papers came with it. We might have been able to escape the Housekeeper's chores, but there was still work to be done. 'Pages from Dad's diary,' I said, holding them up for William to see. 'We need to find somewhere private.'

We ended up in the very back of the greenhouse, sheltered behind a crowd of exotic ferns that hid us from both the outside door and the upper balcony. As William settled himself on a crumbling bench among the broken cobbles, I handed the diary pages over to him one by one. 'The Pastor's daughter, Emily Carol, gave these to me, that night I came back late,' I explained. 'The toad's been working us so hard since then I didn't even think–'

"I'm done keeping your secrets," read William aloud. He looked up at me, eyes wide. 'Where did she *get* these?'

'She wouldn't tell me,' I said. 'But they were definitely ripped out of the back of Dad's diary.'

William nodded, his head bent over the papers as he studied them, lips moving along with our father's words. He came, at last, to the final one, the one that I hadn't been able to read in the failing light of the village, and I leaned over that one myself, hoping to pick out at least some of the words. But with morning sunlight drifting through the greenhouse windows and a clearer head, it only took a little effort to read:

> So I am forced, after all of it, not only to take the blame, but to flee. So be it. I ask for nothing of you, my brother, except this:
> Put her to Rest, Edward. At the very least let her be put to Rest.

It trailed off, illegibly. I looked up from the page to find William staring back at me, and for a moment, it was like looking into a mirror, the surprise and horror that I was feeling at that very moment reflected in my brother's face.

If Dad had written this just before he'd left Ravenscourt, then the only person he could be talking about was Lily. Lily, whose spirit had been stolen. Lily, who was never Rested. Lily, whose murder had been blamed on Dad, even though the real culprit –

'We're trapped in a house with a murderer,' said William, so that I didn't have to. He sagged on the bench, frowning firmly at the floor. 'We should tell Mother.'

'Oh, I'm sure that would go over well,' I said. "Oh Mum? You know Uncle Edward, the person you decided to turn to in our most desperate of desperate moments? Yes, well, he is, in fact, a lunatic murderer, and I think he's out to get us all…"

'Well, we wouldn't say it like that.'

The stained-glass door to the house banged open, and startled, I looked up to the balcony. Thankfully, William was quick. He stuffed the pages away and ducked behind the ferns, pulling me down next to him just as the Housekeeper appeared at the top of the spiralling stairway, her face still half-bent toward the hallway behind her. 'I'm sure they're in here somewhere,' she muttered, turning to look out over the greenhouse proper.

'Come now, children!' she called. 'Come out, come out wherever you are!'

Her bulging eyes raked over the plants and flowers, passing over our hiding place once, twice, thrice, while both William and I held our breaths to avoid making the ferns tremble even the slightest. But she must not have seen us through the crowding leaves: with a huff, she started making her way down the stairs. 'Very well, then. We'll do this the hard way.'

She began combing through the plants, following the crooked paths in wider and wider circles away from the stairs, leaving no corner unchecked. Much longer, and our last chance to escape would be gone: our only hope was to get through the outside door, if we could manage it without falling into the Housekeeper's grasp. There was no way she wouldn't notice us. After all, I'm sure my heart was pounding loud enough to echo.

William nudged me, pointing his chin at the outside door. We'd come to the same conclusion. He pulled a smoke bomb out of his pocket and raised his eyebrows:

Shall I?

The housekeeper swept through the plants two aisles away. This was our only chance. I nodded.

The fuse was lit. William lobbed the firework at the Housekeeper's back, and once again, the air exploded with smoke.

'Run for it!' he hissed.

So we ran. William made a beeline for the door. I followed on his heels, leaping over clawing shrubs and beds of herbs. William ploughed through a bed of rare *Cosmos Atrosanguineus*, the dark red flowers crumpling under his feet.

'William! Those are *endangered!*' I shouted, but the Housekeeper shrieked just behind me, and there was no time to find a way around: I was forced to trample over the flowers myself, though I tried to leap over as much of the bed as possible.

We'd just destroyed a rare species. I was glad Dad would never know.

We ducked under magnolia branches, and now the door was just in front of us. Four yards. Three – the door was almost in our reach. We were two feet away – William's hand was on the knob–

'STOP!' roared a voice, and it was *not* the Housekeeper's.

Immediately, every single one of my muscles recoiled from moving forward, the same way your fingers jump back to avoid being burned by the tea kettle: an automatic reaction, unstoppable as breathing. I nearly toppled over, even as William skidded into a halt in front of me, even as some deeper part of my mind screamed at me to *run*. But no, every bit of me had stalled. Paused. *Stopped*. Just as Uncle Edward had Commanded. And in some dim, back corner of my mind, the realization dropped like one of William's smoke bombs:

Magic.

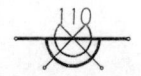

Uncle Edward was a magician – but of course, that was how he'd gotten away with murdering Lily in the first place. Still, it was one thing to suspect a person was capable of magic, and another thing entirely to experience that person taking over your mind. He'd managed to take control of us – of *both* of us – with a single word. And if he could Command our actions with little more than a word, I definitely did not want to think about what *else* he could do. Every single horror story that I'd heard in catechism, every single warning I'd gotten from Dad, all of it came whirling back through my head – about magicians who could drive you insane with an Illusion of pain, or bind you with a lingering Curse that would give you horrible nightmares, or worse, would control your every action, so that you'd be walking around, talking and acting and doing terrible things, except you'd have no memory of it later, or *even worse*, you'd be trapped inside, seeing yourself doing all these horrible things without being able to stop any of it. There was a *reason* Inquisitors hunted down magicians like dogs, a reason that even the whisper of magic could get you locked away or burned.

Dread twisted through my stomach. I wanted to be sick. The Housekeeper finally caught up with us, grabbing each of us by an arm, and I had to swallow against the urge to scream – not that Uncle Edward's Command would let me. And even when the Command lifted, and I realized, suddenly, that I was in control of my own body again, even then, I couldn't stop trembling. The Housekeeper dragged us up the stairs and shoved us into the hall, steering me and my brother after our uncle. We trooped through the corridors – past the gallery of portraits and the twinned library doors, into the dark hall that seemed to go on and on into oblivion.

Though, now that I knew that Uncle Edward was a magician, I also knew it was entirely possible that the hall simply *did* go on and on into oblivion. After all, who was to say that he hadn't placed some kind of Illusion on the hall, to lead anyone who tried to follow it into a never-ending loop? But of course, he'd know how to navigate it.

What would happen to us when we got to the end?

I didn't want to think about that.

Finally (yet at the same time, far too soon), the end came into sight. Uncle Edward pushed open the very last door of the corridor, letting firelight seep into the dark hall from the room beyond. He turned to me and my brother and set his grey eyes on each of us, as if sizing us up. I glared back with as much defiance as I could manage, which was, honestly, not that much, seeing as I couldn't stop my hands from shaking.

'William first,' said Uncle Edward, before sweeping into the room. The Housekeeper shoved William in after him, and the last thing I saw before the door snapped closed between us was my brother's face, drained white as a sheet.

No sound escaped through the closed door, and I didn't dare to lean my ear against it – not with the Housekeeper watching me through those lidded eyes, her mouth set into a gloating smirk. There was nothing for me to do but shift from foot to foot, waiting and watching and wondering what would happen to me – what might have already happened to William.

Finally, the door clicked open and William stepped out, his eyes red, as if he'd been crying, but to my relief, he looked more annoyed than hurt. Before we could exchange a single word, however, the Housekeeper shoved me through the door, and pulled William back into the hall.

The door shut behind me.

I hovered at the edge of the room. It was a sort of office: small but rich, and warm from the fire that crackled in the marble hearth. On one side of the room, a few puffy armchairs stood huddled around a low table set for tea, and on the other side, a heavy desk sat between tall bookcases. A collection of animal specimens, jarred and preserved, stood prominently on the shelves between piles of books. The entire place smelled of leather and antiseptic, and it was a moment before I noticed Uncle Edward watching me from the most imposing of the clustered armchairs, studying my every move.

'Sit,' he said, gesturing to the low sofa that faced him across the coffee table. Of course, sitting down for tea was about the last thing I felt like doing.

'Please,' said Uncle Edward. And while I had been fully prepared to face shouts and accusations and even Commands, that one soft word caught me so off guard that I stepped over to the sofa and sat down before I'd even realized it.

I sank into the overstuffed sofa as Uncle Edward poured two steaming cups of black tea. 'Sugar?' he asked. 'Cream?'

I blinked at him. 'Er... no, thank you.'

'Really? It takes a bit of the edge–'

'No, thank you,' I repeated. I wasn't even planning on drinking the tea.

But he insisted on handing me a cup anyway, with a shrug and a muttered, 'Suit yourself.' I took it in trembling hands, trying my best to keep the cup from clacking too loudly against the saucer.

He stirred sugar into his own cup before settling back into his seat with a sigh. 'Now, Abigail,' he said. 'Would you care to explain to me exactly why you felt the need to attack Mrs. Thompson?'

I opened my mouth to answer, closed it. There was nothing to say to that question, not that I dared say much. I was sitting across from a magician with a teacup full of scalding tea still rattling in my hands. He was staring me down, and I couldn't help but feel that the sofa wouldn't hesitate to swallow me if given half a chance. I set the tea on the table and tried to clear my mind, reaching for the First Defence, pressing my fingers against the cold metal of Dad's ring.

The First Defence is always with you…

Could he read minds?

I would've been surprised if he couldn't. Mind reading wasn't anything to a real magician. And as much as I tried to focus on my defences, I couldn't clear my mind of anything. All of it came rushing through: the fear, the suspicion, the unrelenting questions, and I couldn't manage more than a pale flicker of the warmth to protect myself.

Uncle Edward allowed the silence to linger a bit longer before he spoke again. 'We have talked before about the importance of the rules I have asked you to follow. I would like to hear your explanation for breaking them, but if you would rather we simply meted out punishment–'

'Are you going to *make* me talk?' I said, the words stumbling out of my mouth. 'Or perhaps erase my memory?'

The briefest sign of surprise passed across my uncle's face, followed almost immediately by a laugh. 'Now, dear Abigail. Why *ever* would I do that?'

'I could report you to the Inquisitors,' I said. I wanted it to be a threat. I wanted, however weakly, to scare him.

But all he did was lean forward in his chair, setting his teacup down across from mine. 'Would you really?' he said, almost laughing. Even his voice seemed amused rather than scared.

'I *could*,' I said again, but we both knew that I might as well have been throwing threats at an avalanche, for all the good it would do.

Still, Uncle Edward pressed on. 'And what could you tell them, Abigail?'

The thoughts rose to the surface of my mind, and as much as I tried to tamp them down, I couldn't stop them. There was Dad's old room, decaying on the fourth floor of Ravenscourt House, and Beatrice's warnings. And there was the diary with its pages torn out – pages that I hoped were still hidden safely away in William's pockets. There were the words scribbled down in Dad's shaking hand: *put her to rest*. He'd been afraid. He'd fled from Uncle Edward, from the man who had murdered our grandmother, and he'd been afraid. And when Uncle Edward came looking for him, Dad had kicked him out – their arguments rising against each other in the parlour of the old house, William's sleepy complaints, Dad's shouts. I clenched my jaw, and tried my best to focus on the ring curled around my thumb, on every breath as it passed into my lungs and out my nose: breathe in, breathe out.

'I could tell them you use magic,' I said finally, 'that you used it on us.'

'And let us say, hypothetically, that you did so. What do you think would happen then?'

'*Hypothetically*,' I said, looking up to meet his eyes, 'I think they would have you *burned*.'

Uncle Edward's lip quirked into a half-smile. 'That must be the kindest death threat I have ever received,' he said. 'However, if you are quite determined to hate me, I would rather prefer to know why.'

'You're a magician. Most people would think that's reason enough.'

'Oh, my dear, there are far better reasons, I can assure you.'

I refused to let my eyes drop, but instead of looking ashamed, like any decent person would, he flashed a smile and took a sip of his tea. My stomach churned. Every part of me wanted to flee. He'd already proven himself willing to use magic to get what he needed, and yet, he insisted on toying with me, asking me questions as if he couldn't just rip into my mind and take the answers.

'What do you even *want*?' I demanded.

'Honestly? I want you to trust me.'

'I have no reason to trust you.'

'*Evidently*. However, I would have you know that I am not your enemy.' He stood from his seat, turning his back to me as he drifted toward the fireplace. He sighed. 'I had hoped not to broach this subject with you, but I think... I think at this point it might be necessary. Abigail, your father lies dead, and it is all that I can do–'

I was on my feet so quickly that I almost upturned the table, tea sloshing onto my skirt and spilling out on the carpet. 'How *dare* you speak of my father!'

'Abigail, whatever else you may think you know, I need you to understand that Lewis was my brother, first and foremost. He was as dear to me as he was to you–'

'Well, he hated you! He left *because of you*!' I said, the words spilling out of me so fast that I couldn't hold them back – couldn't change them, couldn't even stop them. They were the only weapon I had left, and I threw them at him as hard as I could, all of the worst words I could think of. 'He knew you were dangerous before he even fled, and when he did, it was to get away from *you*. He hated everything you *are*–'

Uncle Edward spun to face me, and for the first time, I saw that he was truly angry. For all his threats and punishments, I realized that I'd never really believed he had it in him to hit me. But now, his mouth was twisted in rage, his eyes hard and cold in a way that told me he wouldn't hesitate to hurt me, with or without magic. He stepped forward. I stumbled back. 'If anything happens to me... my mother–'

His face lifted in surprise, and immediately the anger melted out of his eyes. His next words were more bewildered than anything:

'Abigail, have I ever done anything to harm you?'

I opened my mouth to retort, but the words weren't there. Because of course he hadn't. Even if he'd forced me and William into obedience with a Command, and even if it was clear that he was capable of much, much worse, I couldn't honestly say that he'd ever actually hurt me. And if he'd wanted to, he could argue that he'd actually helped us – that he'd helped William, certainly – when no other doctor could calm a single one of my brother's fits. I couldn't trust him. I *didn't* trust him. He was a liar and a magician and a murderer and probably so many worse things, but for that moment, he had something of a point.

'Besides,' he continued, 'your mother is as concerned for your safety as I am, and we are both willing to do what we must in order to prevent you from suffering your father's fate–'

'How *dare* you–'

'Abigail, *please*. You must believe me when I say that this is all for your own safety–'

'Safety? My *safety*? You keep talking about our safety – as if there are dangers lurking around every corner. But from what I've seen, the most dangerous thing in this house is *you!*' And before he could reply, before he could respond or stop me or do anything more than shake his head, I turned and fled, racing out the door and past the Housekeeper's protests, through the halls and up the stairs to our rooms.

'Well,' said William as I slammed the door behind me. 'That was bracing.'

By now it was past noon, and William had just started to attack the lunch tray that had been left for us by the maids. He chewed a mouthful of carrot as I sank down onto our sofa. 'You have no idea,' I said, before telling him everything that had happened just before I'd fled Uncle Edward's office. When I finished, he stared at me, wide-eyed.

'And he didn't even deny any of it?'

I shook my head.

William put down his fork. 'That's...'

'Not good,' I finished for him. I sat up on the sofa and contemplated the gravy, but my stomach was still churning from nerves. 'I can't believe I said all that.'

'I don't feel so bad about mine now,' said William. 'I tried to fake cry, but I'm pretty sure he must've seen through it.' He reached into his pocket and pulled out a cube of worn brass – some kind of device, with buttons down the side. 'Did manage to pinch this though.'

I stared at the thing. 'What is that?'

'A voice box. It was sitting on his desk, in the middle of all his notes.'

'And you just *took* it?'

'It looked important,' said William with a shrug. 'Besides, don't you want to hear what Doctor Edward Crowe is recording from his notes? It could be a complete record of his dastardly evil plots...'

I wasn't sure whether to laugh at my brother's brilliance or give him a lecture for being unfathomably stupid. Still, if the voice box held any of our uncle's notes, it might be able to tell us *something*. I took the box from my brother and wound it, pressing the tiny, triangular button on the side to start it playing.

The little thing whirred to life, gears and keys and teeth going to work inside it. As silly as it might sound, I half-hoped that it would start playing a full confession by Uncle Edward, complete with motives, weapons, and weeping admissions of guilt, but, of course it was far more likely to hold little more than medical notes on gout or heartburn, or perhaps a grocery list.

So when a woman's voice poured out, metallic and somewhat tinny from the clockwork, I nearly dropped the box.

Edward, dear, said the voice.

Thank you for the books, they were very thoughtful. There's rather too much time for thinking here, and at least stories provide some distraction. I have been thinking though... about names. I rather like Damon for a boy. It has a nice ring to it, and Tris quite agrees. Of course, depending, I have also always liked the name Lenore – though at this point, that might be a bit too defiant, as far as the Court's concerned.

In any case, it won't be much longer. And then we can leave all this behind – together.

Until then, do try to be gentle with your brother. He means well. And don't anger your mother, or Grahame – they'll be out of our hair soon enough.

Be safe, my love.

For a good minute after the recording ticked to a stop, we were silent. I stared at the box in my hand and waited for it to explain itself.

'Do you think she sent it to the wrong Edward, perhaps?' asked William finally.

Honestly, I didn't know what to think. *It looked important*, William had said, and though I couldn't make heads nor tails of it, I was inclined to agree. The recording must've been at least fifteen years old – it mentioned our grandmother, after all – and the device was worn, but well cared for: freshly oiled, with all its parts in order. Why had it been sitting out on Uncle Edward's desk? And what did it mean, this mysterious woman thinking about names?

Who was she?

The rest of the afternoon passed in a haze. I replayed the stranger's message over and over, listening to it until the sound threatened to lull me to sleep.

Meanwhile, William suggested ways for us to find out more, most of them dangerous and impractical, and always somehow involving fire:

'We could set the sofa on fire. And then, when they're all distracted, we sneak into Uncle Edward's office–'

'Um, no.'

Finally, when darkness fully settled over everything and we sank into bed, I planted the voice box under my pillow. As I drifted off to sleep, I wondered if that was what she was waiting for; if somehow, the woman in the recording would whisper her secrets into my dreams and tell me where to look next.

I woke to a dark room and William shaking my shoulder. 'Abby?'

I muttered at him to go back to sleep.

'Abby, I'm scared. Didn't you feel it?'

Something in his voice worried me. Groggily, I opened my eyes and turned to face him. He was shivering next to the bed, the fear on his face clear even in the weak light of one of his matches. 'William? What–'

A scream cut through the night, answering my unasked question. I sat up in bed, suddenly completely alert. William's nails were digging into my arm, but neither of us dared to move. The match fizzled out. Our breaths echoed in the darkness, the air stiflingly still, both of us tense and waiting. And then–

The scream came again, and this time, it didn't stop.

A sharp, high cry – somewhere between animal and human, filled with horrible pain – the scream tore through the darkness, sharp as nails scraped against a chalkboard, and my hands came up to cover my ears. Still, I couldn't block it out, not completely. That inhuman wail continued to sound, loud enough that I could believe it was coming from someone or *something* just beside me in the shadows, something with broken bones and a twisted body and a voice that threatened to make the air and the walls and the house – the entire world – tremble with the pain of it. The scream shuddered through the air, making every muscle in my body clench with fear–

And then, the world *was* trembling, the windows rattling, the walls shaking, and I was reaching out to pull William close, terrified that he might start seizing. But he simply clung to me, trembling. The scream rose to a shriek–

And then silence.

The air was silent, the world completely still. My book had fallen off the night table, but otherwise, there was no sign that anything out of the ordinary had happened. William was clinging to me, and I was clinging to him, and without so much as a single word, I threw myself out of bed, and both of us stumbled into the sitting room.

I had to pull away from William to open the door, reaching out to turn the knob. But my hands were slick with sweat, and the metal slipped from my grasp. I wiped my hands on my nightdress, even as that awful scream sounded again. I gripped the door handle in both hands, twisted it–

It rattled, but did not turn.

It was like a bad dream. The screams shook the air, but the door stood fast. If I opened the door, the screams would stop. If I opened the door, everything would be normal and still. If I could open the door, I would wake up.

Desperate, I pulled on the door, shook it, banged on it – but no matter what I did, the door wouldn't budge. I turned to William, his face grey in the shadows of the window bars. I stumbled against the door as the tremors began once more, the horrifying truth of the situation crashing down on me in a wave of ice:

'They locked us in.'

KEEPER OF THE DEAD

For what seemed like an eternity, William and I huddled in my room, trying our best to block out the sound of those screams and bracing ourselves against the shuddering walls. At last, long after midnight, the air stilled and the world fell silent, and at some point after that, we both must've fallen asleep, because when I woke up, sunlight was drifting in between the curtains, and a pair of birds were chattering to each other just outside the window. I left William sleeping and slipped out of bed to pad into the sitting room.

Breakfast had long gone cold on the table, but the fire was roaring, and as I tried the door – my heart pounding at the thought that it might still be locked – it opened easily. I poked my head into the hall, but there was no sign of anything out of the ordinary, and so, at last, I settled onto the couch and nibbled on a piece of cold toast. I ignored the congealed bacon. With the bright light of morning drifting into the room and the warmth of the blazing fire, it was hard to imagine that any of the horror of the previous night had really happened at all. It could've been a dream, a nightmare. But the terror of it refused to fade, and as William emerged from my bedroom, his hair sticking up in all directions from his tossing and turning, he looked straight at me and said:

'We have to talk to Mum.'

He disappeared into his room to change. It was as good an idea as any, as far as I was concerned, and so after finishing off the toast, I made myself decent, and together, we ventured out into the house to hunt down our mother.

The halls were quiet and empty as ever, though the drafts seeping in through the floors seemed colder than usual. As we reached the halls branching away from the library, William took the lead, peering up at the doors to try and remember which one she'd shown us, that first night when we'd arrived.

'This one, I think,' he announced, pushing open a door near the end of one short corridor.

A bright, cheerful room lay beyond. As we stepped through the doorway, the familiar scent of lavender and rose tickled my nostrils from where Mother kept them pressed into her clothes. She was sitting at a polished writing desk in the back corner of the room, looking over her scattered papers.

'Well, it's about ti–' she began as we entered, though she cut herself off as she looked up and realized it was us standing there. Immediately, she jumped to her feet and gestured for us to take the settee, hastily stuffing away the papers as she did. 'William! Abigail. Do come in, dears.'

She swept toward us and set a tin of sugar biscuits on the coffee table, sinking into an armchair next to the fire while we settled onto the settee. She rubbed a hand over her eyes and smiled at us, though there was something tense about it. Still, she gave no other hint that there was anything wrong.

'Did you sleep well?' she asked brightly. As if the entire house hadn't been trembling in the night.

William and I exchanged a look. Was it possible that she really *hadn't* heard the screams or felt those tremors last night? Had she slept through the whole thing? Or was she putting on a show, pretending that nothing out of the ordinary had happened, so she wouldn't have to face it? Either way, I couldn't find the words to answer her. Luckily, William came to the rescue:

'Not with the screams, we didn't,' he said.

'Not with...' Mother tilted her head. 'What?'

'The screams,' I said, pressing forward. 'Last night. Didn't you hear them?'

Mother's face pinched into a frown. 'Whatever are you going on about now, Abigail?'

'Are you seriously saying you didn't hear or feel a thing last night?'

'It's an old house,' said Mother. 'There's bound to be places where the wind catches. You certainly shouldn't be losing sleep over it though. I'm surprised you haven't gotten used to it by—'

'This wasn't just the wind catching,' I said. I hadn't gotten enough sleep between screams to justify being polite at this hour. 'These were *screams*. And it's not the only thing that's been strange here. Uncle Edward—'

'Your uncle has been dealing with your antics far more generously than he could be, if we're being honest,' said Mother. 'I would've thought that a week of chores would've been more than enough to encourage some restraint from you two. I honestly can't understand what's gotten into you lately, with how you've been acting up. You should find something to distract yourselves with that doesn't involve—'

'We haven't been acting up!' I protested. 'The only reason I came back late was because Samantha left me in the village.' I stopped myself short of reminding her that the whole thing hadn't been *my* idea in the first place. 'Besides, you can't possibly think that any of it justifies what Uncle Edward did.'

'Oh come now, Abigail,' said Mother. 'He's completely within his rights to assign you chores when you've broken his rules. I daresay–'

'He didn't just assign us chores,' I said, doing everything I could to keep my voice steady. 'Mum, he used a Command on us.'

There it was, the whole nasty truth of the matter laid out between us, shocking Mother into silence. And as she sat there, staring at me, I started telling her the whole story, from the horrid week of endless chores, to our decision to escape from the Housekeeper (I conveniently left out that we'd done so in order to look at Dad's diary pages), coming, finally, to the moment that Uncle Edward used his magic to stop us escaping. As I told her about the Command, I waited for her reaction: for shock or fear, or at the very least, some show of surprise. But all she did was sigh heavily through her nostrils and press her fingers to her forehead in exasperation, her mouth still bent into that grim frown. 'Abigail, you know very well how dangerous an accusation that is.'

I stared at her, lost for words. She couldn't be serious.

'Mum,' said William, 'she's not lying.'

Mother shook her head. 'There is no reason to say such terrible things about those who have done so much to help us–'

'Are you even *listening*?' I burst out. 'He's a *magician*, Mum. He's *dangerous*, and–'

'And even if I *did* believe you, Abigail,' she said, her voice cutting through mine, 'what would you have me do? Call the Inquisitors on the suspicions of two children?'

Heat rose to my cheeks and I had to clench my jaw to stop my tongue. My hands had curled into fists in my lap. I knew, at that point, that if I stayed much longer, I'd end up doing something regrettable. And so, without a word, I stood from the couch, resisting the urge to knock the biscuits off the table as I did. I turned to leave, and without sparing Mother even the briefest backward glance, I wrenched open the door and stormed out into the hall.

I didn't head back to our rooms. My feet were moving on their own and I was two turns past the library before William caught up with me.

'Abby! Wait.'

I halted, the blood still roaring in my ears. I waited for my brother to catch up before continuing down the hall, taking twists and turns at random until we'd ended up in the hall lined all with windows. It was only as we came to a stop in front of the stained-glass door leading down into the greenhouse garden that I realized where my feet had been taking me all along.

'I'm going to talk to Beatrice,' I said.

And without waiting for William's reply, I opened the door, and followed the stairs into the jungle.

We found her crouched next to the bed of crushed *Cosmos Atrosanguineus*, her long, dark fingers sorting through the trampled flowers and straightening out bent stalks. A wooden bucket stood next to her hat and basket, her dirt-stained tools scattered down the aisle. She snipped away crumpled bits and broken pieces, laying the discarded parts in a twisted pile on the cobbles.

She looked up as soon as she noticed us, her golden eyes warming with a smile. 'Good afternoon, young William, Miss Abigail. Lovely day, though someone seems to have trampled my Cosmos.'

The sparkle in her eyes told me she had her suspicions, and my face burned with guilt. 'I – sorry,' I said. 'But it was an accident. I mean... I told William not to–'

'You were right behind me!' said William. 'And we were running from the Toa– I mean, from Mrs. Thompson...' he said, correcting himself hastily with a glance at Beatrice.

But she laughed. 'Oh, I don't blame you,' she said. 'That one has a face known to send grown men into full retreat.'

At least it seemed we hadn't done anything that couldn't be fixed. I knelt down next to her in the dirt. 'Do you need help?'

'I wouldn't mind some,' she answered gently. 'If you can pick up a bucket of soil from the empty bed over that way–' she jerked her chin at the one she meant, 'I'll be able to sort through these before replanting.'

Easy enough. I grabbed the bucket and a trowel and picked my way toward the empty bed, loosening the soil and shovelling it into the bucket by heaping handfuls. It scattered on my skirt and gathered under my fingernails, but it felt good working in the dirt, like returning to an old friend.

Whenever Dad had gone on his collecting trips to Scetis or the Austerland, he'd come back with bruise-purple trumpet flowers and downy pearl thistles, and always, always, a bouquet of floppy wildflowers for Mother (who would greet him with a frown quite as thorny as the thistles – at least until he promised not to leave again for a couple months). Of course, he'd need help replanting his specimens. And since neither Mother nor William much cared for the dirt, that was *our* time: to discuss novels, or quiz each other on different plants, or practice defences.

I was eleven when he taught me the Third Defence. That day, he'd brought back star-thorned mugworts from the Prom Vesperis – fat, thick-headed flowers with prickles that caught me even through my gardening gloves. I remember coiling my breaths to practice the Second Defence and steady my hands, when Dad caught me. 'You're getting better,' he said, his smile lop-sided, as always.

I glared at him sideways. 'How would you know? It's not like I've ever had anything to defend against!'

He raised an eyebrow at that. 'I would think, everything considered, that ought to be a good thing.'

'Well, I mean. It is...' I said. 'It's just... not very reassuring, not knowing whether or not they'd actually work in a pinch.'

'I'm pretty sure they would – maybe not against a proper Command, but still.' He fell silent, his dark eyes contemplating the prickly mugworts. 'Maybe it's about time to start you on the Third,' he said finally.

I sank my fingers into the dirt, trying not to let my grin show. 'Alright.'

The plants sat abandoned as Dad guided me through the first two defences, along the airy path of the First and through the coiling warmth of the Second, to a place in the very centre of it all, that small bright core of light that tells you where your heart is. We built a sanctuary there, protecting it with tall silver hedges and filling it with sky and petals and the warmth of sunset.

'This is your heart and centre,' Dad told me. 'Remember how to find it, and you will never be deceived for long.'

It took weeks of practice, but eventually I learned to find my way there without Dad's help. Whenever the outside world became too much: when the Dame Inquisitor gave me switches for asking the wrong questions, or the town girls asked me if William's 'Curse' was contagious – that was where I'd go. And though I knew, of course, that the sanctuary didn't exist anywhere but in my own mind, sometimes it felt like that twilit garden was more real than any place in the world of things – more real than the old house, than the old town, more real than all of Britannia and the world beyond it, because it was a place that I could *understand*.

And as I sat gathering soil for Beatrice's Cosmos in the Ravenscourt greenhouse, it flashed, briefly, all around me. It was the first time I'd summoned it since Dad had died – the first time I'd been able to. I froze, and even after the sight of it faded, a whiff of cherry blossoms remained, making my nose twitch.

I looked up to find William standing next to me. The bucket was full.

I stood, brushing the soil from my skirt while William picked up the bucket. Together, we carried it back to where Beatrice was still kneeling, sorting through the dying flowers.

'How can you tell?' I asked, watching her hands as they brushed over leaves and stalks. As far as I could see, there wasn't much difference between the ones she snipped away and the ones she left, not until after she'd already snipped them.

'How do I tell which ones won't make it, you mean?' She passed over one with crumpled petals to pick out one with whole leaves, but a bruised stem. 'You listen,' she said. 'Even plants have a bit of spirit. You might be able to sense it if you pay attention.'

I thrust my hand into the cluster of nodding flowers, brushing my fingertips over them, but I wasn't even sure what a plant's spirit was supposed to feel like. 'I don't feel anything.'

Beatrice laughed. 'Most people can't. Those that can have usually studied at least some magic. And yes, Warding counts in that regard.' She smiled at me. 'Sometimes even magic can be put to good use, in the right hands.'

She took the soil and piled it around the flowers, pressing it down to cover the exposed roots and support the drooping stalks. Finally, she brushed the dirt from her hands, wiping her palms on her apron, and stood. 'Well, I think that's about all the repair I can manage,' she said, her eyes settling on me. 'For the plants, anyway. Come. Let's talk.'

We settled down onto one of the benches, and for the second time that day, I found myself trying to explain something that should've been impossible. Even if we knew that Uncle Edward was a magician, there was no spell or Illusion that could've created those tremors, no explanation for those screams that I was now certain had sounded almost every night since we'd arrived.

Beatrice listened, and unlike Mother, she didn't interrupt, or counter anything I said. She frowned darkly when I told her about Uncle Edward's Command, and shook her head when I mentioned the locked door. And finally, when everything had been said, she sighed, heavily, considering her shoes while William and I slumped on the bench next to her.

'Those screams,' she said slowly, measuring out her words, as if they might strangle her, 'have driven many away in the fifteen years since your grandmother died. It's important for you to know that most of those who remain here do so only out of loyalty to your uncle.'

At that, William tilted his head. 'And you?' he said. 'You're still here.'

'Indeed I am,' said Beatrice, her voice eerily level and taut as a stretched wire.

'Why?' asked William. And even though half of me wanted to kick him for not taking a hint, the other half was just as curious to know the answer.

But Beatrice's answer didn't come. For a long minute, while the trapped birds chattered above us and a distant fountain trickled water, she stared down at her shoes, staying silent so long that she very well might have forgotten the question. But then:

'A debt,' she said. 'And a promise.' And her voice did not invite us to ask further questions. 'But you are not me, and you are not *them*. You need not be bound by rules or loyalty or… contracts.'

I looked at William, but he was frowning at the gardener, just as confused as I was. Still, Beatrice was the only one who had listened to us at all, the only person in the whole house who didn't try to tell us that we were confused, or wrong, or *misbehaving*. Maybe that meant she was the only one who could help.

'We found things,' I said, ignoring the way William rolled his eyes and pressing on before I could second guess myself. 'We found pages from Dad's diary and a recording.'

'A recording?' echoed Beatrice.

'There was a voice box in Uncle Edward's office – a woman. She said she was thinking about names, and that they'd be together so–'

I couldn't even finish the sentence before Beatrice had jumped to her feet, her eyes going wide – in horror? In surprise? She pressed her hands to her mouth and started pacing in front of us, while I pointedly ignored William looking at me to say *I told you so* without actually saying it.

Beatrice paused, and her eyes flicked back and forth over the ground in front of her, like a mathematician doing sums in her head. 'You... you found her voice box?' she said, her eyes finally settling on me. 'You listened to the message?'

William decided to leave me to it, focusing fully on the security of his coat buttons. I met the gardener's eyes – she was almost trembling. 'Yes,' I said. 'Do– do you know who she is?'

Beatrice shook her head, suddenly, violently. 'You have to ask the right questions!' She turned away. She took a deep, steadying breath, and I followed her eyes as they went to the stairs. Her trembling hands came to rest at her sides. 'You should be getting back to your rooms,' she said. 'I can–'

William shook his head without looking up. Perhaps it wasn't the best idea to trouble the gardener further.

'Actually...' I began.

'*Please*,' said Beatrice, turning back to me. She was almost begging. 'Please let me.'

I couldn't help it. I nodded.

We followed her up the spiralling staircase and into the house, drifting through the twisting, overwrought hallways toward the library. Forgotten portraits and bent statues loomed in every alcove and corner, but Beatrice barely spared them a glance. At the place where we usually turned left to get to our rooms, Beatrice turned right.

'Er– our rooms–'

But Beatrice shook her head, beckoning us to follow.

William opened his mouth to say something, but I ignored him and continued after the gardener. A few more turns, and we were at the end of the portrait gallery that led back past the library toward the East Wing. Beatrice stopped. She looked up at the portraits of men and women lining the hall. 'I should go,' she said softly. And before I could stop her, she'd hurried off, back down the hall toward the greenhouse, abandoning us among the previous Masters of Ravenscourt Manor.

'So... I'm pretty sure she's nutters,' said William when she'd disappeared into the corridors.

I had to admit he was probably right. I'd been hoping for *something* from Beatrice – some hint or direction or advice. But in the end, even she hadn't been able to help us.

The Masters glared down at us as we made our way back to the room. William pulled ahead of me – I couldn't imagine where he was so anxious to go – and I trailed behind him, peering up at the portraits. We came to the end of the line, and just as I'd noticed on our first night, Uncle Edward's piece of wall remained blank-

But only on the Master's side.

I came to a stop as I set eyes on the final portrait hanging, unpaired, at the end of the line of Ladies. Cold blue eyes stared out of the frame, glittering with something close to life. The voice from the brass voice box echoed in the back of my mind, and I could've slapped myself at the realization.

'William!' I called after him. 'It's *her*.'

'Ariel Raban-Black,' said William when we'd gotten back to our sitting room. 'Born 1851. Died 1877. Sent Uncle Edward a voice letter about names.'

'That's the secret Dad was keeping for Uncle Edward,' I said. 'It has to be. Uncle Edward was courting her in secret and didn't want anyone to find out.'

'But Dad got scared.'

'But *why*?'

The question lingered, and as much as I turned everything over in my head, for the life of me, I couldn't see how it all fit together – how any of it related to Lily's murder, or what it could've had to do with Father's exile… or his death.

William, on the other hand, had come to a conclusion. 'We need to find out how she died,' he said.

I frowned at him. 'But where could we even find that?'

'They'd have those records at the church, obviously,' he answered.

I blinked at him. 'How do you *know* these things?'

'I read books without vampires in them every once in a while,' he answered with a withering look that was better off ignored.

'So we have to find a way to get to the church,' I said. 'Well, Mum did want us to find something to *distract ourselves*.'

William grinned. 'I'd say it's about time I got to visit the village.'

And so, the next morning, after breakfast, we found ourselves making our way, once more, to Mother's room. As much as I knew that we needed to convince

Mother to take us to the village to get any further, I couldn't help the sour feeling that rose in my stomach at the thought of asking her for a favour. I tried to rearrange my face into some semblance of 'staying out of trouble'–

'Abby, you look like you're in pain.'

That earned my brother his first look of the day, but I settled for keeping my face blank as we came to Mother's door. I would try to avoid glowering as much as possible, but if Mother expected anything more pleasant than that from me, she was going to have to learn to deal with disappointment.

I let William do the talking. As Mother ushered us in, and sat us down, and listened to William's proposal of visiting the village, she kept her lips pressed into a thin line – apparently she hadn't forgotten yesterday's confrontation either. I was sure that she'd say no. But then her face softened, and she smiled, and the next thing I knew, she was planting a kiss on William's forehead and flitting up from the couch.

'What a lovely idea, William! Let me get ready. Perhaps we might run into the Carvers as well. Samantha's brother should be returning soon, and it would be good for you to meet him. And you two should bundle up. It's been getting quite chilly!'

Less than an hour later, we were on our way, down the forest road toward the village. The day was overcast but bright, the sun shining through thin veils of cloud. As we pulled into the square, the clock was chiming half past noon, and I eyed the doors of the church, considering how to get myself to the records without raising Mother's suspicions. There was only one option, really.

'Mum, do you think I might call on Emily Carol? I ran into her at the church last time, and I'd… rather like to see her again.' The words came out limp, but of course it was only completely a lie.

Still, I guess that the idea that I might actually be making friends here – with girls of my age, and the pastor's daughter, no less – must've given Mother some hope that maybe, just maybe, I wasn't the uselessly antisocial trouble-making nutcase she had been starting to believe I was, because she positively beamed as she answered. 'Of course, Abigail! Why don't we all–'

William came to the rescue. '*I* want to see the tinker's shop,' he said, not quite whining, but close. 'Abigail said she got to see it while I was sick, and it's not fair.'

I had to marvel at my brother. Mentioning the recovery from his fit was all it took. Mother looked from him, to the church, to me, and back, and the next moment, she was following him down one of the side streets, pausing just long enough to give me a good, solid glare and say:

'If you are not back in this square by four o'clock on the dot, young lady, *I will hunt you down.*'

And they were gone. I turned toward the church, skirting the main steps and following the curve of the wall almost to the cemetery. The door to the sacristy lay tucked away behind a leafless butterfly bush, firmly closed, the windows on either side dark. It didn't look like anyone was there at the moment, though it would still have been polite to knock, just in case.

I tried the door instead.

It opened without a sound, and I poked my head into the receiving room. It was warm, and plush, and absolutely empty. The fire had burned down to embers in the hearth, and the light was low, but the room was bright enough, lined with shelves of books, several doors in the far wall leading further into the church.

I stepped inside and shut the door behind me, pulling off my mittens and warming my hands above the dying fire. Photographs rested on the mantle, pictures of the Pastor and his family. A woman who shared Emily's elegant features peered out of the centre-most picture frame, her sharp eyes dark and piercing, wearing a type of embroidered robe that I'd only ever seen in books and stories about Sina and the Far East.

It was easy enough to find the record room. It was tucked behind the creakiest of the three doors leading out of the receiving room: a small, square space no bigger than a lady's closet, stacked floor to ceiling with ledgers. The towering piles rose, slightly teetering, against all four walls. There was a ladder propped in one corner for the upper stacks, and a single, over-head window let in columns of white light, which filtered down through clouds of glittering dust. Everything smelled of must and paper.

There had to be at least several hundred ledgers, all of them hundreds of pages long. And I had to find one name in all of the names – a single line on a single page. At least with the needle in a haystack, you always had the option of using a magnet – I'd be lucky if I managed to get through even half of these books before Mother came to hunt me down, providing, of course, that no one *else* caught me picking through records before then.

The door to the rectory clicked open. *Rats*.

'Abigail? Abigail Crowe! I *saw* you sneak in here!'

It was Emily, of course. I'd mostly been hoping to avoid her, but if anyone would know how to navigate the stacks, it would have to be Miss Keeper-of-the-Dead.

'In here!' I called.

She poked her pale face through the door. 'So you are. And what, pray tell, are you doing?'

'I need to find a death record.'

'Date?'

'1877.'

Emily's face lit up and she grinned. 'It wouldn't, by any chance, happen to be the record for Lily Crowe?'

'No,' I said. Emily's smile disappeared, replaced by a slight frown, and I had to admit that I felt more than a little proud of myself for taking her by surprise.

But Emily was all business. She stepped into the room properly and strode to the back corner, tossing her coat aside onto one of the stacks. 'Then I'm going to need a more precise date, as well as the name.'

'The name is Ariel Raban-Black, and I don't have a more precise date. 1877's all I've got.'

She sounded out the name silently, her eyebrows knitted in confusion. 'Well, we'll have to start at the beginning then,' she said. She ran her fingers along the spines of several ledgers, pulling two of them down from a low shelf. 'This first one's the aristocratic general registry for 1877,' she said, handing the first one to me. 'And *this* one's the regional death registry for January. You look through that one first.'

I took the book and sank down onto a short pile of ledgers, the books wobbling beneath me as I began my search. I fully expected Emily to leave me to it, but instead of ducking out of the room to abandon me in my research, she sat down next to me with the January ledger and started scanning pages herself.

It was boring work, looking for some sign of Ariel Raban-Black. The woman wasn't in the aristocratic ledger, nor in the registries for January, February, or March. Even though I started out studying each name thoroughly (sometimes checking it twice), before long, I resorted to simply scanning the pages for a capital A or R or B, trying to flip through the pages as quickly as I could.

'William's better at this sort of thing,' I muttered. Ariel hadn't shown up in April, and my legs were starting to go numb.

Emily replaced the ledger on its stack and pulled down two more, handing me June and flipping open July on her lap. 'Your brother,' she said, allowing his existence. 'Is he doing any better since his fit?'

I looked up from June's first page. 'How do you know about–'

'Beatrice told me,' she answered, shrugging without pausing in her search through July. 'She gave me those pages too, if you were still wondering. Though I figured they'd be more use to you than they were to me.'

She continued to flip through pages, and, once again, I found myself trying to figure out whether there was something wrong with the girl, and what, exactly it could be. If she noticed me staring, she didn't seem fazed by it at all, and I still couldn't decide how I felt about her. So I returned to my ledger and continued scanning.

June was short. I finished it, and then August, and picked up October. Every once in a while, I'd come to a stop on a name, catching a large, loopy R or the Pastor's unique A, only to find that it turned into Anna or Agatha or Royce or–

'What kind of a name is *Radagast*?'

'You find all sorts in these,' answered Emily. 'For instance, Mrs. Mews' grandmother – October 13th, 1820 – her name was Mortadella.'

'Isn't that a disease?'

'An Italian meatloaf.'

I tried not to laugh at that. October was done, and Emily was working through November. The only thing left was December. I picked it up and started searching, but we'd almost run out of ledger. Despite all the deaths held in a year of records, we were nearing the end, and there was still no sign of Ariel.

Emily set aside November and stood with a sigh. 'Maybe there are special records in the safe or something…'

I continued flipping through the pages. Had I missed her? Marisa, Lanthir, Cersei, Goyle – I ran my finger along the names as I passed over them.

Ariel.

I came back to the page with a start, halting my finger next to the name. 'She's here!'

Emily paused and came back to peer over my shoulder. I smoothed out the page, leaning close to examine the knotted letters.

Name of Deceased: Ariel Raban-Black | Date: 28 December 1877 | Cause of Death: Fatal Injury | Death Reported by: Lewis Crowe

'Dad was the one who reported her death,' I breathed. I ran my finger along the line again, catching, over and over, on that cause of death: *Fatal Injury*. What kind of injury? How had it happened? But of course there wasn't anything more that the page could tell me. It simply recorded that the event had happened. It wouldn't tell me why, or exactly how, or what anybody felt about it. Still, I couldn't help but look down the page, searching for more information.

I stopped at the next name down. My eye had caught on the elaborate C of a Crowe. I stared at the words written just below Ariel Raban-Black's record, my breath catching in my chest. I'd half expected to see my grandmother's name written there, but the name that stared back up at me was entirely different – but not entirely unfamiliar.

Name of Deceased: Damon Crowe

A YULETIDE CAROL

I stared down at the record in front of me. *Damon Crowe?* It couldn't be. But the name was there, written in black ink on the yellowing page. Emily's skirt rustled as she leaned forward to look more closely at the entry with me.

Name of Deceased: Damon Crowe | Date: 28 December 1877 | Cause of Death: Stillborn (Mother Expired) | Death Reported by: Lewis Crowe

Emily exhaled sharply, her breath tickling my neck. 'Is that...?'

The words from the brass voice box echoed in my mind, making sudden, startling sense. *I rather like Damon, for a boy.*

'Uncle Edward had a son.'

'*Illegitimate* son, judging by the record,' corrected Emily, her voice matter-of-fact. 'And he never lived.'

'He had a *son*. And Dad–' The thought died on my lips as I took a deep, shuddering breath. Dad must've known – about Ariel, about all of it. *I'm done keeping your secrets*, he'd written. And now, finally, I knew which secrets he'd meant. But what, exactly, had he intended to do about all these secrets? Whom had he meant to tell? And most importantly, would Uncle Edward really have let him?

What would my uncle have been willing to do to stop him?

I snapped the ledger closed and set it on the ground. The air felt heavy. 'I– I think Uncle Edward might have killed my father,' I said, finally.

Emily didn't answer. She picked up the ledger and put it back where it belonged, stepping out of the room while I tried once more to straighten out the thoughts in my head. Uncle Edward had been involved with Ariel. They'd had a son. They'd died, and Dad had known. But there was still something missing, some piece of it that I couldn't quite see clearly yet.

Emily returned with a tray of tea, setting it up as a makeshift table on three piles of death records. I took a steaming cup when she offered it, and we sat together in uneasy quiet among the mouldering records of the town's dead.

'Five years ago, half the town, my father included, were convinced that my mother was stark-raving mad,' she began. 'To be honest, you couldn't blame them – she was caught doing some odd things: covering all the mirrors in the house because she was convinced that *they* were watching her; leaving bowls of water out to keep away non-existent shades; and sometimes, in the middle of dinner, she'd go suddenly quiet, looking up into the air, listening for someone – or something.

'Of course, Laurie and I knew she wasn't mad. She was suffering from something, but it wasn't some loose spring in her head, no broken cog – whatever she was experiencing was as real as you and me sitting here now. Still, people started to talk, and eventually the Inquisitors were called. They decided that she ought to be locked up, that she belonged in the prison on Maleth with all the other dangerous witches and sorcerers – for her own safety of course. But before anything could be arranged, she walked out into the snow one morning, and never came back.'

I studied Emily over the rim of my teacup, but her face was a blank page. She might as well have been talking about Mrs. Mews' cats for all the distress she showed.

'No one really cared enough to find out what actually happened to her. Father made a show of trying, of course, but when a few years passed without any sign of where she'd gone, he filled out the death certificate himself. We pretended to have a funeral, and Father remarried, and everyone tried to forget about our poor, mad mum.'

'Why are you telling me this?'

'Because I want to *help* you, Abigail,' answered Emily. 'Rumours are nasty things. They lurk in the shadows and feed off people's worst instincts. But truth... the truth is light.'

If truth was light, I was still fumbling around a dark room. 'I just wish I knew what the truth *was*.'

At that, Emily frowned. 'You said that Doctor Crowe might have murdered your father.'

'Yes. Because Dad knew – he *knew*. About Ariel and about the child. And... and those pages you gave me–'

'They rather suggested that Lily's death might have also been Doctor Crowe's fault,' said Emily, her brow creased in thought now, as she stared at the tea sitting between us. I took another sip from my steaming cup and studied the bits of tea leaves floating just under the surface.

'But it's rather difficult to find anything in the house – there's too many locked doors. Is there any way to find out more about how she died?' I asked at last. 'Ariel, I mean.'

Emily looked up to meet my eyes. 'A pastor keeps records from every Resting he performs. They're not public – my father keeps his in the rectory, and strictly speaking, no one's allowed access.'

'But...'

'But that will have to be where we look next,' said Emily with a shrug. 'Adeline was planning on inviting your family over for Yuletide dinner. We just have to make sure–'

'That we can get to Ariel's record during dinner without getting caught.'

Emily nodded at me, beaming. She leaned forward and reached out, laying her hands on mine – steadying them, though I hadn't even realized they were trembling. 'It won't be easy. It never is. But until then, if you need anything – *anything* – you make sure to ask me.'

'Right,' I heard myself say. I wasn't sure that I understood what had happened. Had Emily and I just become friends? And here I'd thought that I was more likely (and more willing) to be eaten by a shark than to hear even a whisper of friendship from Emily Carol. Though, I guess we weren't exactly planning girls' nights and sleepovers any time soon. 'Right. I will.'

She grinned. 'Good. Now, you should probably let your brother know about recent developments.'

I wandered back into the square to find William tossing scraps of bread and biscuits at the few brave winter pigeons still willing to face the cold. Mother was watching him from the steps of the clock tower, a smile hovering on her lips. The weight of everything I'd just learned pressed down on me, and I lingered at the edge of the square, waiting for the clouds to darken and the storm to break. But the day remained bright, and the pigeons went about their business, and despite all the awful things that I knew to be true, Mother continued to smile.

Of course, she didn't know what I'd found out. She hadn't seen the records, and she trusted Uncle Edward.

What would she do, if she learned the truth? Would she even believe me if I told her?

Or would she wave it off, all so that she could keep smiling?

William caught me staring and waved, Mother looking up and beckoning me over so that we could catch the carriage back to Ravenscourt.

'Did you have fun with Emily, dear?' she asked as soon as we were moving. And though all the truths and secrets I'd discovered were bursting to be said, all I could do was look straight at William as I answered:

'It was *enlightening*.'

The carriage ride dragged on in tense silence, both William and I itching to be away. So when finally the carriage pulled into the drive, and the driver opened the doors, we raced inside and up the stairs and barely managed to slip into our sitting room before it burst out:

'He had a son!'

William stared. 'What?'

'Uncle Edward and Ariel. They had a son. Damon.'

My brother's eyes went wide. 'You mean–'

'They died,' I said. 'Both of them. And Dad–'

'Must've told someone,' finished William for me. 'Because he was done keeping secrets. Or at least threatened to tell.'

'And I don't think Uncle Edward would have appreciated that very much,' I said. 'And we already know that he was capable of murder.'

'You mean–'

'If it came down to it, he might have decided to kill Dad.'

My brother's lips twisted into a frown. 'But why now? Why wait?'

'I don't know,' I answered honestly. Silence settled between us as I turned the situation over and over again in my head. 'And we still need proof. Something to show Mother – or the Inquisitors.'

'So then…?'

I took a deep breath. Emily had already made the plan. I just had to trust that she'd follow through on it. 'Well, Emily thinks that she can find Ariel's resting record. If we can get our hands on *that*–'

'Then maybe it'll tell us more about what happened,' said William. But he was still frowning. 'And if we can't find it?'

It was a fair question. I searched the room for an answer, but all I saw were the iron bars and the wilting flowers and the moth-bitten curtains. We were trapped here, and if we couldn't find the proof we needed–

'Then we find something else. Even a magician makes mistakes. And when he does–'

'We'll be ready.'

Over the next couple of days, the house erupted into a flurry of activity as the staff began their preparations for Yule and Wintersnacht. Whenever William and I ventured into the hallways of the house, we'd catch glimpses of their work – sprigs of holly pinned above windows and wreaths tied to doors, clusters of mistletoe hung like spider's egg sacs from the arching ceilings. Garlands of baubles would sprout along the walls overnight, like holiday fungus, and after one especially awkward lunch with Mother and Uncle Edward, we came back to our rooms to find a bright red bow with noisy bells nailed to our door.

I ripped it off and tossed it in the nearest closet.

But worse than that, ever since that night when we'd woken to screams and tremors, we found our door locked by the time it was eleven, trapped in our rooms until the maid came by to bring us breakfast the next morning. The first couple nights, William had tried to pick the lock, but with no luck. The door wouldn't budge. So even if we'd hoped to find something before Emily's Yule invitation, it was impossible to continue our investigation without being caught by the Housekeeper. All we could do was wait.

Finally, on the morning of the 21st, we woke to a steely sky and a tray of pancakes, and Mother came by with a knock on the door to let us know that we'd be joining the Carols for dinner. 'Do try to make yourselves presentable,' she said.

William and I did our best to keep our faces blank.

When we finally set out at five in the evening, the sky was already growing dark. Heavy clouds gathered overhead, and as Uncle Edward's carriage travelled the worn lane that led south to the Rectory, the first airy flakes of winter flurries began to fall. By the time we pulled up to the Carols' house, the entire world looked like someone had tried to tuck it away under some ratty woollen blanket, except that the hills and treetops insisted on poking through the holes.

We stepped onto the stoop, Mother making last minute adjustments to William's collar and my hair. 'Good first impression now,' she said and rang the bell.

The door burst open, and a towering woman appeared, her glittering dress assaulting us with green. Mrs. Carol's blond hair had been piled high on top of her head in some attempt at a bun, and her fingers sparkled with half-a-dozen bejewelled rings. Her bulging eyes – the same shade of violent green as her dress – were outlined in black, and it took a moment after she opened the door for her to focus on us properly. She shrieked – I couldn't tell whether it was from surprise or excitement – before reaching through the door and pulling both me and William forcibly into the house. Before I could manage to dodge it, she'd also given me a sharp pinch on the cheek, and I glanced sideways to see William pressing his hand against his own pinch-marked face, horrified.

'Come in! Come in! The gentlemen are already waiting.'

She led us through several hallways with low, cream-colored ceilings and bright-painted walls. Pastel portraits and watercolour prints of drooping children and wide-eyed animals peered down on us as we made our way through the halls, and though they were far from the twisted statues and grim paintings of Ravenscourt's galleries, I couldn't say they were much of an improvement. Certainly, if you had to find a house that was the perfect opposite of Ravenscourt, the Carols' rectory would've been it. I got the feeling that neither dust nor cobwebs would ever have dared to grace the corner of a single one of Mrs. Carol's flowery-scented rooms. And yet, I almost found myself missing the soot-stained tapestries and the peeling wall paper and the sinister seeping drafts. At least with Ravenscourt, you could tell the place was being honest.

Mrs. Carol led us into the parlour, a small, cosy space with pink walls and green-cushioned chairs and edges lined with frilly lace, where Uncle Edward already sat, talking to a thick-faced gentleman who must've been Pastor Carol.

'It's not a decision to be made lightly, Edward,' the Pastor was saying. 'Of course, if you've already decided on it – '

He cut off as we entered. Both men looked up at us, and Pastor Carol's face immediately broke into a wide grin, not so different from Emily's, as he bounded over to greet Mother with a bow.

The adults settled into their seats, leaving me and William pretty much to ourselves. William immediately started inspecting all the knickknacks that Mrs. Carol had scattered throughout the room, bending down to peer into vases and poking at picture frames and figurines. I hovered while the adults talked and laughed and gossiped, or at least, while the women and Pastor Carol did. Uncle Edward, on the other hand, seemed more interested in the fire than the chatter, staring into the flames with all the broody silence of a penny dreadful villain.

Mother and Mrs. Carol hadn't even managed to get to the half-way scandalous gossip before Emily and Laurie appeared, followed by the Carols' butler, who ushered us into the dining room for dinner. Emily manoeuvred her way to my side as we made our way out of the parlour, taking my arm and leaning close so that she could whisper her plan to me.

'I managed to track down the resting records,' she said, her words barely more than breaths against my ear. 'Father keeps them in one of the cellars. We'll have to sneak away after dinner, if we can manage it.'

'We'll manage it,' I whispered back, as we entered the dining room, and Mrs. Carol set me and Emily down on opposite sides of the table. The Pastor took his place at the head of the table, Uncle Edward and mother to his right, while Mrs. Carol and the twins sat to his left. I ended up sitting across from Laurie, while William sat at the very end of the table, all my hopes of figuring out a plan with Emily lost to the seating arrangements. But at least I had a distraction: dinner was served. There was a mountainous roast that made my mouth water at the smell of it, dishes piled high with carrots and greens, as well as three kinds of potatoes, all served with butter and tureens of gravy and sauce. Of course the Carols' would have a better cook than Ravenscourt. After all, who has the energy to prepare a proper roast when they've been kept up all night by ghastly wails?

The Pastor said a brief grace, raised his glass, and with that, the table went silent, everyone too focused on the food to spare their mouths for useless things like talking.

After the first furious round of serving and eating and passing plates and pepper and gravy around the table, the hum of conversation bubbled back up again, the Pastor trying and failing to get Uncle Edward to share more than two words, while Mother and Mrs. Carol continued exchanging news about everyone in town. Emily had mostly finished her plate, and she caught my eye across the table, slowly mouthing a few words in the hopes that I could make them out:

We'll – have – to –

But she was cut off by Mrs. Carol, who interrupted suddenly, reaching over to place a hand on her step-daughter's arm.

'Now take this one, for example,' said the woman to the entire table and giving Emily a pointed glare. 'Been out in society for almost a year now, haven't you, love?'

Emily looked at the hand on her arm as if it were a venomous spider and said nothing. But Mrs. Carol continued on unfazed. 'Hasn't made any progress, of course. Can't find a single decent boy willing to deal with her. Both you and your brother nearly sixteen, and no prospects whatsoever.' She tsked.

For the first time that I'd seen, Emily actually looked uncomfortable. Her cheeks had turned an unnatural shade of pink, and she bit her lip, sawing into the bit of roast left on her plate with a vengeance.

'But how about yours, Maris, love?' continued Mrs. Carol. 'Can't be much longer before–'

'Oh, Adeline,' said Mother with a delicate laugh. 'It'll be a couple years before she's ready. She's only thirteen.'

'Oh, but it's never too early to start preparing, you ought to know. She'll need a dance instructor, and tutors: art, music, French, of course. And the event itself, why, you might need an entire year to–'

She continued outlining my societal debut, while Mother nodded along, with the blank, staring look that you only ever saw when she was overwhelmed. Emily caught my eye from across the table and shook her head, before she began miming the actions of hanging herself. By the time her step-mother got down to the details of dresses and shoes, Emily had hung herself, shot herself, slit her wrists, slit her throat, and drowned herself (or, at the very least, I *think* that one was drowning herself) in mime.

'It's something to consider, you must admit,' ended Mrs. Carol. 'Especially if you want to find her a good match – and it won't be cheap.' She took a sip of her wine, her lips leaving blood-red marks on the glass. 'Speaking of which, we haven't yet talked about your own prospects, Maris, love.'

The entire table went silent as I choked on my potatoes.

'You mean…' attempted Mother, before abandoning the question.

'Of course, I'm not suggesting you be too hasty, or anything. By all means, take your time to mourn. But don't fool yourself into thinking that you'll be a widow for the rest of your life. After all, what's that they say? Other fish in the sea, and all that?' She smiled, and I had to drop my silverware to clench my fists against the urge to land a punch on those paint-cracked lips of hers. 'There's always a better prospect,' she said.

'Are you serious?' The words were out of my mouth before I could stop myself. And though the entire table turned to me, not even their glares could stop the rest of the words from coming out. 'My father is not some worn out cog to be replaced at our earliest convenience!'

'Abigail,' warned Mother, but her voice was soft. Uncle Edward leaned back in his seat and lifted his glass of wine to his lips, smiling, but I tried my best to ignore that, and the appalled stare of the Pastor too. Instead, I focused my entire glare on Mrs. Carol, who, instead of looking ashamed or surprised, was positively grinning with amusement.

'Oh, love,' she said. 'I meant nothing of the sort. But of course you'd be too young to understand the needs of adults.'

'I think I understand plenty, thank you very much.'

'Well, then surely you wouldn't want your mother to be alone for the rest of her life?'

'She's not alone. She has us.'

At that, Mrs. Carol burst out laughing. 'Hardly the same, young Abigail!' she said. 'Hardly the same. Two children are more of a burden than anything, and without a husband, why, you'll be lucky to avoid a workhouse yourself.'

'I can take care of myself.'

'Oh, I think you'll come to see differently in a few years.' She tilted her glass to her painted lips, draining the wine from it in one long swallow. 'But of course, that's not the point,' she said and set the empty glass on the table. 'The point is, your father's absence is a problem easily solved, if you simply accept certain facts as true.'

'I'm sure you would think so, being the replacement wife of a widower.'

At last, I'd wiped the smile off her face. Mrs. Carol's poisonous eyes went wide. I wanted to laugh, and for a brief moment, I almost could have, before I realized exactly what I'd done:

I'd just insulted the Pastor's wife. In front of the Pastor himself. In his house. At his dinner table.

Mother was not going to let me survive this.

I took a deep breath through my nose, and though my face felt hot enough to fry eggs, though my hands were trembling, I stood from the table with as much calm as I could muster. I folded my napkin onto my chair. And without so much as a backward glance, ignoring every single one of the shocked stares, I crossed the dining room, exited into the hall, and let myself out the back door, into the Carols' garden.

The night air was clear and cold, stars glittering above, and I set myself down on a boulder at the edge of the lawn, dusted with snow, though of course I didn't have my coat. The frosty air stung my lungs as I breathed it in. The lights of the Carol house cut through the darkness. Maybe if I just stayed out here long enough, they'd forget all about me, and I could run off and join the circus, or something, as one of their freak shows: Abigail, the Witless Wonder. Watch her put her foot in her mouth! See her awkward attempts at humour!

I sighed, my breath coming out in a cloud of steam. How long could I stay out here before they sent someone to fetch me? How long did I dare to avoid them?

The back door of the house opened, and someone approached across the lawn, the snow crunching under her feet.

'Emily?'

She drifted over to join me on my boulder, and I saw that she was smiling – a slight, hovering smile so different from her usual bare-toothed grin. 'I just wanted to thank you,' she said. 'You have no idea how many times I've wanted to slap that woman.'

I released my breath, and suddenly the weight on my shoulders didn't feel so heavy. Chill air whispered through the trees, and Emily traced her fingers over the stone.

'She deserved it,' said Emily.

'I know she deserved it,' I answered, because she did. 'But still, I'm–'

Emily stopped me, pressing her ice-cold fingers to my lips. 'Don't you *dare* apologize,' she said. 'Not to me and not to the Replacement. If anyone should be apologizing, it's her.'

I shook my head. 'But how do you deal with her?'

'I try not to,' said Emily with a sigh. 'I mean, it was hard when Mum disappeared. And then… well, I like to imagine that Father was overcome with grief when he decided to marry that witch.' She sighed again. 'But time helps things… cures most wounds, as it were. Or, at the very least, it makes you forget how much they hurt. It is absolutely *astounding* how much you can get used to.'

We sat, our breaths steaming the air.

'Besides, I don't think even Laurie could've engineered a better excuse for our absence,' said Emily suddenly. She looked at me, and I saw her grin was back: bright and full of mischief.

'The Resting records?' I said.

'The Resting records,' she answered. 'But we still ought to be quick about it. Come on.'

We slipped back into the house like thieves, trying our best to silence our footsteps as we avoided passing anywhere close to the dining room, where the others were still chatting. We made our way to the foyer instead, and down a short side hall, to find a door that looked just like all the others in the Carol house: plain and wooden and unimposing.

But Emily drew a key from her pocket, unlocked the door with a click, and pushed it open to reveal a stone stairway leading down into the basement.

A chill drifted upward from the basement below, damp and shivering cold, and Emily didn't wait to see if I was with her, but started down the steps, never questioning the fact that I would follow.

I closed the door behind me, trusting my feet to the single flickering lamp beside the door. At the bottom of the steps was an iron gate, barely visible in the scarce lamplight. Emily unlocked it with another key, large and heavy, the gate clanking as she undid the lock. And then, the gate was open, and the resting records were there, waiting for us.

I'd been expecting a room rather like the church's registry of births and deaths – a collection of ledgers and paperwork, musty with the weight of old books. But the resting records were something else altogether. The windowless room lay dim and lightless, except for the soft, silvery glow of the records themselves.

There were rows upon rows of them, a labyrinth of shelves, all of them weighed down with glass vials, glittering and brilliant, though there were no lamps and neither Emily nor I had thought to bring a candle. No, what little light we needed to see came all from those glass vials, each and every one of them with the glimmer of a pulsing star in its heart.

'Emily?' I whispered. 'What exactly are Resting records?'

She turned to me, her face turned to shadows in the eerie glow of the records. 'Every time a spirit is rested, the pastor invites it to leave a bit of itself behind, for the records.'

My skin turned prickly with cold. 'Then these are—'

Emily grinned, her teeth all that I could see in her shadowed face. 'Ghosts,' she said.

She led the way through the records, and I caught glimpses of the labels attached to each glowing vial: Rosemarie Gallant, Lanthir Navarre, Thomas Peverell. And as I turned my gaze to each bit of spirit, and read the names of those who had passed, it seemed to me that they glowed brighter – that somehow, they were reaching out to me, calling for my attention.

A thought occurred to me. 'Would Damon's record be here as well?' I asked.

But Emily shook her head. 'Records aren't kept for children... or the unborn.'

Which I supposed made sense. How much could a baby really leave behind, without any time to learn language or experience anything of the world?

We came to a shelf tucked away in the back of the room, and Emily slowed to a crawl, bending forward to examine the labels more closely. Apparently, the records were arranged alphabetically by name: we'd found the shelf full of R's, including Vladmir Royce and Horatio Radagast.

'Arial Raban,' announced Emily, plucking one of the vials from its place on the shelf. She held it out to me. 'The honours, I think, are yours.'

I took the vial. It was small and round, almost small enough to wear as a pendant, with a narrow neck stoppered by a cork. It burned like ice in my fingers, and looking closely, I saw veins of some dark metal tracing the shapes of wards through the depths of the bright, clear crystal. The spirit trapped inside – Ariel's spirit – flared brighter as I picked at the cork, though the vial only grew colder. I pulled the stopper free.

The spirit burst from the glass, the entire room thrown into harsh illumination, a dark landscape suddenly revealed by lightning. I half expected to see her, to come face-to-face with her fully-formed spectre, but the only thing left of her was a hovering ball of light and her voice – that sweet voice that I'd heard once before, warped by the gears of a voice box.

'It takes some measure of desperation to seek a ghost,' said Ariel's voice. 'Perhaps, what I warned you of has come to pass? No, but you are not who I expected.'

That brilliant light swirled in front of me, the spirit's glow touching my face. 'I–' I wasn't sure what to say to her, whether she would even hear me. 'My name is Abigail–' I tried.

Her response cut me off: 'Oh, I've no patience left for names. No, you came because you wish to know something from me. I'm afraid it's useless for me to know anything of *you*–'

'But can you answer my questions?'

'I can try.'

'May I ask how you died?'

The voice went silent, as if thinking, and the air snapped with cold, my breath rising in a luminous cloud between me and the spirit. 'A brother overcome by fear. A mother trying to protect her sons. But I...' She trailed off, the light dimming a little, pulling into itself, pulling away from me. 'Oh, but words are so... difficult... it has been so long.'

I looked to Emily, who was frowning into the light, and she turned to meet my eyes. 'Ask her to show you.'

'Show me?' I echoed.

'Shall I?' asked the spirit. 'Yes, perhaps that...'

I turned back to the light. 'You can *show* me what happened to you?'

'I can. But you must let go of your defences.'

I looked down to where my fingers had started twisting my ring – I'd been setting my First Defence without even realizing it. With a nod, I relaxed my hands. 'Show me,' I said.

The light flared once more, and a single tendril of bright spirit drifted forward to brush my eyelids, like gentle fingers urging my eyes closed. And though I was strangely conscious of my feet planted on the floor of the record room, and of the glass vial growing warmer in my hands, I felt myself falling forward, the light of Ariel's spirit rising up to carry me away, leading me through a cold, empty place filled with grey light, and further, into a raging stream of sound and feeling.

Images rose up to assault me, half-formed faces with nothing but black wells for eyes, the halls of Ravenscourt house turned into an inescapable labyrinth, echoing with voices. As I drifted through the warped halls, figures emerged from the darkness – there was my uncle, the grey gone from his hair, his face untouched by the decades of lines and worries. He sat next to my father, at Ravenscourt's dining table, both of them looking up as I stepped into the hall. Father stood to pull out the chair next to him, and as I sat down, Uncle Edward smiled across the table – a real smile, warm and almost charming.

The hall fell dark, and the world shifted around me, a dizzying whirlpool of secret glances and smiles and clasped hands, the house falling into the cold of winter. Once again, the halls of the house fell into place around me, and I saw my father, his shadow rising against the wall, and Uncle Edward facing him, their shouts making the air tremble, the words broken and twisted until they were almost unrecognizable –

'You can't ignore this any longer!' exclaimed Dad, his words suddenly clear. 'It's dangerous– Edward– '

My uncle turned to face his brother. 'You would endanger her for this?'

'You would endanger all of us for her?'

The two brothers faced each other in harsh silence, before Dad's eyes shifted to the hall, and found me–

The walls folded in, and once again, the world shifted, faces rushing past, the scene twisting into the shape of a shade-filled wood dusted with snow, a woman with white skin and a curtain of midnight hair leaning forward to look at me, the empty holes where her eyes should've been threatening to pull me into yet deeper nightmares.

'I take it Lewis told you?' The words escaped my lips in a voice that was not my own, Ariel's words hanging in the air between the woman and me as she smiled gently down with those blank eyes.

'He told me everything I needed to know,' said the woman, and with a jolt, I realized I recognized her. This was Lily Crowe – my grandmother, the woman whose spirit had disappeared, her body lying whole and uncorrupted in the vault beneath the Corvick cemetery. And as a sudden, hot shock lanced through my gut, I looked down to find her hand holding a blood-stained knife, red spreading across my vision before the world faded to grey–

'Abigail!'

The air shook, and I felt myself thrown suddenly backward, opening my eyes to the record room with a horrible lurch – Emily's hand was on my shoulder, but all I could focus on was Ariel's glowing light, and the sickening realization of what had happened–

'It was Father,' I said to the light. 'He betrayed you – he told Lily. He's the reason you–'

'Abigail!' yelled Emily snatching the vial out of my hands. With a whisper to the ghost, the spirit, the record – whatever it was or wasn't – she urged it back into its crystal cage, stoppering the light once again. I stared at her, uncomprehending, and she gripped my shoulder tighter.

I felt sick, shaken, and the floor beneath me was shuddering. It took me a moment to realize that it wasn't just my own light-headed horror. The vials on the shelves had begun to tremble, and as Emily looked up toward the ceiling of the record room, her face went grim. 'Something's wrong,' she said.

Another tremor shook the shelves, and my blood went cold as I realized–

The tremors weren't coming from the records. The tremors were coming from above: from upstairs, from the house.

'William!' I shoved past Emily, bolting for the stairs, racing to find my brother, even as the walls began to shake in earnest.

I stumbled into the upstairs halls, picture frames and windows rattling, the chandeliers shaking above me, an open threat. Down the main entrance hall, into the dining room – it was empty already – I threw myself through the door into the sitting room. My eyes tore over the room, torn doilies and shattered plates, broken glass and books scattering devastation across the floor. Movement, a yell–

Everything went suddenly still.

The Carols stood frozen in shock in one corner of the room. In another, Mother leaned against the wall for support. She pressed her limp hand to her chest, as she watched Uncle Edward bent over my brother in the middle of the room. And William–

He lay unconscious, Uncle Edward towering over him, the needle still pressed into his neck. I couldn't even see whether or not my brother was breathing, he'd gone so still–

I rushed to his side. 'I thought you'd cured him!' I yelled at Uncle Edward.

But he ignored me. 'Charles,' he said to the Pastor. 'If you please, I need to take him back to the manor immediately.'

'I– I'll ready the carriage,' said Pastor Carol, and he left the room.

William *was* breathing. His breaths were weak, almost nothing, but they were there, his chest rising and falling ever so slightly as we waited for the Pastor to return. Uncle Edward paced in front of the fireplace, and Mrs. Carol ventured some soft words of comfort to Mother. At last, the Pastor stepped back into the room and without waiting for anyone to say a thing, Uncle Edward scooped William into his arms and made his way through the entrance hall to meet the waiting carriage.

I was close on his heels. 'I'm coming with you.'

Uncle Edward said nothing, simply climbing the steps into the coach and setting William down on the hard seat. And as I made to climb in after them, Uncle Edward pulled the door shut in my face.

If he thought I was going to abandon William so easily, he was sorely mistaken. I wrenched the door back open and clambered in. 'I'm coming with you,' I said again, and planted myself in the opposite seat. Uncle Edward exhaled heavily in exasperation, but didn't protest further. He stayed still and silent as a prehistoric monolith the entire tense ride back to the manor.

As we pulled into the drive, the Butler came out to greet us, helping Uncle Edward carry William into the house. They started down one of the side halls, and I was determined to follow them to the end, but then Uncle Edward paused, and turning to me, he stopped me with a look that said all it needed to:

You have been warned.

I watched them disappear into the hall, carrying my brother away to some unknown fate. I didn't want to think what Uncle Edward would do if he found me following. It was clear he expected me to stay away, and I already knew what he was capable of.

But of course, the decision had already been made when I followed him into the carriage. I wasn't going to abandon William. And so, twisting my ring and taking a deep breath to summon my defences, I did the only thing I could.

I slipped down the hall after them.

Curiouser and Curiouser

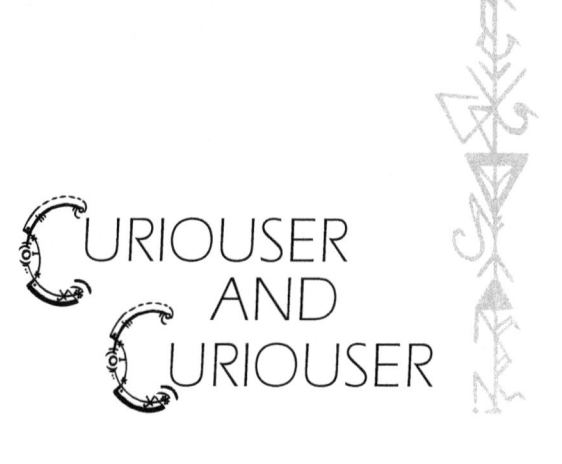

Uncle Edward and the Butler made their way down the halls of the West Wing, passing closed doors and water-stained portraits, their shadows thrown against the walls by the flickering gas lamps. The Butler led the way with William in his arms, while Uncle Edward followed more slowly, leaning heavily on his cane. Neither of them took notice of the way the shadows shifted and bent, and so, slipping from darkness to darkness, I followed them through the maze-like passages, to the very end of a crooked hall, where a large, metal door stood closed.

Uncle Edward pushed the door open, and the men disappeared inside. I darted past the door to duck around the next corner of the hall, and taking deep breaths, I waited.

Some ten minutes later, the men stepped out of the room once more.

'Send for the Carvers. I want this taken care of as soon as possible,' said Uncle Edward. At the mention of the name Carver, my heart stopped. Why did Uncle Edward want to talk to Mr. *Carver*? Why did he need a *mortician*? He couldn't possibly mean…

I didn't let myself follow the thought any further.

'Of course, sir,' answered the Butler.

'If Silas can't come, at the very least make sure Isaac does,' continued Uncle Edward. 'Also, if the girl is not in her room, I want her found immediately.'

The Butler bowed his head in understanding and turned to take his leave. I held my breath–

'Oh, and one more thing, Galen?'

'Yes, sir?'

'Check on Maris for me.'

'Of course, sir.'

At last, the Butler disappeared down the darkened hall, and Uncle Edward ducked back into the room. This time, it was several minutes before he came out again, and he immediately set off down the hall, leaving the door ever so slightly open behind him.

I waited until his uneven footsteps had faded and pushed open the door. It was heavier than it looked but opened easily, and I stepped into the room, making sure to close the door behind me. The room was a laboratory, a round space that felt just a bit too clean, lit with electric lights, their cold glow, so unlike lamp or firelight, casting everything in blue. Chemical bitterness filled the air, mixed with the bloody tang of metal – it was everywhere: the curved walls, the floors, even the ceiling had been cast from the same unidentifiable metal as the door.

William was nowhere to be seen: the room was empty but for the metal counter that wound its way around the left half of the room, topped with scattered papers, fountain pens, test tubes, and flasks. Opposite the counter was another metal door left ajar. The only other thing in the room was an ornate mirror, looking quite out of place. It stood tucked away behind the main door – as if no one could find a proper place for it – and it reflected the entire room back at me, almost as if there were a third doorway leading out of the laboratory.

William could only be behind the second door. I leaned on it to push it open, and it gave such a harsh screech that for a moment, I was sure someone would hear it. I froze, my heart pounding, but everything stayed silent. There were no sudden screams or alarms or footsteps in the hall. I slipped into the room beyond, fumbling blindly along the walls to find a light switch.

As I found the switch, the lights flared to life, electric and cold. The room lay exposed in front of me, and I had to swallow against the sudden urge to vomit.

It was an operating room. The walls gleamed with that same bare metal, the sheets on the operating table a blinding white. And there was William, lying on the table, his face as white as the sheets, and again, I had to cover my mouth, fighting down my nausea. He was alive. At the very least, he was alive, his chest moving with every shallow breath. But needles speared his wrists, pumping strange liquids into his veins from snaking tubes, and wires wove around his head, hooked into machines that clicked and chattered. I stood, light-headed, staring at the pumps and machines, my stomach churning.

Was there any way to get him away from here? Was there any hope of escape?

The sound of heavy footsteps in the hall answered that question for me. Unfortunately, it was a resounding *no*.

I ducked out of the operating room, flicking off the lights, though I didn't dare to close door. Its screech would betray me – I just had to hope that Uncle Edward wouldn't notice. But where ever would I hide?

The footsteps grew louder – not just one pair of feet, but three. There wasn't any furniture in the laboratory: no tables or wardrobes, only the counter on the other side, and it was far too exposed. Even the mirror wasn't big enough to hide me, assuming I could manage to duck behind it, and now a hand was closing on the doorknob. The footsteps paused; there were voices. The doorknob turned, and I darted behind the door just as it swung open, stumbling backward, into the mirror –

Not *against* it, you have to understand. But *into* it, as if it were a pool of water.

The world slipped strange. My skin prickled with eerie cold as I fell through the clear glass, the world on the other side opening its jaws, inside turning outside, outside turning in. I was falling, but instead of falling down, I was falling sideways, everything shifting. At last, my feet found a solid floor, and I looked up to find myself on the other side of the mirror, staring back through the heavy brass frame into the laboratory, just as my uncle stepped into the room and shut the door.

I'd just stepped through a mirror. It shouldn't have been possible, and yet–

I reached forward, to run my fingers along the mirror's brass frame. It felt real enough: solid and cold and smooth, the twisted brass gleaming in some impossible light. My reflection, however, was nowhere to be seen. Searching the glass, all I saw was the laboratory – Uncle Edward's laboratory, with its metal walls and its crowded counters – and in the middle of the room, Uncle Edward himself, explaining the situation, while Mr. Carver and another man (if he were even old enough to be called such) listened attentively.

'...he has been comatose for nearly an hour,' Uncle Edward was saying, while Mr. Carver nodded.

'And the strength of the fit?' asked the younger man.

'I would say...'

Their voices carried into the room – I couldn't imagine how, though at the moment that was, perhaps, the least concerning impossible thing on a very, very, *very* long list of impossible things. After all, I'd just fallen through a mirror, and now, looking at the place that lay on the other side of my uncle's laboratory looking glass, I was starting to think that most mirrors probably had a very good reason for keeping people out.

Not that the room was all that different from the laboratory – at least on the surface. Here, too, there were two doors leading out of the room – one right next to the mirror, the other one on the other side – and a counter, though it ran along the right side of the room instead of the left, which I guess can only be expected from a reflection. Still, I couldn't shake the strange, creeping sense that the edges of the room were shifting, that as soon as I looked away from anything – the doors, the counter, the mirror – that thing would change into something *else*, only snapping back into place when I looked at it again. Even the brass frame of the mirror, identical in every way with the one on the other side, somehow felt like it was welded together from all the wrong angles.

'Shall we take a look at him, then?' asked Mr. Carver, drawing my attention back to the other laboratory – the *real* laboratory.

'Of course,' answered Uncle Edward, pushing the door to the operating room open and ushering the two men inside.

The door screeched closed behind them, leaving the laboratory empty. I could sneak out now. I could sneak away and act like I hadn't seen anything, and maybe I could come up with a plan to rescue William–

But what *was* this place? It couldn't be magic – at least, not any magic that was supposed to be possible. As far as I'd ever heard, the only thing that you might expect to find waiting for you on the far side of a mirror was the realm of the Fey: that shadow world haunted by the trapped Raven King and all those shape-shifting cannibals you heard about in stories. But could I really have just stepped into the Feyrealm? The thought that I might've was equal parts terrifying and impossible – except, of course, that I was standing on the wrong side of a mirror, which implied that there were at least a few things that were rather less impossible than I'd been led to believe.

I wasn't sure how many impossible things I'd have to add and multiply before reaching a conclusion that made any sort of sense. And that, more than anything was the reason why I didn't move, why I didn't escape, why I didn't sneak away from the laboratory when I had the chance. Because not even five minutes later, while I was still trying to figure out where I was and how I'd managed to get there, the operating room door screeched open again, and the younger man stepped out, careful to pull the door closed behind him.

He made his way toward the mirror and leaned in to examine his reflection. To be fair, he had the kind of face that most people wouldn't have minded looking at, with bright, blue-green eyes and blond hair pulled back into a ponytail. He peered into the mirror, straightening his collar and smoothing out his fringe. I rolled my eyes.

There went my escape. I wasn't sure how much longer I'd have to stay in this strange mirror room with its uncomfortable angles, but there was no way I was going to be able to leave while Mr. Afternoonified insisted on preening himself. At last, he seemed satisfied with his appearance: he straightened up. And then, as I watched, his image shifted, shimmering–

He stepped through the mirror.

He did it as easily as stepping through a doorway. First, the tip of his shoe poked through, the rest of his foot reaching through the frame to find the floor on the other side, the flat image of him beyond the glass turned suddenly real. He ducked his head through next, and the rest of him followed, and in the space between breaths, his reflection had disappeared, and he stood in front of me, raising an eyebrow as his eyes met mine.

I waited for him to turn around, to duck back through the mirror and into the real laboratory, to push open the operating room door and call for my uncle. But when almost a minute had passed and he still showed no sign of ratting me out, I decided that I could try being friendly.

I waved.

'Er, hello,' he said. 'You... must be Abigail.'

'Abigail Crowe,' I said with a curtsy. 'Sorry, but I've no idea who you are.'

He gave a small laugh at that, 'Well, I daresay my sister doesn't mention me all that much, and I'd be surprised if you actually talked to my father–'

'You're–?'

He sank into a low bow to match my curtsy. 'Isaac Carver, at your service.'

Of all the places I'd expected to meet Samantha's mysterious brother, I could definitely say that around the back-side of a reflection in a strange-angled mirror-laboratory wasn't one of them. Yet here we were, the other, younger, and objectively better-looking Mr. Carver straightening up from his bow to study me through those blue-green eyes of his. I had the uncomfortable feeling that he was waiting for me to say something – to explain myself, probably, except that I had no explanations. I didn't have much of anything else either – all my words seemed to have flown away.

He let the silence linger a moment before pressing on. 'May I offer to escort you back to your rooms?' he said, holding out his hand. 'As I think you've realized by now, you've poked a bit too much into things you ought not to be poking into–'

'You mean this... place,' I said, ignoring his offered hand. I had to look up at all of it again to stop the edges from melting, though I knew the walls were still changing behind my back. At least with the other Mr. Carver here, they couldn't shift too much without one of us noticing. 'This... mirror laboratory. Except... well. I'm not sure what that means, exactly. I've never even heard of magic like this.'

The other Mr. Carver dropped his hand and lifted his eyes, to the ceiling that I hadn't even thought to look at, teeming with shadows so thick and heavy and dark that I had to look back down or start feeling dizzy. 'I doubt that's true,' he said. 'I think everyone's heard stories about this place.'

'You're trying to tell me that my uncle keeps an entrance to the Feyrealm in his laboratory?'

'Doesn't everyone?' answered the other Mr. Carver with an ironic smile.

'Well, I don't know about you magicians, but most of us, no,' I said flatly.

He lifted an eyebrow at that. 'You're assuming a lot, Miss Crowe.'

'You're honestly going to tell me that you're not some kind of magician? Here? Now? While we're standing in the Feyrealm?'

'The evidence does rather seem to be stacked against me,' he admitted. 'But truly, Miss Crowe, I can assure you that I'm no more a magician than you are.'

'Right. And next, you're going to tell me my uncle has never uttered a spell in his life, is that it?'

'Well, no. Doctor Crowe is definitely a magician, and perhaps one of the most powerful in Britannia, if we're being honest.'

That brought me to a stop. I blinked at the boy in front of me, his eyebrow still quirked in a question. 'Give me one good reason why I shouldn't turn him in to an Inquisitor then, *if we're being honest.*'

The other Mr. Carver seemed to reconsider me. 'Is there a particular reason you should want to submit your uncle to Inquisition?' he asked.

I could think of at least a few, all my suspicions and the fractured memories of Ariel Raban's resting record swirling through my head. Still, if I could be sure of anything, it was that Isaac Carver was by far the worst person to confide those fears to. 'He's a magician,' I said. 'I should think that's bad enough.'

Isaac shook his head. 'I get the feeling you don't have a very high opinion of magic.'

'There's a reason it's illegal.'

'People are always afraid of what they don't understand.'

'Of course they're afraid!' I said. 'People shouldn't be allowed to control others!'

'And yet they do, every day, with or without magic.'

I frowned at him, to hide the fact that he had a point. 'Are you sure you're not a magician?'

'I'm training to be a neurologist,' he said. 'A brain surgeon.' His pale lips twisted into a bemused smile. 'Whatever you may think of magic, I think even you must realize that it's hardly the only way to control others – or hurt them.'

'Perhaps, but it certainly makes both of those things easier.'

'If one has the inclination, true,' he conceded. 'But you, of all people, ought to know that Doctor Crowe has no interest in doing either.'

But I shook my head. That didn't at all fit with what I'd seen of my uncle. 'How can you be so sure?'

'In the time I've known your uncle, I've learned to trust his judgment,' he said simply. 'Perhaps he's a bit... intimidating. But there are monsters in your uncle's past that would've destroyed a weaker man. People don't come out of that unscathed.'

Ariel, I thought, the memory of the resting record rising in my mind once more. He was talking about Ariel and Damon, about everything that Uncle Edward had lost because of Dad. 'But that's no excuse for using magic.'

'Perhaps not. But magic is nothing more than a tool, like any other. You can choose how you use it. Restraint is as important as ability, and whether or not I agree with your uncle's decisions, restraint is something he has certainly mastered.'

'And do you agree with his decisions?'

'Not always,' admitted Isaac. 'But most of the time, yes.' He offered his hand once more. 'Still, if I may offer to discuss this with you another time, Miss Crowe, it really would be best not to linger.'

I looked down, to where I'd started twisting my ring in my fingers. 'He called you in because of William's fit, didn't he?'

'Yes, he wanted to make sure there wasn't anything seriously wrong with William's brain.'

'Can you promise me that my brother will be alright?' I asked finally.

'I can promise that I will do everything in my power to make sure he recovers as well and quickly as possible,' said Isaac. 'And I can promise you, if you really are concerned about it, that I will let you know if Doctor Crowe makes any decisions I don't agree with.'

His eyes glittered in the strange light of the mirror laboratory as we considered each other a moment more. 'You swear you won't let anything happen to William?' I said.

'I solemnly swear that he will be returned to your care unharmed,' answered Isaac, drawing an x over his heart with one finger. And with a bow, he held his hand forward for me to take.

This time, I took it.

We stepped through the empty mirror, the passage between places sending tingling needles all up and down my spine. The younger Mr. Carver led me back out into the hall, through winding corridors of the West Wing, and back to the darkened foyer.

'This is where I must take my leave,' he said, with another low bow and a small salute. 'Goodnight Miss Crowe. Try to get some sleep. And remember that your brother is in very good hands.'

I gave a silent nod, watching as he disappeared back into the shadows of the house. And it was only after his footfalls had faded to nothing that I turned to take the stairs back up to my room, holding off the storm of strange thoughts just long enough so that I could climb into bed, before letting my exhaustion do the rest.

For two days, William remained quarantined in the West Wing. Meanwhile, I was left to myself; neither Mother nor Uncle Edward bothered to disturb me, though the Housekeeper made sure to poke her head in whenever the maid brought up my meals – solely so she could allow herself a gloating smile when she found me miserably picking at my books and food.

More than anything, I wanted William there so I could tell him what Emily and I had learned from Ariel's resting record, because without anyone else to talk to, the truth of what had happened to her – and Damon as well – ate at me like acid. It was the first thing I thought about as I woke up, and it gnawed at me throughout the day, making me sick to my stomach every time I considered what it meant:

They were dead because of Dad.

Uncle Edward had lost everything because Dad had betrayed him, and Ariel and Damon had paid for it. The monstrous, twisted logic of it all turned my stomach – after all, what other explanation could there be? For Dad's death, for being trapped here, for everything? Why else would Uncle Edward have shown up on our doorstep, fifteen years after the fact? What else could he have wanted, after losing everything? There was only one answer:

Uncle Edward had wanted revenge.

And his magic gave him the power to get it.

Still, though I knew that answer, even with Ariel's record, there was no *proof* – no real evidence of Uncle Edward's involvement in Dad's death. Because that, after all, was the most important thing: if anything was going to be done about Uncle Edward, we needed to find a way to convince Mother that it was necessary. And that meant finding solid proof of Uncle Edward's anger and his desire for revenge. The only problem, of course, was the fact that as far as we'd seen, *there wasn't any*.

I drifted toward the window and stared out over the Ravenscourt lawns, willing some answer to reveal itself, but of course, answers being the tricky things they are, none of them did anything of the sort. Last night had been the first heavy snowfall of the season, and everything was white and still and soft –

Someone was crossing the lawn, a lick of shadow hurrying across the world of white. I pressed my face to the glass of the window to try to get a proper look at whoever it was and caught a glimpse of flyaway hair escaping the dark hood.

It was Beatrice.

I was out the door before I could think twice, grabbing my coat and racing outside. The snow slowed my steps, and before I'd even reached the rose hedge maze, Beatrice had plunged into the Blackwood. But she'd left a clear set of footprints in the snow, and I followed them to the forest trail, just in time to catch her before she disappeared completely. I slipped after her, the forest path bare and dry under the thick trees, trying my best to keep my feet and my breaths from catching her attention.

At a bend in the path, she turned and started cutting her way straight through the brush. I waited a moment before following, cursing silently at every broken twig and rustling branch that got in my way. But if Beatrice noticed me, she gave no sign, simply drifting further and further into the pathless wood, until, at last, she stepped into a clearing, a single yew tree standing tall in the centre of the snow. I shrank back into the trees, watching, as the gardener pressed her hand against the trunk of the tree.

'There's no reason for you to hide from *me*, Miss Abigail,' she said without turning. 'So you might as well come and have a look.'

Only then did I realize I'd forgotten my defences entirely. I stepped out of the trees. If Beatrice were angry at being followed, she didn't show it. And yet, I couldn't shake the feeling that I'd stepped in on something private. I crossed the snow to join the gardener at the tree and saw, at last, the plaque that had been set into the roots:

For Ariel and Damon, that their spirits may find rest.

Beatrice knelt to lay a dead rose at the foot of the tree, and I reached out, to run my fingers over the scaly bark, remembering, suddenly, that it was the 23rd of December. 'This would've been the day they died,' I said. Beatrice had bowed her head, eyes closed as she paid her respects. 'Ariel… and Damon,' I said, pressing on. 'We found things, after – after you showed us her portrait. Her death record, and her resting. We saw that she'd had a son. And… and she showed us how she died. That Dad had told Lily, and Lily…'

I fell silent.

Beatrice tilted her head toward me, and her eyes held a curious light. 'You figured all that out by yourself?'

'Well,' I said, 'William helped.'

Beatrice laughed. 'I would not like to be your uncle, while he has you two to contend with,' she said, and she leaned forward, catching me with her eyes. 'You've got the gist of it, child, but this is very important. *They are not all lost*. You may yet be able to–'

She cut off, her eyes darting toward the trees, every muscle suddenly tense, and the next moment, she was ushering me toward the edge of the clearing, toward a path that opened from the other side. 'Your uncle's near,' she said. 'Head back to your room directly. I don't want to have you sticking around to get caught.'

'But wait! What's he…?'

'Go, child!' and she very nearly shoved me out of the clearing, shuffling her feet to mix up the snow as she made her way back toward the tree. It wasn't a moment too soon. Footsteps crunched over the leaves and branches of the wood, and I had just enough time to twist my ring and wrap myself in my defences before he stepped out onto the white snow.

Beatrice had told me to go back to my room, but that wasn't going to happen. Not when there was even half a chance of finding something out.

'I expected you earlier,' said Beatrice, her voice chilly and light as the breeze. She was still pacing the snow, hiding my footprints, though Uncle Edward hadn't missed them. His eyes followed her feet, and he peered into the trees – almost directly at me, my breath catching, even as I focused on keeping my defence steady.

At last he let down his guard, turning toward Beatrice and the tree. 'The boy suffered another fit,' he said.

'William?' asked Beatrice, so softly that I almost missed it.

'William,' confirmed Uncle Edward, and his face was grim. He stepped up next to the tree, to face Beatrice directly. 'Ellen tells me you've been making friends with the girl,' he said.

'And has Mrs. Housekeeper Ellen Thompson, by any chance, told you she's been making enemies with the same?'

'This is no time for games, Beatrice.'

'I never assume you're playing,' answered Beatrice primly. 'I just thought you ought to know. However much friends may encourage, nothing spurs a person to action more than an enemy.'

But Uncle Edward's voice had gone dangerous. 'How much have you told her?'

'Edward, you know that I–'

'How much have you told her?'

'Nothing that she could not learn from others,' said Beatrice, as if reciting a bothersome rule.

'Beatrice, how long have we known each other?'

The gardener muttered numbers under her breath. 'Let's see... today's fifteen years since her death, and I was seventeen when they signed me over. Your father's been gone now since '81 and that would make it, oh, about nineteen years total.'

'Long enough to find some loopholes in a contract, would you say?'

'Right. My *contract*. How very Inquisitorial of you,' huffed Beatrice, turning away. She kicked at the dirt under her feet. 'I don't suppose you've decided what you're going to do about the Court?'

Uncle Edward hesitated. Finally, he said: 'I have sent Rosalind an invitation for the party.'

'Rosalind? *Lady* Rosalind?' exclaimed Beatrice, turning back to face Uncle Edward. 'You'll be lucky if that woman doesn't stab you in the back!'

'If I need a backstabber, I always have *you* close at hand,' said Uncle Edward.

'You flatter me.'

'Hardly,' said Uncle Edward. He exhaled heavily. 'I do not like the idea any more than you do. It is dangerous having one of them here, but Rosalind might be convinced to strike a deal–'

'And deals with the Court *never* go wrong,' muttered Beatrice.

'And in any case,' continued Uncle Edward, ignoring her, 'we need information – Lewis' death has set too many things in motion–'

'There are others who could give you information. Bentridge–'

'Anyone who we can trust completely is unlikely to have current contact with the Court. I need to know what is happening *now*. And I need someone who is willing and able to negotiate on the Court's behalf, because if we can find something of worth, we may be able to make a trade for Lewis's spirit.'

I couldn't stop myself from gasping at that: a small sudden sound that escaped me before I could clamp my hands over my mouth to silence it. I froze and waited for the adults to look over, to drag me out of the bushes and convict me of eavesdropping, but they were completely involved in staring each other down, the rest of the world forgotten. I waited for my heart to calm, taking shallow breaths through my nose and willing my Defences stronger, but Beatrice's words were echoing in my mind, over and over:

They are not all lost…

Everything I'd suspected was true. Uncle Edward had killed Dad, but his spirit had never been lost: Uncle Edward had *stolen* it. He'd kept Dad's severed spirit, and now, he planned to trade it to the Court.

'Beatrice,' said Uncle Edward, his voice shattering my thoughts. 'I need your support when it comes to Rosalind.

The gardener shook her head. 'And Maris,' said the gardener. 'You still intend–'

'It is the only way I can ensure their safety. As dangerous as it is, it is necessary.'

'You will, of course, do whatever you think is best.'

Uncle Edward exhaled heavily, leaning his weight onto his cane. 'Beatrice, I–'

'Standing here, *now*, you still–' Beatrice was pacing now.

'Beatrice–'

'You refuse to listen to anyone but yourself,' she continued.

'*Beatrice.*'

The gardener shook her head and laid a hand on the yew tree. 'This was supposed to be a *reminder*, Edward. How many more mistakes have to be made?'

Silence pulled taut between them, and I didn't dare to breathe.

When Uncle Edward next spoke, his voice was soft, but there was no mistaking its tone. '*Leave.*'

Beatrice nodded, bowed her head, and turned toward the wood. Her shoulders dropped, and she made her way toward the path. I pressed myself out of the way, her footsteps slow and heavy.

Uncle Edward hesitated. And then, 'Wait, Beatrice.' The gardener paused, but didn't say a word. 'Can I trust you in this?' he asked. And in the silence that followed, I was sure my heartbeat was loud enough to give me away.

'You ask that as if either of us has a choice in the matter,' said Beatrice at last.

I ducked into the trees, as far back from the path as I dared to without making too much noise, and swallowed my breaths as Beatrice stalked past. Her face was impossible to see under the shaded trees, but I wasn't sure I wanted to see it. Beatrice had told me to go straight back to my rooms, and now I knew why. She hadn't been looking out for me: she'd wanted to stop me from seeing what I'd just seen. Beatrice knew more than she'd ever been willing to tell us. And I knew now, that whatever else she said or did, Uncle Edward trusted her, and she was loyal, first and foremost, to him.

It was only after her footsteps had faded into the wood that I realized my fingers had gone stiff with cold. Uncle Edward lingered by the yew tree and showed no sign of leaving. It was time for me to go. I sneaked away from the clearing and down the forest paths, heading back toward the house across the gardens. Besides Beatrice's betrayal, her mysterious words and Uncle Edward's plan continued to haunt me, because now I knew the truth of what Uncle Edward had done–

And more, I knew what I had to do to stop him.

If Uncle Edward was keeping Dad's severed spirit in order to trade it to the Fey, then that meant Dad was still here, in Ravenscourt, *somewhere*. All we needed to do was find him, and then everything would be set right. He'd be able to tell everyone what happened. We'd be able to rest him properly. And I–

Despite the horror of everything that Uncle Edward had done, despite Beatrice's betrayal, despite the fact that William was still quarantined somewhere among the sick rooms and laboratories of the house, still, I couldn't help but feel like I was walking on air. For the first time since Dad's botched funeral, I knew what I wanted, what I had to do.

I was going to see my father one last time. I'd be able to say goodbye properly. And he'd make everything right, the way he always did.

I drifted upstairs to the second floor, pushing open my door, but as soon as I stepped into the sitting room, I froze.

The Housekeeper stood in front of the fire, turning something over in her gnarled fingers. As soon as she saw me, her gloating face lit up. I couldn't tear my eyes away from the thing in her hands, the thing that we were definitely not supposed to have, the thing that William had stolen from Uncle Edward's study.

The voice box.

Before I could run, she'd crossed the room to grab me by my hair, and she started dragging me out the door and down the hall.

'I bet you think you're clever,' she hissed. I struggled against her grip, but it was hopeless. Every move I made, she yanked my hair harder, and my head burst with pain. 'I bet you think you can get out of anything. Perhaps, you even think that there's not a thing I could do to actually harm a single hair on that clever little head of yours.'

She turned toward the dark hall.

'But let me assure you. I may not be allowed to leave marks, but I am *anything* but powerless.'

She pulled her keys from her belt, unlocked one of the black, featureless doors of the hall, and wrenched it open. A small, bare closet lay beyond, and I took a sharp breath before she shoved me into it, slamming the door, and locking me in. The darkness was complete.

'Enjoy your evening,' said the Housekeeper, her voice echoing from miles away. Her keys jangled as she left.

I scrambled to my feet, lunging forward to beat my fists against the door–

But the door wasn't there. My fists met a blank wall of stone, solid and cold. I ran my hands along it, along the other three walls, searching, but there wasn't so much as a gap or a crack in those walls, and when I reached upward, my hands immediately met the rough-hewn ceiling.

I had to sit down, my head going dizzy with confusion, putting my hands over my mouth to calm my breathing. I had to think. What was happening to me? Where, exactly, had the Housekeeper put me? And *how…*?

Water lapped at my ankles.

Or, at least, I hoped it was just water.

I reached forward, searching the floor and walls again, searching for any escape, but all I found was a trickle of water running down the walls, pooling on the floor around my feet.

'Oh, no, no, no.'

Desperately, I ran my fingers across all that blank stone again and again, searching for any crack, any crevice, any place where I might hope to find light or air or escape. But there was only the water, rising now to cover my ankles, and that awful silence. I took a deep breath, willing myself to stay calm. After all, it wasn't like I was *definitely* going to drown in this airless stone closet without any hope of escape.

I could always suffocate first.

The water kept rising. Now it was at my knees.

When I was ten, there had been an incident in our village, where a woman had been caught by the Inquisitors and sentenced to death by drowning. All the girls in the catechism class had gone to watch, and they'd dragged me along with them. The Inquisitors put the woman in a boat, and took her a little bit out to sea before tossing her into the waves, while we all watched from the rocks. And though she struggled at first, eventually she went still, and the water took her under. She looked as if she were going to sleep.

But when Dad found out later where I'd gone, he told me the truth: that when you drowned, you didn't just pass out into blissful unconsciousness. No, overwhelmed by the water, your body immediately responded to the lack of air: your throat closed off, preventing your straining lungs from taking in anything, and while you sank, weakening, into the dark, your heart slowed, and slowed, until, finally, your stomach spasmed, your throat opened, and your lungs took in *everything* – water, spit, and vomit – and you ended up smothering yourself in your own bile.

The water rose to my waist.

Things could be worse, right?

Of course, Dad had explained the process in more scientific terms, but the fact remained that drowning was not a pleasant way to go. I would much rather have been facing the prospect of being mauled by bears, or drinking a gallon of lye, and it didn't help that my breathing was already becoming difficult.

I had to control myself. I had to–

Perhaps…

As the water rose up to my shoulders, I twisted my father's ring beneath the surface. As difficult as it was, I slowed my breaths and focused all my thoughts on my lungs, and on the ring around my finger, wrapping myself in the First Defence, coiling the Second around my heart. I closed my eyes as the water lapped against my neck. I needed the Third Defence. Even if it couldn't change anything, even if there was no way for it to make air where there wasn't any, or to banish water from a stone prison, at the very least, it would save me from having to feel myself drowning. It was some small comfort. I took one last deep breath. And as the water closed in over my head, I summoned the garden of my sanctuary.

It burst to life all around me: the blossoming cherry tree growing from a still pool, the tall hedge, the darkening sky filled with stars and touch-me-not petals floating through the air–

But something was wrong. Pieces of the hedge lay tramped and broken, and water was pouring through, running in rivers among the grass and flowers. I reached out to touch the splintered branches, the realization hitting me like a punch in the gut.

An Illusion. The Housekeeper had tricked me.

Closing my eyes in concentration, I willed the silver hedges to knit back together and stem the flood. I felt the branches straightening under my touch, the water slowing to a trickle, and then to a drip, before drying up altogether. The touch of the sanctuary's breeze grazed my cheeks.

I opened my eyes, and with a sigh of relief, I found the water was gone, and the impossible stone walls gone with it. I was still sitting in a closet, but it was just a regular, wood-panelled storage closet, dry and dusty, with dim light drifting through a keyhole. I sank to the floor, exhausted, and kicked my feet against the door.

Footsteps sounded down the hall. I kicked the door harder, and called out, hoping whoever it was would stop for me. The door opened, and I stared up into the face of my rescuer.

It was William.

'Good Will and Charity'

'We have to tell Mum,' said William.

He knelt by the fireplace, attempting to rekindle the smoking embers while I sagged on the couch, sipping a cup of lukewarm tea. The Housekeeper's punishment had left me drained and empty, like a worn-out rag wrung dry and left to hang on the line, and I wasn't sure that telling Mother was any sort of solution for it.

'I don't know–' I said.

'But she locked you in a closet,' said William, fumbling with his matches. He didn't look any worse for wear after his three days of quarantine (or was it four? I'd lost track of time while I'd been stuck in the closet – already, the night sky had started to brighten a little at the horizon). Still, I could tell that the latest fit had taken its toll. He was sagging too.

'I know,' I told him. 'But she didn't believe us last time. So why–'

'She locked you in a *closet*–'

'Yes, thank you! I'd forgotten!' I snapped. I immediately regretted it. 'Look, William–'

But he threw down the matches and turned to me, and I can tell you now that I'd never seen my brother look so angry in his life. 'No, you look!' he said. 'Do you think this is all just going to go away? That somehow, we'll find something, and all of a sudden, Mum will believe *everything*? Because that's not going to happen. We've done everything except try to talk sense into the one person that could help us. Dad's *dead*, Abby, and that isn't going to go away. We need *help*. We can't do this by ourselves. We've tried. And Mum is the only one—'

At that I shook my head and stood. 'She's not the only one,' I said.

But William frowned. 'If you mean Beatrice—'

'No, not Beatrice either,' I said. 'I don't think she could help us even if she wanted to. But William, I overhead them talking, in the woods, before—' Before the Housekeeper had locked me in an illusion of terrors, I wanted to say, but the words couldn't quite find their way out of my throat. 'Anyway, Beatrice told me they're not all lost. And Uncle Edward…' I took a deep breath. 'He's got Dad's spirit. He kept him. He's trapped here, somewhere, and if we…'

'…can find him, then he can help us fix everything,' finished William for me. His face had finally gotten back some of its colour; his matches lay forgotten. 'But how do you know he's got Dad?' he asked.

'Because he told Beatrice that he was planning to trade Dad's spirit… to the Court…' I trailed off, watching for William's reaction to that last part, to see if he would dismiss the thought of Fey, or miss it all together.

'The Court?' he said. 'You can't mean…'

'The Fey Court, yes,' I said. I chewed my lip. 'I think there might be something to it,' I explained at last, and without letting him interrupt, I told him everything I'd discovered since the night of the Carols' Yule dinner – explaining what Ariel's spirit had shown me and telling him about Isaac Carver and the mirror in the laboratory, and how stepping through it had taken me somewhere that sounded very much like a place that trapped Fey Kings would've been very happy to haunt. 'And Uncle Edward said he wanted to make a trade with them – with the Court anyway. That's the exact word he used. He invited a woman named Lady Rosalind to the Wintersnacht party because he said she'd be able to negotiate a deal for the Court...'

'We can't let him make the trade,' said William. He was no longer sagging. He stood alert, like a hound that had suddenly caught the right scent. At last, my brother was back. 'We have to–'

'–make sure that *we're* the ones who get Dad's spirit instead,' I said with a nod. It sounded so simple as I said it, as if it could happen just like that, quick and painless. 'It won't be easy. If she's really Fey–'

'It can't be worse than what we've been through already,' said William. He had a point.

And despite the strange and desperate circumstances, despite the exhausting hour and the fact that I hadn't slept in the last twenty-four, and despite having no idea what we'd be facing when we went to the Wintersnacht party to find a representative of the Fey and steal our father's spirit back from the magician who had killed him, despite all that, I almost felt like smiling. We knew what we had to do. Now we just had to make sure we did it.

So dawned the 25th, Wintersnacht morning. Somehow, despite all of Ravenscourt's darkness, the manor staff had managed to fill the Great Hall with something close to cheer: they'd hung the walls with garlands and lined them with lamps, wreathed the chandeliers with holly and mistletoe and burned pine cones in the hearth so that the entire place smelled like Yule. The staff had just finished their last decorating when the first of Uncle Edward's guests began to arrive.

Mother whisked us away upstairs before we could catch a glimpse of any of them, handing William over to her maid while she dragged me into my room to get me dressed and take care of my hair. It was more attention than she'd given either of us in the past two months, and that, more than the new, too-tight dress or even the endless hair-styling, made me uncomfortable. It didn't help matters that the entire time she was trying to smooth out my curls, she avoided catching my eyes in the mirror, leaving me to wonder what she wasn't telling me.

It took an hour for us to get ready, and every minute of it, I was listening for the faint sound of the front bell, hoping that none of the scattered guests trickling in one and two at a time was the Lady Rosalind, ready and eager to meet Uncle Edward to discuss business. Finally, Mother was satisfied. She put one last pin in my hair, and at last, she found my eyes in the mirror and smiled.

William was ready as well, and we met him in the sitting room just as the maid stepped out the door. He'd been done up in his best mourning suit, and his face had been cleaned and scrubbed until it was raw and pink. He looked almost as annoyed as I felt.

'Let's take a look at you then,' said Mother, straightening us out in front of her. She adjusted William's collar and replaced the pin she'd just set and pecked each of us with a kiss on the forehead. 'That'll do well enough, I guess, though the important part is that you'll be on your best behaviour tonight.'

William and I exchanged a look at that. 'You say that as if you expect one of us to set someone on fire,' I said.

'Honestly, I wouldn't be surprised with the way you two have been acting lately,' muttered Mother. 'And don't roll your eyes at me, Abigail, that is exactly the sort of behaviour I'm talking about.'

I hadn't even noticed that I was rolling my eyes, but apparently she had.

'Anyway, enough of that. I'm sure you two will be your usual pleasant and charming selves, and that we won't have to worry about a single thing when it comes to the guests. There are a lot of important people here, you should know. Your uncle has so many connections. It would be good for you to make a good impression.'

I wondered if she had mixed us up with another pair of children, because whenever Mother thought of us, I doubted that 'pleasant', 'charming', and 'usual selves' were ever combined into the same sentence. 'Right,' I said. 'We'll be careful to consider our impression while sulking in the corner.'

Mother tsked, though it was half-hearted. She reached out to straighten William's collar again. 'I– I know this is difficult, dears. It's been difficult for all of us, and there's nothing I can say or do to change that. But I just need to you to know... this is all for the best, really.'

This time, I made sure to catch myself as I rolled my eyes, so I could make the gesture as big and obvious as possible.

Mother sighed, and turned away. 'Take all the time you need, Abigail. You can come down when you're ready to behave.' She pulled open the door and stepped out into the hall. 'All I'm asking,' she said over her shoulder, 'is for you not to embarrass me tonight.'

And with that, she was gone, the door clicking shut behind her.

It took every bit of willpower for me to stop myself from grabbing the vase on the mantle and smashing it on the floor. It would serve Mother right if we *embarrassed* her, as if she'd need us to do the job for her. She was the one who was making a fool of herself, refusing to listen or recognize any of the problems we'd found ourselves in. She, of all people, had the least right to ask *us* to behave – as if we'd been pulling petty pranks on the house staff, instead of, you know, trying to solve a murder mystery and save Dad's spirit.

William tapped me on the arm and gave me a meaningful look that said all it needed to. Whatever Mother's attitude, it didn't change anything. We still had work to do.

I took a deep breath and flashed my brother a smile. 'Up for a party?'

We made our way toward the grand staircase and the entrance to the Great Hall, where the trickle of guests had grown into a proper flood. Crouching at the top of the upper landing, we watched. The front doors lay wide open, spilling lamplight and firelight onto the front lawn as carriages pulled up, spit out their guests, and clattered on. There were far more of them than I'd expected: women in gowns of lace and tulle carrying Sinean fans, men with shiny shoes whose coattails flapped behind them as they entered the hall. A trio of grey old scholars whose philosophy argument echoed throughout the foyer greeted Uncle Edward warmly, followed by several gentlemen who wouldn't have looked out of place in Parliament. Behind these came more nobles, a gaggle of stiff-backed matrons dripping with pearls, and a lady in sky-blue silk, accompanied by an awkwardly tall manservant.

'Pleeeeease...' droned the manservant as he bowed his lady through the doors.

'Is– is that a golem?' whispered William into my ear.

I leaned forward to get a better look at the creature below. Strictly speaking, golems – which were basically dead bodies brought back to life by just the tiniest bit of spirit, allowing them to walk around and follow basic commands and, to a very, very minor extent, talk – were the definition of illegal magic. But of course, that didn't stop the richer nobility from owning one or two of them as servants. After all, you never had to pay or feed a corpse.

In Caledonia, William and I had been sure that the old Countess who lived on the outskirts of town kept three of them. I'd never gotten more than a passing glance, but everyone knew that the young lady who did her washing was mute, and that the man who drove her carriage through town on Sundays had a habit of staring straight through people. Every time I'd seen them, they'd given me a sickening sense of dread, and it was the same with the manservant in the hall now, as he jerkily took the lady's coat, a chill of horror running down my spine.

'My Lady Rosalind,' said Uncle Edward with a deep bow. So *this* was the Lady Rosalind that Uncle Edward had invited to deal on behalf of the Fey. She was nearly as tall as her golem manservant, with olive skin and wide dark eyes, and she wore her black hair pulled back into a bun. Her sky-blue gown shimmered in the lamplight. She peered imperiously down upon Uncle Edward as he stood from his bow and finished his greeting: 'It is such a pleasure.'

'The pleasure, Doctor Crowe, is all mine. It has been far too long,' she answered. Her words came out deep and rich and definitely not quite fully Anglican – wherever she came from, it sounded as if they spoke in music and not in voices. She smiled, and her eyes shifted to Mother, filled with all the glitter of an eager viper. 'And if it isn't the lovely Maris Astor – too long by far!'

The Lady darted forward to kiss Mother's cheeks three times before proceeding into the hall. At once, William and I were moving, dashing down the stairs to follow her, leaving Mother startled and bewildered at the doors.

The hall beyond had been completely transformed, swept clean and clear of cobwebs, while the largest, grandest Wintersnacht Tree I'd ever seen stood in a corner, tall enough to brush the Great Hall's ceiling with its starry crown and so wide that you felt you could get lost under its branches. Every inch of it was dripping with tinsel and candles and glittering ornaments, and for a moment, the brightness almost blinded me. I had gotten too used to Ravenscourt's usual darkness, and the shimmering room in front of us held not a single shadow, every corner filled with light. Guests spun across the dance floor, while a string quartet wove a waltz, sheltered in one of the Hall's shallow alcoves.

It was impossible to see all of it at once: the guests and the decorations and the musicians and the food and the lights. William and I paused, trying to take it all in.

'This is... not what I expected,' I said.

William nodded slowly. 'I know,' he said. 'I mean, who would've thought that Uncle Edward had this many *friends*?'

I had to remind myself why we were there, and searching for the sky-blue silk of the Lady's gown among the dancers, I spotted her, leaning against the wall on the other side of the room with her manservant close at hand, watching over the heads of the rest of the crowd but refusing to take even a single step toward the dance floor. She lifted a glass of champagne from the tray of a passing servant, sniffed it delicately, and with a wrinkle of her nose, passed it off to her golem, who downed the entire thing in one gulp.

'Miss Crowe,' said a voice, drawing my attention back to the scene just in front of me. Isaac Carver parted from the crowd, stepping forward to greet me with a bow. He stood and flashed a brilliant smile, his blue-green eyes glittering in the lamp light.

Cocky jerk.

'And how are you finding this year's Wintersnacht party?' he asked.

'It's... something.' I said. I don't think I could've managed a lamer reply if I had actually put in the effort to. Heat flushed my face, and I willed the floor to swallow me, turning my attention to William in an effort to hide it. 'What do you think?'

But that didn't help. William caught my eyes, shooting me a quizzical look before he brightened with realization. Great. Now they'd both be against me.

'It's quite... *scintillating*, wouldn't you say?' said William. Both Isaac and I gave him a look. Isaac raised an eyebrow.

'What? It means brilliant,' explained my brother.

'Uh, right...' said Isaac. 'In any case, I've been meaning to ask you, William, how are you feeling?'

William shrugged. 'Better,' he said. 'You and Uncle Edward seemed to patch me up pretty well.'

'Hopefully well enough,' said Isaac. 'Do make sure to take your medicines, and let us know if anything feels out of the ordinary. We wouldn't want you to run into trouble. Speaking of which...' He reached into his coat and pulled out a lumpy package wrapped in cloth, handing it over to William. 'I believe these are yours.'

'What are those?' I asked, even as my brother's face lit up, and he took the package in both hands.

'Definitely not smoke bombs,' said Isaac with a wink.

'I thought I'd lost these!'

'Your uncle was rather alarmed to find them when you came back from the Carols',' admitted Isaac. 'And as far as he knows, I never gave them back to you.'

William grinned as he stuffed the smoke bombs into his coat. 'Now you need to get Abigail a present,' he said.

Isaac shifted his attention to me, and I had to glare at William to hide the fact that my face was probably flashing just about every possible shade of red. The last thing I needed was a Wintersnacht present from Uncle Edward's assistant. I just wish that my face understood that as well as I did. 'I don't need anything from you,' I said, perhaps a bit more coolly than I should've.

'Oh come now, there must be something you want.'

'Not that you could give me,' I said, meeting his eyes at last. Even if it was harsh, it was true. Everything that I wanted right now was impossible. there was no magic that could bring Dad back from the dead, not fully.

To his credit, Isaac seemed to understand what I meant. 'I suppose that's only fair,' he said. 'I wish I could say that things get easier from here, but that would be a lie.'

At least the boy was honest.

Thankfully, we were interrupted by Emily Carol, who stepped up next to Isaac and handed him a drink. 'Good to see you made it back,' she said in a flat voice, though she wasn't looking at him as she said it.

'Well, I would hate to miss this, wouldn't I?' said Isaac, taking the drink. They clinked their glasses.

'Not as much as Samantha would,' said Emily. 'I swear, if I had to choose between getting my eyes gouged out and listening to your sister croon on about ladies' dresses for the entirety of this party, I'd choose the former.'

'But then you'd be blind for a lifetime,' said Isaac.

'Worth it.'

'And what would you gouge out during the next party?' teased Isaac.

'Someone else's eyes,' replied Emily, looking out over the crowd. 'In any case, if you feel like actually catching up at any point, you know where to find me.'

And with that, she walked off, leaving the three of us to stare after her as she left. I looked up to check on Lady Rosalind, just as a brave young soul dared to ask her for a dance, the poor man's face reddening at the Lady's reply, before he scurried back into the crowd. All good there. Samantha Carver had parted from the crowd, and rushed up to us, crooning non-stop about the party, just as Emily had warned.

'It is such a lovely party everything is so bright and have you seen—' She went on so long that I started wondering how it was possible for her to keep running on so little air. I finished my drink and checked the Lady Rosalind's alcove to make sure she still hadn't moved—

Only to find it empty.

William had noticed as well. We exchanged a panicked look, both of us wondering, *now what*?

I scanned the room, peering into every alcove—

There.

A flash of sky blue at the other end of the hall slipped through one of the doors to the main courtyard. There was no time to excuse myself to the Carvers. Straight across the hall, I ploughed through the dance floor, dodging weaving couples and darting through the crowds, not even pausing to apologize as I trampled over polished shoes and trod on the lacy hems of skirts. One or two ladies gasped as I raced past and hurtled through the outer door, into the main courtyard of the house.

The night air was freezing and wet, and it didn't take long for the cold to seep into my fingers, fat flakes of snow drifting down from above. There was no sign of the Lady: no whisper of skirts among the silent stones, not a glimpse of sky blue silk. Instead, as I wandered through the bushes, I found Emily sitting in the very centre of the courtyard, on a covered bench, staring out at the moonlit snow. Her face was blank and still as an icy lake, without sign of chill or chatter.

'Emily?'

The girl stirred, her dark eyes settling on me, a chill of strange discomfort running down my spine as she did so. 'Odd,' she said in a light voice, 'how pretty everything looks in death.'

The bushes rustled, but when I turned and looked, there was nothing there. And Emily was still staring.

'Are... are you alright, Emily?' I asked finally.

Emily's laughter broke the heavy silence, high and strangely jarring. 'Come now, Miss Crowe. I know you didn't brave to cold just to check on me. So, be honest: what are you looking for?'

Her eyes dared me to lie, so I told her the truth. 'There was a lady wearing a blue gown, and I think she came out here. Have you seen her?'

Emily tilted her head, her brow furrowed in thought. 'No,' she said. 'I don't suppose I have. You're the only one who's ventured out here all night, aside from myself, of course. It's just us and the hawthorns.' She gave a pointed look at the surrounding bushes. 'Though I must ask what you hoped to do when you found this... lady.'

I gave the courtyard one last searching glance, but it was well and truly empty. I was certain I'd seen the Lady disappear through the outer door, though where she could've gone from here, I had no idea. The entire situation made me uneasy. But if there were a single person in this house that I could trust who wasn't William, it would be Emily.

'Her name is Lady Rosalind. And... Uncle Edward invited her here tonight because he's planning to make a trade with the Court.'

'The Court?' said Emily. Her face had broken into a smirk. 'Are you certain?'

'Yes, and I can't– I can't let it happen, Emily. You have to help me. Because he wants to trade them Dad's spirit. So please, Emily, if you've seen her...'

Emily gave me an unreadable look. 'I haven't seen her. Not exactly. But that doesn't mean I can't help. I *can* help.' She stood from the bench, that strange smirk still on her lips. 'After all, what are friends for?'

The bushes rustled behind me, and I turned just as Lady Rosalind's golem manservant pushed his way through the hawthorns, blocking my path back to the hall. My heart pounding, I turned back to Emily, but it wasn't Emily standing there anymore. The air shimmered, bending and wavering like light through a prism, and I could almost feel the strange scene in front of me twisting, until Emily – her pale face and her dark hair and her grey dress – had been pulled away like a veil, revealing the Lady Rosalind standing there instead.

Facing her now, I wondered what I could've possibly thought I could do against a member of the Fey. The Lady towered over me, and her golem manservant was probably stronger than he looked, and they had me trapped between them – no escape. And I knew, I *knew* that every single fairy story made it clear that you weren't supposed to mess with the Court, and even Uncle Edward had regarded them with caution and even fear, but still, I'd gone after her, and now she was staring down at me through her large, dark eyes, daring me to run. And the worst thing wasn't that she'd trapped me so easily, or even the fact that she'd been able to Illusion herself to look like Emily – no, it was something about her eyes, about the way they seemed to see everything all at once, dark and deep and hungry–

'Pleeeeease,' moaned the golem suddenly. I jumped, startled, and the Lady laughed – a musical sound, just slightly out of tune.

'Now come, little girl. Did you think I wouldn't notice you staring at us all night? Enough starting and startling, we might as well talk.' And with her cold, mesmerizing smile, she waited for me to break the silence.

'Who are you?' I said at last.

'Lady Rosalind D'Argens Morose-Gael, which you seem to know well enough.'

'Wrong question then. *What* are you?'

'You're the one who likes listening at doors and corners. You tell me. What am I?'

'My uncle invited you here because you're part of the Court.'

The Lady's eyes lit at that. 'Oh, little girl. Who's been telling you monster stories?'

But I wasn't going to let her get the better of me. I wrapped my arms across my chest to fight my shivers. 'But that doesn't explain anything. I don't understand what you would want with my father's spirit – or what the Court even *is*. What the *Fey* are.'

The lady bared her teeth. 'We're the monsters under your bed, the shadows in the corner of your eye, the faces half seen in mirrors, what need have we for reasons?'

'But you're not even supposed exist. Those are all just *stories*–'

'And so we are. But just because we are made of fiction does not mean that we are lies, little girl. It's an important thing to learn the difference.' The Lady began pacing in front of me. 'As for your father, it has always been the domain of the Court to ensure the… sanctity of certain powers. It is not always a pleasant task, but rest assured, I've no intention of striking any deals tonight. Your father's spirit will likely remain safe and sound right where it is–'

'That's not good enough,' I said. 'You may be willing to leave Dad with my uncle, but I'm not. I want his spirit back.'

'Why ever would you want a silly thing like that?'

'It's not silly. He's dead. My uncle killed him – *murdered* him and–'

'And? Taking his spirit won't bring him back.'

'I know that! But he ought to at least be Rested. And I just – I *need* to talk to him. I have to! Just once more–'

'Oh little girl, do you think that you're the first person in this world to lose someone? You're not. But clinging to memories, to spirits, to remembrances? You'll only give yourself more pain.' She leaned forward, until her eyes were even with mine. 'Regret is far less satisfying than *revenge*.'

'You're no better than my uncle–'

'And yet, I can offer you something he can't. Help me tonight and I can take you away from here – you and your mother, and dear little brother–'

'I can't help you.'

'Oh, but you *can*. See, all I need is an invitation. Four little words: *go where you will*.'

I didn't know what she meant by that – she'd been greeted by Uncle Edward already – but I'd heard enough fairy stories to know that if the Lady was offering to take us away from Ravenscourt, she probably didn't have our best interests in mind. I shook my head, steeling myself as I turned away from the Lady to face her golem manservant. I was ready to flee if I had to – or fight, if it came down to that, though winning was doubtful.

But the golem merely stepped out of the way, leaving the path unguarded. I glanced back at the Lady over my shoulder, but only for a moment. There was always the chance, while I was still out here, that she could change her mind. Quick steps brought me toward the warmth and light of the hall. I opened the door.

'We could help each other, Abigail,' called the Lady.

I stepped into the hall and let the door swing shut behind me.

The closing chords of a minuet faded into silence as I found William sitting with Samantha and Laurie at one of the tables at the edge of the dance floor and took a seat next to them. The chatter of the guests swelled up to replace the music, and at the front of the hall, near the stage where the musicians sat tuning their instruments,

Uncle Edward rose, chiming his wine glass for attention. Bit by bit, the hall fell silent, rustling silk the only sound left, as all eyes turned to the stage.

'Thank you,' said Uncle Edward. His voice rang out across the vast room, clear in every corner and alcove. 'Thank you, dearest friends, and dearer family, for your attention, and your presence here tonight. As many of you know, this season, which should be a time of joy for us all, has been marred by the loss of one of our own – my dearest brother, who passed not two months hence. He was a devoted husband and father, and truly, the loss of his brilliance darkens all our worlds. Alas! Lewis – may we all remember him!'

He raised his glass in a mourning toast, and I had to clench my jaw to stop myself from leaping up right then and there and calling out everything I knew about the man in front of us – not that it would've made much difference. These were Uncle Edward's friends, weren't they? Would they even be surprised to find out that he was a magician and a murderer?

Would they even care that he had killed my father?

The man was a snake, worse than a snake, and here he was pretending to honour the memory of the brother whom he had hated, whom he had killed, whose spirit he planned to *sell*. I was so focused on trying to keep my trembling hands steady that I almost missed what happened next.

Mother had stood, joining Uncle Edward at the front of the hall, and a strange, horrifying dread began to sink into my stomach. Uncle Edward continued to speak:

'But even in these dark times, we have found hope. Dearest friends, through tragedy, we have come together, supported each other, and found solace in each other. Today, I am delighted to announce to all of you...'

Mother was smiling, her face a mask of delight, as she stared out over the crowd. Uncle Edward took her hand, and even through the horror, the fog, the buzzing in my head, his next words rang loud and clear as he dropped them, one by one, into the hall.

'We are to be wedded!'

And that's when I fainted.

Smoke and Mirrors

For more than a minute after I opened my eyes, I couldn't remember where I was, or what I'd been doing. All I knew was that someone had tucked me into my bed, the fluffed-up pillow a comfort against the pain throbbing through my head. Light was flickering everywhere, and I couldn't quite decide if it was the fault of the sputtering candle on the table next to me, or mine. I gave the room a minute to stop spinning. Finally it did. My shaky vision cleared too, and I found myself staring into the blue-green eyes of Isaac Carver.

'Good,' he said. 'You're awake.'

It took me another moment to realize that William was sitting on the bed next to me, and that Samantha and the Carol twins were hovering next to the door, watching me as if waiting for me to burst into flame.

'You gave everyone quite a scare,' said Isaac.

I blinked at him. 'What? Why? What happened?'

Everyone exchanged shifty glances, and I had to close my eyes as the room insisted on taking another spin. But when three minutes had passed and no one had said a word, I opened one eye to glare at each and every one of them. *'Well?'*

Emily scrunched up her face. 'I guess the first question would be... how much do you remember, exactly?'

I tried to think back, though it felt like reaching for something buried in the mud. 'Well, we were at the party, weren't we? And then...'

Oh god. The Wintersnacht party. Uncle Edward's announcement. And *Mother–*

Pain shot through my head, and the room decided to try its hands at a pirouette. I attempted to sit up, but instead the bed decided to swallow me whole, my half-hearted attempt at a curse coming out as a strangled cry. Both Isaac and Emily reached forward to make sure I didn't topple off the edge of the bed, but I threw their hands off... or tried to.

'I'm going to talk to her. This is insane. This... this is *ludicrous*!'

'Abigail,' said Isaac. 'I think you need to calm down–'

'Calm down? I'm not going to *calm down*!' I managed to bat his hand away, though Emily was still cradling my shoulder. I pulled myself away from the pillow and swung my legs over the edge of the bed. 'It's been barely two months! She's insane. She needs to be stopped. I'm going to talk some sense into her.'

I waved Emily's hand away, pushed myself off the edge of the bed, planted my feet firmly on the floor... and promptly collapsed.

'I don't feel so good,' I said from the floor. It took the combined efforts of Emily, Isaac, and William to get me back into the bed.

'All right, Abigail,' said Isaac. 'Right now, I would really suggest that you get some rest. So... why don't you stay here, and we'll go and get you something to drink?'

As much as I wanted to protest, the fact that I couldn't even stand was about enough to convince me that maybe Isaac had a point. 'Fine,' I said. 'I'll wait here. And if you see my Mother, please slap some sense into her?'

'Will do,' said Emily. And with that, the two Carols and the two Carvers trooped out of the room, leaving me and my brother alone with the sputtering candle. William sat twisting his coat buttons, while I closed my eyes in an attempt to relieve the pain behind them. I couldn't get the image of Mother's face out of my head, as she stood hand in hand with Uncle Edward. She'd been smiling, *actually smiling*, more brightly and more happily than I'd ever seen her smile before.

'I can't believe it,' said William finally. 'You wouldn't think–'

'I know,' I said.

'I just don't understand how she could possibly–'

'I know!'

'And yet...' he trailed off into silence, and I opened one eye to glare at him.

'What?' I said. 'What were you going to say?'

William looked down at his coat buttons. 'She looked happy.'

She had. That was the worst bit of the whole affair. It was bad enough that it had all worked out in Uncle Edward's favour – after all, what better revenge could there be for Ariel's death? He'd not only murdered Dad: he'd trapped his family, stolen his wife, and planned to trade his spirit to the Fey. But *worse than even that*, he'd managed, somehow, to convince our mother that it was the happiest choice she'd ever made.

The thought stuck in the back of my throat, lingering like a sour aftertaste. There was only one thing we could do now.

We had to fix it.

'We have to get Dad's spirit back,' I said. 'That's the only way to fix all this; it's the only thing that matters.'

'But we don't even know if it's still *here*,' said William. 'I couldn't exactly keep track of Uncle Edward or the Lady when you decided to go and faint.'

I gave him the look, and without waiting for him to apologize for his rudeness, I pushed myself up in bed once more, and tried my feet again. This time, they held me, so I grabbed the sputtering candle and made my way to the door. 'Then we'd better go and find them before it's too late.'

We hurried through the corridors, slipping from shadow to shadow, past the carved library doors, through the portrait gallery, and toward the Grand Stair. A cold draft seeped in through the floorboards, and shivers ran up my legs as we made our way through the East Wing. We'd just reached the Dark Hall running through the centre of the house when I signalled for William to stop, pausing at the end of the hall. I'd heard something like a long, low creak, except that it wasn't just a creak. There were words in it. I held my breath and listened.

'Pleeeeease…'

I looked back at William, whose face had gone white – and *he* hadn't even had to see the golem manservant up close. Goose bumps crept up the back of my neck. I wasn't eager to come face to face with that thing again.

But if the golem was there, then that meant that the Lady couldn't be far off. We crept slowly down the hall, trying our best to avoid any creaking floorboards and listening, listening, until at last, we heard another voice, muffled by one of the hall's plain black doors. But it wasn't the Lady speaking; it was Uncle Edward:

'…certain that the proposal is more than fair.'

The Lady answered him. 'A book of power in exchange for the spirit of a murdered brother. Perhaps it is a fair trade. But as far as the Court is concerned, the deal is far from appetizing–'

'What more use is it to you? What else could you possibly–'

'*Information*, Edward,' said the Lady. I could hear the smirk in her voice. 'The most valuable thing in this world. It's the only thing that opens doors and lets you see past the smokescreens and mirrors. Why, imagine if I'd come to Ravenscourt without information? I might have gotten completely entangled in your Wards, or never realized the existence of a certain pair of *children*.'

'You–'

'Most interesting, however, is what I now know about the deranged soul locked up in that tower of yours–'

'So *that* is what you are after,' said Uncle Edward. His tone was no longer conversational. 'Rest assured, my Lady Rosalind, you will *not*–'

He cut off at the sound of a low, rumbling, '*Pleeeeeeease*.' There was a smash and a thump, and the next moment, the door had blown open with a resounding bang. Out popped the Lady Rosalind, who raced away, fleeing down the Dark Hall in a flutter of sky blue silk. Uncle Edward and the golem emerged next, rather too preoccupied with each other to notice me and William standing next to the remains of the door.

'Beatrice!' Uncle Edward managed to yell before the golem closed its hands around his throat. He attempted to hit the creature with his cane, but they stumbled together, Uncle Edward nearly collapsing–

A pair of dark hands reached out of the room, grabbed the golem's head, and gave it a sharp, sudden twist. The next thing I knew, the golem had tumbled to the ground, lifeless.

'Pleeease…'

Beatrice stepped through the door and kicked the twitching golem out of the way. 'What did I tell you?' she said as she helped Uncle Edward to stand.

He looked down at what had once been Lady Rosalind's golem manservant and straightened his jacket, peering down the corridor where the Lady had fled. 'If I am unable to catch her,' he said, 'you will have to cut off her escape.' And with that, he ran off down the hall.

'As much good as that'll do,' huffed Beatrice. She shook her head and turned to us, still standing next to the door and staring.

'Beatrice?' said William in disbelief.

The gardener grinned, and she laughed. 'Why, hello Young William,' she said brightly. She nodded at me as well, 'Miss Abigail. I'd follow the other two if I were you. They promise to be much more exciting than my Wardwork.' And with a wink, she pushed past us, to make her way toward the other end of the hall, heading back toward the East Wing and the servant's stair. 'They're headed for the laboratory, by the way,' she called back over her shoulder as she disappeared into the darkness. 'I'm sure you know where that is.'

Without another word, we were off.

We'd only made it a little way down the Dark Hall – just barely to the place where you had to turn left to get to the Grand Stair – when it happened: all of a sudden, the Dark Hall went even darker, the scattered torches all extinguished at the same time. William and I were thrown into complete darkness, without even a candle to guide us. We slowed to a stop, William rustling in his pockets for his matches. But before he could quite manage–

'OW!' There was the sound of him slamming against the wall, as someone heavy bowled him over.

'William!'

'Abigail?' said another voice.

'Samantha?' said William.

'Ow, sorry, just a moment, everyone,' said Laurie at last.

A click, and the hall blazed with light, revealing where Laurie had landed on top of William on one side of the hall, while Samantha stood on the other side, shaking her head. I had to hold up a hand against the blinding light, while Laurie jumped up, helping William back onto his feet and sweeping the light in his hand over the rest of the hall to make sure there wasn't anything else lurking in the darkness.

'That thing you've got is useful,' I said.

'Electric torch,' answered the boy, holding up the device.

'Yes well you might have thought to use it a second ago when we were stumbling up those stairs with only the lamps and then everything went dark–'

I didn't wait for Samantha to continue her potentially never-ending thought. As soon as William seemed sure of his feet, I grabbed his hand and made to set off down the hall once more. Except, of course, that Samantha grabbed my arm to stop me.

'Where are you going?'

'Laboratory. Got to run. It's really none of your business though.'

Samantha's eyes went wide. 'Well fine be that way,' she said.

'I will!' I called over my shoulder as I ran.

'Fine then,' said Samantha, crossing her arms.

Finally, she'd gotten the hint.

Or so I thought, until some five doors later, while I paused to let William light another match, Samantha caught back up with us, Laurie in tow.

'Well you need the flashlight anyway even if you won't admit it,' she said, waving the thing in front of her.

It was true that William's matches were probably running out, but still, I wasn't going to admit anything. So we continued down the hall, Samantha following closely to light our way with Laurie's torch. We turned off the Dark Hall, taking a stairway down and then a turn left, then right, then left again, weaving through the maze-like corridors of the West Wing until finally, we came to the dead end where the metal door to Uncle Edward's laboratory stood wide open. I peeked through the door. It was empty. Slipping inside, I motioned for the others to follow.

William was close behind me, but Laurie and Samantha paused at the door.

'This...' said Samantha. 'Abigail I don't think that this is really the smartest–'

'Samantha?'

'Yes?'

'Do shut up.'

She huffed, but stepped through the door with Laurie, shivering a little at the cold and the silence and the clinging smell of alcohol. I urged the door closed a bit, to peek at the mirror behind it.

'Miss Crowe–?'

I shushed Laurie, stepping fully in front of the mirror, and with one deep, measured breath, I counted to three and stepped through the mirror. Those strange, tingling goose bumps washed over me, just as they had the last time, the world shifting, and again I felt myself falling sideways before stumbling into the mirror laboratory on the other side. I looked back to see William, Laurie, and Samantha staring, shocked, at the spot where I'd just been standing, but there were more important things to worry about than Samantha's disbelief. Unlike the laboratory, the mirror laboratory was *not* silent. Instead, footsteps and shouts were echoing from the door next to me – the mirror version of the door that, in the real laboratory, led to the rest of the house. I poked my head through the mirror.

'Back in a moment,' I said, before bolting through the laboratory door, not even waiting to see who followed.

I raced up the narrow stairs, which curved up and up, an endless spiral with close, dark walls. As I climbed, Uncle Edward's voice grew clearer, the Lady's protests louder and nearer with every step. At last, I reached the landing: the walls fell away, and there, across the open floor, I saw them:

The Lady had almost made it to a second set of stairs, which spiralled upward into the rest of the tower, but Uncle Edward was close on her heels, and as he reached for her, she turned to land a vicious kick to his chest. He staggered backward, clawing the wall for support. The Lady had made it, she climbed, she was almost out of sight–

'STOP!' Commanded Uncle Edward.

The Lady stumbled, though she didn't stop, not completely. But that single pause was all Uncle Edward needed. He leapt forward, grabbing the Lady by the arm, and wrenched her back down onto the landing.

'*Back off!*' hissed the Lady, and even though the Command hadn't been meant for me, the force of it pushed me backward. But Uncle Edward didn't so much as flinch. He dragged the Lady away from the stairs. By the time she'd managed to free herself, landing another kick that almost knocked his legs out from under him, it was too late. He'd backed her against the wall, inches away from a glass-less window, with no hope of escaping to either stair.

'Thieves are not welcome here,' he said, grabbing her wrist. As he twisted her hand, she dropped something, a coin of amber, gleaming dully. It clattered onto the stones, skittering away across the floor, and I just managed to catch a glimpse of the Mark carved on one face: the crescent topped with a dot. It was the Wardstone that had rested above the doorway in Beatrice's cabin. The Lady stared at it, wide-eyed, as the shadows at the edges of the room bristled.

'Please,' she gasped. 'Edward!'

But Uncle Edward's eyes were cold. He reached forward–

The next moment, the Lady Rosalind had wrested her gloved hand from Uncle Edward's grip, and with her other hand, she shoved him back. She kicked him once more, this time in the stomach, before tumbling backward out the window, her sky-blue gown fluttering like a flag in the wind. Uncle Edward lunged forward. She was gone, but without a single second of hesitation, he jumped over the sill and out the window, plummeting after her.

That was it. They were crazy. Also probably dead, but mostly crazy. I ran to the window and leaned my head out, scanning the ground below and expecting to see the broken bodies of an insane murderous magician and his insane Fey contact, but there was no sign of them: just the plain snow surrounding the tower and in the far distance, the trees of the Blackwood wavering in the wind. Just as William, Laurie, and Samantha reached the landing from the stair, I turned and started running back down.

'They're outside! They just fell!' I yelled, leaping down the stairs two and three at a time.

Out the door, through the mirror, and into the twisting halls. I had no idea where they'd gone, but at least now, I knew where the mirror led. It was the only entrance to the South Tower, the highest tower of Ravenscourt, which sat, like a black rook, at the very back of the house, almost at the edge of the Blackwood. And if they'd fallen from the tower...

I tore my way through the West Wing and out one of the side doors, out into the blustery night, the wind kicking up flurries of new snow. I rounded a corner of the house and skidded to a stop at the base of the tower. Those glass-less windows opened like black jaws up the side of the tower, and at the very, very top, there was just the faintest glimmer of firelight. I circled back and forth around the base of the tower, searching for any mark on the fresh-white snow, but there was nothing: no sign of my uncle, or of the Fey Lady. Not even a footprint.

'Abigail!' called William as he and Laurie finally caught up, Samantha lagging behind, her breath coming short.

'What do you think you're doing are you mad what did you–' Samantha stopped. She was finally out of breath.

I shook my head. 'I saw them fall,' I said.

William and Laurie exchanged a look. 'Abby, if they fell...' William didn't finish the thought, and he didn't have to. The clean, white snow below the tower said all that needed to be said. But I knew what I'd seen – or did I?

I sank onto my knees in the snow. It seeped into my skirts, but I didn't even feel the cold, all my thoughts focused on figuring out what could've possibly happened. I tried to see the scene again in my head: the Lady backed against the window, the stone on the floor. Uncle Edward reaching forward, and then the Lady had kicked him, and she fell–

But she'd fallen from the tower on the *other side* of the mirror. I couldn't begin to imagine where they'd ended up.

William held out a hand to help me up, and he and Laurie made sure I stayed standing. My face burned with the thought of the questions Samantha might start asking – but no, she was the last person that needed an explanation at this point. We stood in silence, as the wind twisted through the darkened trees, making the naked branches rustle. For the briefest instant, I thought I could hear voices in it.

No, I *could* hear voices in it.

Fear pricked at the back of my mind, and I turned to the forest, straining to see through the gloom. But there was nothing there – only the trees and the shadows and the sense that someone very far away was whispering words to the wind. 'Do you hear that?' I asked the others, ignoring Samantha's huff of annoyance.

Laurie pointed his flashlight toward the trees, but its beam couldn't touch a thing in the darkness. The shadows beneath the trees thickened, and the air went suddenly cold. All at once, the flashlight went out. The night swallowed its light whole, leaving us blind. I reached out, searching for William's hand, or Laurie's, or even Samantha's.

The whispers grew louder, and now I could hear words in the noise, scattered, broken, and glued back together. They rose into voices, rose into screams, and I had to cover my ears against the harsh cries, sharp as broken glass. The cold was overwhelming and so was the fear, as those things teeming beneath the trees surged forward like insects, swarming in for the kill. There were more than shadows in those woods. Hadn't Beatrice told us as much, when we first met her in the Rose Hedge Maze?

These were shades.

The shades' cries rose again, but as much as I tried to block my ears, I couldn't keep them out. The screams weren't in the trees or in the air; they weren't anywhere in front of or outside me – they were *in my head*, piercing through my skull and tearing my thoughts to shreds. I realized that one of the voices was mine, screaming against the pain in my head, and I gasped for breath–

My defences. I sucked in another harsh breath, steeling myself against the pain and cold, and as the shades continued to scream, I tore my hands from my ears, clasping them in front of me and focusing on the weight of Dad's ring on my finger.

The First Defence is always with you, but this ring will help you remember it.

The warmth of the Defence flickered over me, dulling the shades' voices and letting me take another breath. The chaos calmed, and I stood fast against the shades, the darkness lifting, just the slightest bit. I could do this. Breathe in, breathe out.

The Second Defence is self-control, and you must master your breath to maintain–

A harsh, icy wind grabbed hold of my throat, and I choked on air. My fragile Defence shattered, leaving only the cold and the screams and the darkness. The world faded into nothing, and I felt myself cut adrift, floating in a place without earth or sky, no up or down, no sideways, no light.

And as suddenly as they had attacked, the shades fell silent.

I opened my eyes to find myself lying with my cheek pressed into the snow, one of my hands splayed in front of me, unnaturally white. William lay nearby, crumpled into a motionless heap, but I couldn't see Samantha or Laurie. The shadows were still too thick.

And the shades were still here. Though I couldn't see them properly, I could *feel* them. They crawled over my skin, the touch of their inky fingers like spider's legs, sending shudders of horror through me, but I couldn't move, couldn't brush them off, couldn't so much as *shiver* properly. Their hissing whispers twined through my head.

Intrudersss... Their voices were harsh as gravel, thick as tar, completely inhuman – and entirely delighted. I didn't know what a swarm of disembodied and corrupted spirits could possibly consider delightful, but whatever it was, I was sure that it meant bad news for us. *Yesss... We shall have a feassst tonight...*

Definitely bad news.

I tried to push myself up, but none of my muscles wanted to obey me. Even my fingers rebelled against me, refusing to so much as twitch as I focused all my efforts on moving them one by one. I was frozen in place, even though I'd gone far beyond feeling the cold at this point.

Ahhh... sighed the shades. *But these are little more than children...*

Ssstill, they are intrudersss, the voices answered themselves. *They are promisssed usss.*

'No!' I managed at last, my voice coming out harsh and ragged around the edges.

The shades quieted, and like icy needles pricking my skin, their attentions settled on me, one by one. I wanted to be sick. But they were all focused on me now, and at the very least that meant they weren't feeding on the others.

What isss thisss one? They clustered around me, turning the world dark. I closed my eyes. At least that was a darkness I could control. *Ahhh... thisss one hasss the blood, but it isss not sssupposed to be here.*

I opened my eyes and focused my attention on my hand, still lying limp in front of me in the snow, my arm numb and unmoving from cold. Dad's ring glinted on my thumb, and taking a deep breath, I tried once more to summon my defences.

A scream from the shades, and all the warmth drained out of my body at once. The shades chattered and shrieked, their inhuman laughter pounding behind my eyes. *Ssso weak, itsss defensssesss!*

I wanted to scream at them, but my voice wasn't nearly strong enough for that. I could do nothing but lie there with my body pressed to the ground, wondering what they were waiting for and how long they'd let me stay alive–

Ahhh, you will ssstay alive. We wouldn't dare touch one with the blood – even if it isss tresssssspasssssssing.

Of course they could read my mind. I gritted my teeth, and with monstrous effort, I pushed myself up from the ground. I was safe then, it seemed, though what that meant for the others...

The intrudersss will be taken care of–

'You leave them alone!' I said. 'They're not intruders!'

The shades bristled, and I braced myself against their next attack, but it didn't come. Instead, they whispered among themselves, in those half-heard broken words. And then–

Would it like to extend them invitationssss? they asked.

'Yes, anything, whatever. Just leave them!'

A breath of wind gusted over the lawn. And the next moment, like steam evaporating into the cold air, they were gone, leaving behind only the cold, white snow, the empty trees, and the weak moonlight. I pushed myself to my feet and hurried to William's side, shaking him awake. He stirred, groggy and disoriented, but none-the-worse for the shades.

'Abby? Wha–' He blinked and shook his head to clear it, alert as he scanned the woods. But there was nothing there anymore.

'Help me wake the others,' I said.

I couldn't get Laurie to move an inch, though his flashlight had sputtered back to life, flickering weakly in the snow. Samantha wasn't much better, her eyelids fluttering while the rest of her lay still and heavy as stone. The only thing I could be thankful for was that they were both still breathing. That, at least, meant they were still alive – or, at least, that their bodies were.

No, I wouldn't let myself think that.

'We have to get them to the house,' I said. William nodded in agreement, though we both avoided voicing the question we were both thinking: *how?*

Snow crunched behind us, and I lunged for Laurie's flashlight, turning it to cut through the shadows of the wood, just as someone emerged from the trees. The intruder held up one hand to shield his eyes.

It was Uncle Edward.

Through the Looking Glass

William and I watched from the doorway of the house while Mother and Uncle Edward loaded Samantha into a coach with her family. Laurie had already been sent off – he'd managed to come to for the moment, and Emily had made it her personal duty to get him back to the Rectory in one piece. Now the adults turned their attentions to Samantha, who still hadn't recovered a bit. She drooped in Uncle Edward's arms as he lifted her into the Carver's coach, Isaac immediately bundling her into a blanket and pulling her close. Still, she didn't stir. The men exchanged a few short words, and Mr. Carver shut the door. With a snap of the coachman's whip, the horses clattered off, the sound of their hooves on the gravel fading into silence as the Carvers disappeared down the drive into the Blackwood.

Mother turned toward the door. She and Uncle Edward exchanged a look – the sort of look that only adults seemed capable of, full of things that I couldn't even begin to guess at – and without so much as a nod in our direction, she hurried past us and into the house. We were left facing Uncle Edward, and unlike Mother, he was focused fully on both of us, his grey eyes full of questions and measurements.

But in the end, he also made his way into the house, tipping his hat to us as he hobbled by. And that was that. The only things left were the empty drive and the gusting wind, and the snow. William and I slipped through the doors and up to our beds, too exhausted to even wish each other a Happy Wintersnacht.

Despite the unfortunate events of the evening, the Wintersnacht party continued into the early hours of Wintersday, the strains of music and laughter drifting up to us until well past three in the morning. But at long last, the guests said their goodbyes, the house went dark and blissfully silent, I managed to sink into a deep and dreamless sleep, and by the time I woke up, it was well past noon. I slipped out of bed and into the sitting room, where presents had been piled up next to the fireplace during the night. Breakfast lay waiting on the table as well, and knocking on William's door, I made sure he got up so we could set to work on these two very important things.

We'd gotten a good number of new books: novels and plays and a thick tome of Roman history for William, whose eyes lit up when he saw it, the way other boys' eyes light up at candy or treats. He'd received a few new toys as well, including a set of smart-looking tin soldiers that moved by clockwork as well as a wind-up mouse, the same one that I'd seen scurrying through Laurie Carol's tinker shop.

'Here, Abby, this one's from Isaac,' said William, grinning as he handed over a small, flat package tied with blue ribbon. I stuck my tongue out at him and opened the box, revealing a few dozen chocolates and a folded note. Handing the chocolates over to William, who immediately started wolfing them down, I focused on the message:

Dear Miss Crowe,

Merry Wintersday.

   I hope this present finds you in good cheer, though I can guess that you have more than the holiday on your mind as you read it. Doctor Crowe has told me his plan to announce the engagement at tonight's party.

   As I've told you before, while I do not always agree with your uncle's decisions, I have come to trust his judgment. I'm sure that the announcement has come as something of a nasty surprise, but I must assure you once again that Doctor Crowe never does anything without a good reason.

   If you ever need anyone to talk to, please consider coming to me first. At the very least, do let me know before you go poking into any more doorways or mirrors. These things are always a bit safer with someone to watch your back.

   I hope you'll find that your brother is doing better.

                              As ever and always,
                                At your service,
                                Isaac Carver

Well, that stung. To think that the boy had known all that time, and hadn't thought to mention a thing? I crumpled the letter into an angry ball and handed the chocolates over to William before digging back into the pile.

There was a present from Emily too, half-buried at the bottom. It was smaller than Isaac's gift, and heavier, and the note tied to it with a piece of string had been scribbled on a ripped sheet of paper, hastily folded and sealed.

Abigail,

After everything that has happened, I know there's nothing I can say that will make any of it better. So instead, please find my present attached. I managed to catch Laurie breaking curfew with the help of the enclosed gadget. I have no idea how it works, but it seems to be quite good at opening things.

In any case, I figured you'd find better use for it than sneaking out after hours to meet Samantha Carver, of all people, so I hereby gift it to you.

Good luck with those locked doors.

Ever and Truly Your Friend,
Emily

P.S. If you need anything at all, you know where to find me.

P.P.S. I am going to murder that Carver boy. You can be certain he knew about that announcement and he's a right prat for not warning you.

I considered the oddly-shaped gift, turning it over in my hands before finally tearing away the paper. What I found was a large and intricately designed key, built of brass, with a thick, heavy handle full of springs and gears. It looked like it would fit most of the locks in the house, except for one tiny detail, which made the thing pretty much useless: it had no teeth.

William had caught sight of it, and his face scrunched in confusion. 'A toothless key?' he asked.

I handed it over to him so he could take a look, reaching for Isaac's chocolates just as the clockwork mouse that Laurie had gifted William scrabbled over the wrapping paper, bumping into the box, and rolling to a stop in front of my brother's feet. He shook his head and handed the key back over with a shrug. 'No idea,' he said.

I turned the key in my fingers, examining every bit of it. There were slits in the sides, I noticed now, and also, at the top, a tiny hole, just big enough to allow a toothpick or hairpin. As I frowned at the puzzle in my hands, William scooped up his clockwork mouse and began winding it. I looked up as he removed the winding key and let the mouse scurry across the room once more.

If the key was clockwork, then of course it needed to be wound! 'William, can I see the winding key for that mouse?'

He handed it over: a small, flat piece of metal that was still too big for my key. I handed it back to him and instead removed one of the pins from my hair, sticking smooth end into the top of my key.

It caught the mechanism, and with a twist of my wrist, I wound it.

The key burst to life, teeth sprouting up and down the length of it in a dizzying array of different shapes. William's eyes went wide.

'I think Emily just gave you–'

'–the best lock pick ever,' I finished for him with a grin.

We'd reached the bottom of the pile, with paper and ribbons and clockwork gadgets of every type scattered across the floor of the room. There were a couple potted plants for me, far too many silk ties and pairs of new socks and fancy handkerchiefs which all ended up piled and forgotten in the corner, and at least one box of sparkling jewels that I knew I would never wear. The last present was small, wrapped in a delicate brown paper thin as skeleton leaves. Carefully, I pulled away the wrapping, revealing something round and heavy folded in a silvery grey cloth. A note had been penned on the underside of the paper:

> A light against the darkness.
>
> A costly light, but that cannot be helped, you will need it to find answers. Not even your blood will defend you in the place he has protected.
>
> Best of luck, Miss Abigail
>
> *Beatrice LaNoir*

I didn't even need to try to decipher the looping signature at the bottom of the message to know that Beatrice had sent me a present. I unfolded the grey cloth to find a flat coin of amber with a Mark engraved into its smooth surface: a thin crescent moon topped with a dot. The power of the Mark pulsed against my eyes, and not for the first time, I wondered what the gardener was playing at. It had been Beatrice who first told us about Dad's exile, Beatrice who pointed us to Ariel, Beatrice who had always been willing to listen to us, and to tell us more than the others. But I'd seen her talking to Uncle Edward in the woods, and if her actions proved anything, it was only that she was loyal to Uncle Edward. It was hard to believe that she'd ever truly been a friend at all. Perhaps it had all just been part of another game. And yet –

The stone felt warm in my hand. This was the stone that Lady Rosalind had dropped in the tower, when

Uncle Edward had caught her. And when she'd lost it, the look on her face had been more than fear: she'd been terrified. But why? What did the stone protect against? It wasn't just a Ward – that much I had already figured out myself. After all, Wards were meant to protect a place, to define boundaries and keep out trouble. No, the stone was likely some sort of *enchantment*, a spell bound to the amber stone with the Mark, though what it was meant for, I couldn't imagine.

Still, if we were going to break into the tower, we'd need all the help we could get, magical or otherwise. And of course, we *were* going to break into the tower: it was the one thing I was completely certain of, now. I turned to William.

'We need to talk about what happened last night,' I said.

'Which part?' he asked, looking up from his presents. 'The fact that Uncle Edward just announced that he's marrying Mum, the weird tower that happens to be in a mirror, the attempted murder by means of defenestration, or that swarm of shades that came out of nowhere?'

'Defenestration?'

'Throwing a person out a window.'

I shook my head at him. 'Well we're going to have to do *something* about Mother. I mean, the whole thing doesn't make sense. There's no possible way she could believe this was the right thing to do.'

'Uncle Edward must've convinced her somehow.'

'Maybe he put a Curse on her,' I said. It would've made sense. He was a magician, after all, and if he was willing to steal and trade a murdered spirit, placing a Curse on his dead brother's wife could hardly be considered worse.

But of course, Mother had been the one to bring us to Ravenscourt in the first place. She had to have known how Dad felt about his brother, even if she didn't know the details. And yet, she'd agreed to come. And now…

If it was a Curse, then at least it meant Mother wasn't completely insane. But it also meant that she was under Uncle Edward's complete control – and some Curses could kill their victims if they tried to do something the magician had forbidden. Would it even be possible to get her away from Ravenscourt at this point? On the other hand, I didn't want to think about what might happen if she stayed.

'We have to get Dad's spirit back,' I said finally. 'I don't think there's any other way for us to fix this. And there there's only one place it can be. Lady Rosalind needed the stone to break into the tower, and now we have it.'

'He's expecting us to do something, you do realize,' said William. He picked up the clockwork key and held it out to me. 'But at least we can sneak out of the room now when they think it's locked.'

I took the clockwork key, holding it in one hand and weighing the amber stone in the other. A charm for locked doors and a light against darkness. It would have to be enough.

'Tonight, then,' I said, wrapping the stone in its grey cloth. Immediately, the touch of its power dulled, and I stuffed both it and the clockwork key into my sock. 'Tonight, we get our Dad back.'

Night had fallen, and as the snow and wind continued to bluster outside, I lay in bed, reading one of my new novels by candlelight. The plan was to feign sleep until it came time for them to lock us in. We'd wait a couple hours more, and then, once the adults were sure to have gone to bed, we'd use the clockwork key to escape, and make our way to the tower behind the mirror. It was a simple enough plan – elegant, really. The only problem was the waiting. It had been an hour and a half since the Housekeeper had come around with the keys and locked our doors, but the clock had just barely chimed midnight, and I wanted to wait just a quarter hour more, to be sure.

It was a good thing I did. Just as soon as I thought it was probably safe, footsteps sounded in the hall, followed by the jingle of keys. I snuffed my candle and buried myself in my covers, hoping that William had enough time to do the same in his room.

The door to the sitting room creaked open, and I focused on my breaths, doing my best to keep them deep and even. My door creaked open, and someone stepped into the room. I dared to open my eyes the tiniest bit – a shadow swept across the room, light steps carrying the person back into the sitting room. The door swung silently closed, and I let myself take a deep breath of relief before creeping to the door and pressing my eye to the keyhole. Mother drifted through the room beyond, opening the door to William's bedroom and peeking in on him too before leaving the room in a few quick steps. A key turned in the lock, trapping us once again.

Mother's footsteps faded down the hall, and I slipped into the sitting room. William appeared at his door too. 'I think it's time for us to do this,' he said.

I nodded. I pressed my ear against the main door, listening for any sign of life on the other side, but the halls lay silent as death. I set the clockwork key into the lock and with a small wish for good luck, I jabbed my hairpin into the top to wind it. The key came to life, whirring and spinning, until the key found a fit and the lock sprang open with a click. I pushed the door open.

We threaded through the labyrinthine corridors of the house toward the laboratory, the moonlight drifting through the windows and turning us into ghosts.

William lit his matches to guide the way, our feet freezing in the drafts that crept in under doors and windows, the floorboards like ice beneath our slippers. We pushed further and further into the house, through the Dark Hall, all the darker without its weak gas lamps, and then, at last, a few more turns, and the door of the laboratory loomed in front of us, emerging from the darkness like an iron side through sea mists.

I wound the clockwork key again, and the door screeched as I pushed it open. Without waiting to find out if we'd been heard, we ducked inside, stepping through the mirror into the other laboratory, the prickling feeling of passing between places sending shivers over my skin. But then I was on the other side, and William was there too, and the door to the tower lay open in front of us. We scurried up the steps.

By the time we reached the landing where Uncle Edward had faced down the Lady on Wintersnacht, I was out of breath. William paused next to me as I recovered, clutching his arms around his chest against the cold. The stairs continued on the other side of the landing, sprouting from the wall like toadstools and leaving a steep drop on one side. I looked up to see where they led, but the top of the tower was invisible – the stairs simply spiralled further and further away before disappearing into complete darkness. The tower wasn't nearly as tall from the outside, but who knew what strange tricks could be played on this side of the mirror?

I pulled the amber stone from my sock and freed it from its cloth, its power surging to life in my hand, like a small coal, warm and bright. It was glowing, but not with any sort of light that I could see. It was the same sort of light that I knew was there when I used my defences, invisible but warm, unfurling in a golden thread that flitted forward toward the stair, urging me to follow it upward into a place just out of sight.

William grabbed my hand, and together, we made our way forward.

Despite the light of the amber stone, darkness bristled in every window and alcove, and I refused to look down at the steep drop to our right. At last, we reached a narrow landing, and I leaned against the wall to catch my breath. A torch burned next to the open window, its flame dancing in the draft. As I stepped forward to take the next stair, it sputtered, flickering three times and threatening to go out completely, before suddenly flaring back to life. For some reason, it made me shiver. We continued on.

There was a second landing, and a third and fourth, and still the stairs continued. I looked up as we reached the fifth landing, but the stairs still disappeared into darkness – there was no end in sight. While William sank down onto the steps to rest, I studied the walls, looking for any sign of how much further we had to go. But the landing was just like every other one we'd found: a ledge spanning half the tower, with the stairs continuing upward in front of us and a torch flickering next to one of the tower's glassless windows.

The torch sputtered in the draft. I watched as it flickered – twice, thrice – and then, with a sudden flare, it recovered. *Déjà vu.*

No, not *déjà vu*.

'William!' I said, reaching down to shake his arm. 'It's an Illusion!'

He looked up at me, 'What?'

'The staircase! It's not real – it's…'

His eyes went wide. 'It's an infinite loop,' he said, jumping to his feet. He reached out to touch the walls, though they felt solid as any real wall. 'But, then how do we get to the top?'

'I… I think I can break it,' I said, though even as I did so, I wondered if I really could. After all, I'd only managed to break the Housekeeper's Illusion by accident, and I didn't know if I could do it again, much less do it for both of us. Still, I had to try. 'Here, just take my hand.'

We clasped hands with the amber stone nestled in our palms and stood together on the landing. I closed my eyes and ran my thumb over the band of Dad's ring. With deep breaths, I pulled the coils of the Second Defence into my chest and imagined the garden flowering around me: the scent of it, the touch of the breeze. The tree and the hedges of my sanctuary wavered behind my eyes, halfway between reality and dream, the grip of William's hand turning into something imagined, the strange, unseen light of the amber stone growing bright and blinding. Something flared up in my chest – something icy and burning at the same time, knotted tightly into the threads around my heart. I reached out with it–

The Illusion cracked and faded away, and I opened my eyes to find that we were standing, not on a narrow landing, but at the top of a short set of stairs, a smooth, blank floor in front of us. At the opposite side of the tower, a single, shimmering mirror stood: an open doorway suspended in a silver frame between two glassless windows.

'Whoa,' said William, and I laughed with relief. Just a few more steps and we'd finally have Dad's spirit back – we'd find out the truth of everything. I hurried toward the mirror, ignoring the strange shadows twisting in the corners of my eyes, but William paused.

'Abby?' he said.

I turned to find out what had spooked him, but there was nothing there: nothing but the trembling shadows. The light floating in through the glassless windows grew dim, and a sudden wave of absolute, numbing cold washed over me. The shadows at the edges of the room began to whisper, and quickly as I could, I pulled William close.

The shadows in the tower clustered around us, heavy and clinging, and the world itself faded, the room swallowed by the thickening darkness until, at last, we were left floating in a shapeless space of absolute empty black. The only way I knew there was still floor under my feet was because I could feel it through my slippers – there was none of it left to see. The voices of the shades rose to a frenzy:

Who daresss disssturb usss?

William clung tight to my arm. I wasn't sure how much he remembered from the last time we'd had to deal with the shades – whether he'd felt them the same as I had, or had heard their awful voices echoing in his own mind. That time, they'd let us go because of my blood. I had to hope that would be enough, but the amber stone in my hand told me that it probably wouldn't be. Its warmth had flared into a steady burning heat, and I clutched it tight as I raised my Second Defence, refusing to let my voice waver as I faced them.

'I wish to pass,' I said.

The shades chattered with laughter, like small, awful animals that feasted on dead meat. *And why would it wish to do that, little one? Thinksss it can go anywhere it pleasesss now?*

'Why are you talking to them?' whispered William. 'I thought this was what the stone was for.'

I shushed him and gripped the stone more tightly. 'We have the blood and we wish to go forward,' I said. 'You've no right to stop us.'

The shades hissed, and it was safe to say that it was not a happy hiss. It was more like a very, very, very angry hiss, their voices rising into a howl like a violent wind. *It presumesss much, if it thinksssss it can tell usss what to do.*

I held William closer against the darkness as it shifted, growing solid in front of us, pushing us back, away from the mirror, toward the stairs – no, toward the empty window–

I planted my feet, leaning forward into the wind.

It mussst not passsssss! The voices deepened, and the shades were no longer hissing. No, their voices rolled through the tower in a thunderous roar: *It is oursss!*

I raised the amber stone, holding it up as a ward against the darkness. What it had been meant to do, I still didn't know, but I'd left it too late, almost certainly I'd left it too late. Perhaps it wasn't even meant to stop the shades. What if it was just another of Beatrice's tricks, a promise that meant nothing?

The stone burst to life.

Light erupted from it – bright, blinding, pure white light that I still couldn't see but that I could feel in every single atom of my body and mind, a brilliant light that could banish any darkness. The festering creatures broke and scattered, screeching as they fled, and for a moment, we stood in the centre of that sphere of sheltering light.

The magic flickered bright around us, and I felt it winding through me, touching those threads of warmth that coiled around my heart, twisting among the shades and shadows. The power of the stone was everywhere, and I knew that it wasn't just protecting me, but that I could *use* it–

My magic flared through the amber stone, bursting outward in hundreds of tendrils of light and power, tangling the shades in its grip. I could feel their twisted, decaying spirits struggling against me, and with a single word, I knew how I could banish them:

'Sleep,' I Commanded.

With a sigh, the shadows melted into nothing. The unnatural darkness lifted. The mirror gleamed in front of us and my magic curled back into my chest, leaving me breathless. I dropped the stone.

It clattered against the floor, and I reeled, dizzy and lightheaded, William's hand the only thing keeping me from falling after it. Was it dangerous, what I'd just done? I'd used magic – not just defences, but real, controlling, powerful *magic* – and it was not so different, it was not so difficult. Despite knowing that everything the Inquisitors had ever taught us was mostly wrong, that magic didn't turn your spirit into some dark and twisted thing, that it didn't send you straight to the devil, I also knew everything that Dad had taught me, about the dangers of power, the temptations of controlling what you had no right to control. Magic might not corrupt the spirit, but it could still be dangerous. It could still be *wrong*.

I picked up the amber stone and folded it into its cloth, stuffing the whole thing back into my sock. The power had been the same as my defences – and was it truly so bad, what I had done? If I hadn't used magic, then what would've become of me – of William? Or was all this simply the first step on a slippery slope toward Cursing random passers-by?

'Abby?' said William softly. I looked at him, staring at me wide-eyed. 'That... that was awesome.'

Well, if William was alright with it...

Across the bare floor, we came face to face with our reflections, the tower landing warped and strange in the glass behind us. With one last deep breath, we stepped through the mirror.

The room beyond was larger than I'd expected, a wide, round space filled with light and warmth. A single unbarred window looked out over the roof of the rest of the house, a fire burning in the hearth next to it, while above, an iron chandelier hung dripping with candles. There was a chair too, and a small table, but I didn't pay much attention to any of it, because the single, most glaring thing in the room wasn't the furniture or the lighting: it was the cage.

We stood on one side of the room, next to the window, but the rest of the space was fenced off by a wall of dull, iron bars, curving up and out like the spokes of some giant bird cage. Beyond the bars lay a handsome desk and an impressive number of tall shelves stuffed with books, a standing screen hiding part of the room from view. But among all the rich furniture, two things stood out. The first was a brazen chair, equipped with straps and things designed to hold a person down. I didn't want to know what it was supposed to be used for.

The other thing the cage contained was a boy.

THE IRON CAGE

I couldn't move. I didn't dare to speak. It was impossible to do anything but stare, as the boy slept, one arm sprawled across the wooden desk, his fingers twitching in some sort of dream. Uncle Edward was capable of terrible things, that much I'd already known. He'd been willing to murder, to steal spirits, to make deals with the Court – but *this*? I couldn't guess how long the boy had been here. By the look of his face, he must've been at least a couple years older than me, but he was thin – too thin – making him look young and weak and frail. Skinnier than William, even. Pin-line scars traced his sunken cheeks, his dark hair cut ragged and short.

'Abby?' said William, his voice little more than a breath. 'Abby, what do we do?'

Part of me didn't want to know that this boy existed. Part of me wanted to step back through the mirror and forget that we'd ever found him. But I couldn't – and more than that, I couldn't leave him like this, not now, not when we'd found him here, locked up by our uncle. I drifted closer to the cage, reaching out to touch the bars. A tingle of electricity made me pull my fingers back, all the hairs on my skin standing on edge as the shock pulsed through me.

The boy shook himself at the same time, jumping up from his seat to face us, nearly toppling the chair he'd been sitting on. His wide eyes were a shocking shade of blue, and something unpleasant twisted in my stomach as he focused them on me.

'Is this some kind of trick?' he hissed, his lurid eyes never breaking from my face, never even blinking. 'Because I told that miserable mortician, and now I'm telling you: if anyone tries to cut me again, I'll bite their nose off!'

'I–' There were no words, no words for this impossibility. We'd fought through Illusions and shades in the hope of finding Dad's spirit, and here, now, instead, we'd found… I couldn't even say what we had found. 'We don't want to hurt you,' I said. His eyes were unnerving, a frigid, unnatural blue, unblinking. I realized that I'd seen those eyes before – I *knew* those eyes. They'd been the part of his mother's portrait that had seemed most alive. 'You're Uncle Edward's son,' I said.

The boy laughed, a wild sound, like the cry of an injured animal. 'Damon Crowe, at your service,' he said with a mocking bow. 'So you are our dear cousins who have been causing so much trouble! Tell me! How did you find me?'

I told him. Starting from the day of Dad's funeral, I told him everything: about Beatrice's story and our discovery of Ariel Raban, our search through the church ledgers and the resting record, all the way up to the Wintersnacht party and what had happened then. And the entire time, those blue eyes barely moved, barely blinked, focused entirely on me.

'We… we thought he must be keeping Dad's spirit here, so we had to find out,' I finished. 'But we didn't know… we didn't think… *you*–'

'Well you might as well come to terms with it!' snapped Damon, finally looking away. He paced back and forth beyond the bars, shaking his head as if trying to empty it. The nagging fear in my stomach was telling me to flee, but I knew I couldn't do that. William and I had found this – had found *him* – and though the situation was monstrous, we couldn't turn away now. I edged closer to the cage, and Damon stopped his pacing to set his eyes on me again, wary and watching.

'The records. They said you died,' I explained. 'We couldn't have known. And we didn't think… even with everything, we didn't think Uncle Edward could–'

'You don't know my father very well, do you?' said Damon. He shook his head again, as if shuddering. 'Dr. Edward Crowe always knows what's best. Dr. Edward Crowe doesn't have to follow the rules, because he can do better. Dr. Edward Crowe would go to any lengths to be certain that no one could ever find out about his sickly, illegitimate son.' He lowered his eyes, his fingers curling into fists at his sides. 'And I'm sorry that your father had to pay the price for that.'

I'd heard enough. 'How do we get you out of here?'

He gestured toward the opposite wall, at the alcove that held the window, just next to the mirror behind us. 'There's some kind of control hidden in the wall, but I don't know how to open it. They'd never feel safe if they thought I knew.'

William was already on it, his fingers searching the wall for any sign of the hidden panel. 'Here!' he said, fiddling with something half-hidden among the stones. I joined him in the alcove to see what he'd found: a pair of gears set into the wall, with numbers engraved along their edges, and a switch set beneath them. Could it be this easy? I flipped the switch.

A bright arc of electricity shot between two of the cage bars, and hastily, I flicked the switch back into place. 'Sorry!'

'Let's not do that again, shall we?' said Damon.

'There are numbers here, but I don't–'

'Quiet!' hissed Damon suddenly. We froze, and I realized that footsteps were echoing through the tower, the sound seeping into the room from the mirror. It couldn't be anyone but Uncle Edward, and there was no way for us to escape unseen. Thankfully, we were hidden away in the alcove, but only for a minute more at most–

William reset the panel, a sheet of stone closing over it, and without a word, he threw open the window, letting the cold air whirl into the room. As he clambered out onto the roof, I looked back at Damon, and met his eyes.

We'll come back for you, I mouthed silently.

He nodded.

I leapt out onto the rooftop and pushed the window closed, ducking under the sill just as a shadow fell over the room behind us. I'd never realized, until that moment, the terror that a mere shadow could invoke – worse than shades, or even the Illusion of darkness. I shivered as our uncle stepped into the room.

'Hello, Damon.'

No. *Not* our uncle. The voice that drifted through the window was young and bright, and I couldn't help myself – I had to poke my head above the sill to make sure that I wasn't hearing things, that what I heard was true. And sure enough, there he stood, prim and confident as ever, his pale hair perfectly arranged.

It was none other than Isaac Carver.

I sank back below the window, the chill of fear turned into something harsher, something that burned. As little as I knew about Isaac, I couldn't help but feel betrayed – after all, he was the one who had told me that he wouldn't let anything bad happen to William. He was the one who had told us to trust Uncle Edward, and he'd known the entire time what Uncle Edward was hiding. What else did he know? And what else was he hiding from us?

William tugged on the sleeve of my nightdress, his eyes darting toward the other side of the roof to say that we should make a run for it, but I shook my head. If Isaac Carver was involved in this – if Uncle Edward had sent him, then I wanted to know exactly what it was that Uncle Edward had trusted him to do.

'Well, look who's back,' said Damon, the sarcasm in his voice only barely muffled by the glass of the window. 'Whatever did we humble peasant folk do to be graced with your ever-so-honourable presence, Mr. Carver?'

Isaac brushed off the question. 'You're awake late,' he answered, his voice flat as an icy lake. 'Edward told me you've been having trouble sleeping.'

'Of course. My dear father tells you everything–'

'When was the last time you slept through the night?'

A pause. 'At least four months ago,' answered Damon finally.

'Since starting the new round of medications,' mused Carver. His voice was so soft I almost missed it. Next to me, William gave an unwilling shiver, and I pulled him close. 'Perhaps we'll have to add a sedative to the formula–'

'And here I thought I was just missing you while you were away,' said Damon.

Isaac didn't even pause. 'I'll have to run tests as usual, of course.'

'Oh come on, Carver. You've lost your sense of humour.'

Isaac chuckled at that. 'And your insults have seen little improvement.'

There was a pause, and Isaac's shadow fell across the roof. I had to fight down the urge to peek over the sill again as his silhouette lingered there, considering something on the sill – had he noticed some sign of our escape? I pulled my nightdress close, William trembling uncontrollably beside me, and we held our breaths. At last, the shadow drifted away.

'What are you waiting for, Carver? Surely you don't still need that witless butler to take care of little old me.'

'Don't worry, Galen will be here soon enough.' The top of his shadow floated back and forth over the snow in front of us. He was pacing the room.

Damon huffed. 'Really, Carver. You used to at least be entertaining. What happened?' When Isaac didn't answer, he continued, lowering his voice to a whisper. 'Did she reject you again?' Isaac's shadow paused, and Damon pressed forward: 'To be fair, you ought to have learned *something* from the last time.'

'It's times like this that I wish I could just press a button to knock you unconscious.'

'I mean, how many times has it been that you've asked now? Four? Five?'

'Three.'

'Oh, but you do seem to be such a *glutton* for punishment. Have you considered–'

'Shut it,' said Carver, his voice rising at last. 'You shut it now.'

Damon let out a bark of laughter. 'That's the Carver I know! But really, you should know that I'm rooting for you. You're like a brother to me–'

'*Shut it!*' snapped Carver, just as the sound of heavy feet fell onto the tower steps. 'That'll be Galen,' he said with obvious relief. Within a minute, another shadow had fallen over the room – tall and heavy as the butler himself – and within another two, things had been set down and there was the sound of gears creaking and grinding within the tower, the Butler's shadow receding as he stepped away from the window.

'Don't touch me!' spat Damon – there was the butler's heavy footsteps, the crack of something, a scream. 'BACK OFF!' yelled Damon. 'SLEEP!'

The Commands trembled through the air, but there was no reaction from the butler: no sign, no sound. I couldn't help it, before William could stop me, I'd stood and turned to lift my head above the window sill again. The butler was there, wrestling our cousin into the brazen chair, the bars of the cage sunk into the stone floor while Isaac–

Isaac was looking directly at me. His eyes widened–

And before he could do or say anything at all, I'd grabbed William's hand. We ran. Across the roof and toward the back doors of the greenhouse, we ran, trusting the clockwork key to save us. We fled Isaac, and we fled the tower, and we fled the screams that followed, trying not to hear them, even as they followed us into our rooms, as they found us under the covers of the bed – even as they echoed through that sleepless, dreamless night, a nightmare that we couldn't escape.

When I woke, William was still sleeping, dozing beside me. Somehow we'd managed to sleep, though how it was possible and how long we'd managed, I couldn't tell. Wintry light poured in through the window, and I slipped out of bed to find breakfast waiting in the sitting room. Mother had tucked a note under one of the teacups:

> *Carols coming at noon.*
> *Make yourselves presentable.*
>
> *Much love*

I didn't think I could stomach even a single bite of potato at the moment. Instead, I turned the note in my fingers, drifting to the window to watch the snow moving over the frosted grounds. I couldn't get any of what I'd seen or heard last night out of my head. All of it played over and over: Damon's barking laugh, his pale eyes, the power of his failed Commands, and Isaac standing there–

But worst of all were the screams. Because now we knew – those screams didn't come from a spirit or ghost. They came from Damon, from our living, breathing cousin: screams of terror and pain, the memory of them as fresh and horrifying as the blood of a new wound.

The floor creaked, and William stepped up beside me.

'Get any sleep last night?' he said.

'Must have. You?'

'Same.' I turned back to the window, trying to figure out exactly how we'd gotten to this point. So many things that should've been impossible – Dad's death, Uncle Edward's deals with the Fey, Damon's imprisonment – all of it was now laid out in front of us, and I couldn't have even started to make a list of the countless things that were wrong with the whole situation. Besides, making a list would be pointless. There was only one thing to do now:

'We have to fix this.'

'But how?' asked William. 'What can we do?'

I looked down at the card in my hand. *Carols coming at noon*. Emily had once promised she'd do anything she could to help. 'I think it's time to call in a favour from Emily,' I said.

'You think she'd actually be able to help?'

'I don't think it would hurt to ask.'

William nodded and made his way over to the table, scooping bacon and potatoes onto a plate and shuffling back over to hand it to me. At this point, though, I was sure that it wouldn't end well if I tried to eat anything, especially Ravenscourt's bacon. After all, you never could tell what might be in it.

'I'm not hungry,' I said.

But William insisted. So I swallowed a few potatoes before retreating to the bath to wash and dress, making sure I was ready well before the clock chimed half past eleven. I wasn't sure how much Emily would actually be able to help – I just hoped she'd be willing to listen to me, at least.

Finally, the tower bells rang out for midday, and took a deep breath to steady myself before I had to face Emily. I opened the door–

And found myself face-to-face with the Housekeeper.

'And just where do we think we're going?' she croaked, a nasty smile smeared across her face.

'We're going to wait on the Carols. Mother said–'

'You'll be doing no such thing,' sniffed the Housekeeper. 'Neither of you are to step foot out of the East Wing, Master's orders.'

'But Mother–'

'Is hardly the highest authority in this household, little girl. Now, if it's all very well and good, you'll be getting back into your room now.'

When I tried to push past her, she all but lifted me off my feet to set me back on the other side of the door, slamming it closed and jamming the keys into the lock. I nearly broke the handle trying to wrestle it back open, but all my kicking, yelling, and banging was in vain. I might as well have been trying to force my way through a cliff wall.

'Let us out of here you wretched, old, toad-faced–'

William pulled me away from the door. 'Let me handle this,' he whispered. 'Er, Mrs. Thompson?' he said, speaking through the keyhole.

'If you think I'm going to let *you* out here, you brat, you are sorely–'

'Well, no, I don't expect that,' said William. 'But, er… just to let you know, they didn't send any of my medicines up with breakfast.'

'So? What do you want me to do about it?'

'Well, Isaac and Uncle Edward said that I have to take them every day.'

'*And?*'

'And, well, I was kind of hoping you could let them know that I haven't got them? I'd… really rather not like to have another fit.'

Silence buzzed on the other side of the door, the Toad no doubt contemplating her options. Part of me raged at the thought that the Toad might very well be willing to let my brother seize, if she had to. But at last, she sighed. 'Oh, very *well*. I'll tell your uncle about the miserable medicines, but I swear, if I come back to even a single bit of funny business, I'll make sure that you're locked in a closet for a week!' And double locking the door with a click, she took the keys and started down the hall.

We both winced at that. Her footsteps faded, leaving the hall on the other side of the door silent once again. William mouthed for me to fetch my hand mirror, and poking it under the door to look both ways down the hall, we made sure that the coast was clear.

'I'll have to stay here for when she gets back,' he said, 'but get the clockwork key and go quick!'

He didn't have to tell me twice. I set the key in the door and wound it, the mechanism fitting to the lock with a click. I slipped out into the hall and tucked the key back into my sock, hurrying toward the foyer and hoping that I hadn't managed to miss them.

Thankfully, when I got to balcony overlooking the entrance hall, the Carols were just coming in. I ducked into the shadows of the upper foyer, watching through the banister as the butler ushered them into the house, the Pastor and his wife removing their hats while Emily supported a drooping Laurie on her arm. If the boy looked any better than he had two nights ago, after the shades had attacked us, it was only because happened to be upright and standing – which I guess was an improvement in itself. But he was still bone-white, his eyes staring blankly at everything and nothing at the same time, his thick hands shaking a bit, even as Emily held him steady. I swallowed the pang of guilt that bubbled up from my stomach.

Uncle Edward entered from the West Wing, Mother close behind, and I had to clench my teeth to stop myself from groaning at the situation. While Mother greeted Adeline and the Pastor, Uncle Edward bent down to give Laurie a once over, before gently removing him from Emily's arm and turning to lead him toward the West Wing.

'I hope you actually know what you're doing this time, Dr. Crowe,' said Emily before he could quite escape.

But Uncle Edward gave only the briefest pause as he answered, 'You have nothing to fear about that, my dear,' and led Laurie away down the hall. Mother ushered the Pastor and his wife toward one of the East Wing doors, and Emily was left watching both of them, debating which group to follow.

I whistled from the top of the stair.

Emily's eyes rose to meet mine. She stood, still as stones, until the foyer was empty, and then immediately hurried up the stair to meet me. 'Abigail – what in–'

'Wait until we get somewhere private!' I hissed at her. 'We can't be caught!'

She huffed, but followed me silently into the West Wing, as I took as many turns as we could until we'd found a place where neither Uncle Edward nor the Housekeeper would find us: a close, dusty, lonely hall, the back lawn stretching away through the line of windows on the right. At last, in front of one of those windows, I paused and turned to look Emily in the eye.

'So it seems like you're the only one who knows what happened to Laurie,' she said before I could say anything. 'Or at least, you're the only one who might be willing to tell.'

'We were attacked,' I said. And all of it came tumbling out: Uncle Edward's argument with the Fey Lady, the chase to the tower to find out what he was hiding, the way the adults jumped and the search for them in the snow. 'And then these shades came out of nowhere, and they were everywhere, and I didn't know…'

'Shades?' said Emily. 'A *swarm* of shades! We're lucky he wasn't killed!'

I shook my head. 'They seemed to listen to me – at least a little.'

Her eyebrows furrowed, her eyes running over me, head to toe, as if re-measuring me. 'You– you talked to a swarm of shades?'

I shrugged.

'And have you been back to the tower since?' pressed Emily.

All I could do was nod, the words sticking in my throat. Even now, I couldn't bring myself to describe what we'd found, even though I knew she needed to hear it – that if she was going to help, she needed to know. 'Yes, we broke in last night,' I managed finally.

'And?' Emily was focused entirely on me now, her dark eyes intense and searching. 'What did you find?'

The words trembled there, right in my chest, and I had to take a deep breath to loosen them. 'We… we found his son.'

'YOU FOUND HIS WHAT?'

I had to clamp a hand over her mouth. 'Shhhhh! If anyone hears us–!'

'*Uuuuufffndddithhhwhhhgggt?*' repeated Emily through my palm

And out came the rest of it, everything we'd discovered just last night, though I stopped myself short of mentioning Isaac Carver. I still couldn't make sense out of that part of it, and something about the whole situation told me that Emily wouldn't appreciate hearing it from me. 'He's *alive*, Emily. And they've been keeping him locked up...' the words failed me again. 'We need your help,' I said finally.

Gently, Emily took my hand and lifted it away from her mouth. 'That boy,' she said. 'Damon. Damon Crowe. He... he *wasn't dead*?'

I shook my head. Emily hadn't blinked for the last minute or so, and her eyes had gone wider than should've been possible. 'But then... the *screams*... why everyone leaves...' she said, half to herself. She shook herself and started pacing, her hands clasped in front of her, thinking. 'Alright. Alright. We can figure this one out. We can handle this...'

'We need to get him out of here. But more than that, we need to find somewhere that he'll be *safe*.'

She looked at me, but there was no hint of her usual grin – no flash of teeth. Her face was grim, and her sharp eyes met mine. 'Beatrice,' she said finally. '*This* is what Beatrice wanted us to find – wanted *you* to find.'

The gardener's whisper as she stood next to Ariel's grave rose up in the back of my mind: *they are not all lost*. Everything the gardener had done, she'd done to save Damon – to help him. It had never been about us at all, never been about Dad, not really. *Damon* was the reason she'd given us the stone, the reason she'd told us about Lily's death and Dad's exile. Damon was her reason for telling us everything–

But no, it hadn't been everything. And if she'd been so desperate to save him, if she'd really wanted us to find our cousin then why:

'If she knew, why didn't she just *tell* us?' I said. More than that, I wondered: why had she needed our help at all?

Emily shook her head. 'I don't know. But I don't think there's anyone else who could help him – who *would* help him. Not against your uncle.'

That, of course, was the truth. We couldn't trust anyone else. Not a single one of the house staff would take our side, and Emily's parents never struck me as the type to step into situations like these. We certainly couldn't trust the Carvers, least of all Isaac.

I wasn't even sure we could trust Mother.

'You're right,' I told Emily finally. 'I have to talk to Beatrice. If we're going to get him out, she has to be the one to know.'

We made our way back toward the main halls of the house, heading down one of the stairways that opened onto the Dark Hall and hurrying down the Dark Hall itself. I had to get to Beatrice, which meant braving the outer gardens and perhaps even the Blackwood, if she wasn't in the greenhouse. We came to the place where the Dark Hall met the main second floor corridor, when voices reached us from down the hall–

'You lying little *brat*!' screeched the Housekeeper, and for a moment, I stood frozen, horrified that she'd somehow managed to find us, here, now, until I saw them–

'*William!*'

Before Emily could stop me, I was racing toward them, barrelling toward the Housekeeper and her shouts as she dragged my brother down the Dark Hall, William struggling against her clawing grip. They were heading away from the stairs, the opposite direction from Uncle Edward's study or anything in the West Wing, and though William was fighting her every step of the way, it wasn't difficult to see that she was too strong to let him escape. And if she wasn't taking him to Uncle Edward, then–

I was not going to let that old Toad lock my brother in a closet. Not now. Not *ever*. I pushed past them to block her path. As her lidded eyes settled on me, her face lit up and her wide mouth curled into a wicked grin.

'So there's the little jail-breaker,' she croaked.

And before I could say a single thing, her hand shot out to grab my hair, pulling it so that I had no choice but to look up into her hideous face. 'Sneaking out and around all over the place – I might not know how you managed your little disappearing act, but rest assured, little girl, that it *won't* happen again.' She started down the hall again, ignoring my swipes and punches, as if they were no more than bothersome flies. 'You know,' she said as she dragged us toward the closet at the end of the Dark Hall, 'Your father was another one who thought the rules applied to everyone but him. And look where that got him – pity old Master Crowe never quite got over having to banish him–'

I aimed a punch for the area just above her apron waist, but she stopped and, with a jerk on my hair, she wrenched my head back so that she could glare straight down at me again. 'Good girls do not try to punch people. Naughty girls have to be punished.'

My eyes watered at the pain as she twisted my hair into a knot. I tried to kick her. She jerked me off my feet.

'William! William– *fire*–'

I didn't even have to look to know that he understood. There was the snap of a match being lit–

The Housekeeper tugged me up onto my feet, and pushed William forward, his smoke bomb and the box of matches spilling out of his hand, her foot coming down to extinguish the one he'd lit. And now there was nothing we could do as she dragged us down the hall, toward some horror that we couldn't even imagine yet

– even if I broke the Illusion again, I couldn't know how long she'd leave us there–

There was the scrape of a match against the wall, and a sudden hiss of flame. The Housekeeper froze. She turned, and we turned with her, looking back, to where Emily stood, contemplating a lit match in one hand, and the hem of the nearest curtain in the other. She looked up at the Housekeeper and grinned.

The curtains caught light in no time, and the Housekeeper shrieked, letting go of us to rush forward to try to put out the flames. We were free, and Emily's hand was reaching for mine, William latching on to me from the other side. We fled back down the hall, through the twisting passages toward the greenhouse door.

'I'll handle things here,' said Emily as we reached the greenhouse. She bowed her head to William and ushered him through the door before turning to me, refusing to let go of my hand. 'Let Beatrice know what's happening. Get him safe.'

And with one last bare-toothed smile, her fingers squeezed my palm. The next moment, she was gone. William and I exchanged a nod, and with that, we were on our way, down through the greenhouse, out into the gardens, and forward, into the Blackwood and the bitter cold.

By the time we'd reached the tiny cabin by the stream, we were shaking with shivers, the rattling branches giving way to the neat lawn of the gardener's cottage, where even Beatrice's wildflowers had wilted in the winter wind. I knocked on the frost-rimed door, but there was no answer.

'Beatrice?' I called, her name shattered through my chattering teeth. I tried the door handle, but it was locked. I fished the clockwork key from my sock, and worked the door open.

I poked my way into the cabin, William close behind, but it was empty – cold and bare without any sign of

Beatrice to give it life. Embers smouldered in the hearth and the windows were grimy: it was only barely warmer than outside. It had the feeling of a place that had been abandoned, but something strange was tugging at the back of my mind, and looking around the cabin, I realized that the curtain in the back had been pulled aside, the door behind it slightly open.

I drifted into the back room, to find Beatrice lying there under a pile of blankets, her skin turned dull and sick-looking in the weak sunlight that filtered in through the room's single, frosted window. My stomach clenched at the sight. Everything in the room was so, so utterly still. Only the dust swirled in the thin light, and if it weren't for the way the glittering motes moved ever-so-slightly as the gardener breathed, I would've thought she was dead.

I sank onto the floor at Beatrice's bedside and took her hand, pressing it in mine and waiting – waiting for her to move, to stir, to wake up so that I could apologize for mistrusting her, apologize for everything–

But the gardener didn't wake.

'What do you think happened to her?' I whispered to William.

It wasn't William who answered.

'To be honest, that's a question I think we'd all like to know the answer to.'

I stood to face Isaac as he stepped into the room, placing himself firmly between us and the door. His eyes flicked from me to William and back again, before settling, at last, on Beatrice's face. 'Miss LeNoir was well enough until yesterday, when she must have done something quite desperate – something she was forbidden from doing. Suffice to say that, unless Doctor Crowe figures out exactly what that something was, he won't be able to lift the Curse at this point. It will kill her.'

'The Curse?' I echoed, the word twisted like a knife into my chest. How stupid must I have been not to realize it? Beatrice had been *Cursed* – it explained why she hadn't been able to tell us everything, why she'd had to keep things hidden. Hadn't she said as much in the woods, when she'd confronted Uncle Edward about Lady Rosalind? But now...

'What's Uncle Edward waiting for? He should know how to break his own bloody Curse!'

'It's not that easy,' said Isaac with a sigh, and he stepped forward, pausing as I flinched away from him. 'If you'll allow me to explain–'

'You can explain from where you're standing,' I said.

'Have I done something to offend you, Miss Crowe?'

'You know well enough what you've done.'

Isaac bowed his head, as if to say, *fair enough*. 'I can't change what you've seen. All I can do is try to get you to *understand*–'

'If you think there's *any* explanation that could convince me that what you're doing is right, then you're worse than Uncle Edward. And stupider.'

'I would never presume to put myself on the same intellectual level as your uncle. That said, you have to understand that there are bigger things at play here: despite what your cousin might have told you, he is no tortured little boy, and your uncle has every good reason to lock him up as he's done.'

'It's revolting–'

'It's a *necessity*,' said Isaac, looking me in the eye and daring me to look away. I didn't. 'And I need you to understand that, Miss Crowe, because I don't want to have to tell your uncle that you've been in the tower–'

'You... haven't told him?'

Isaac shook his head. 'I promised you that I'd do everything in my power to keep your brother safe. And that includes this: I'm giving you a choice. Let this go – forget what you've seen and believe me when I say that this is something that needs to be done. *Trust us*. Because if you insist on interfering...' He shook his head again.

'That situation is one that all of us want to avoid. All I'm asking is for you to trust us. To trust *me*.'

I studied the boy in front of me, the way his eyes were pleading, his hands clasped in front of him in a picture of earnesty, and I had to admit, I didn't trust him a single bit. But if convincing him that I did meant avoiding Uncle Edward, then there was only one thing to do. 'If we walk away, you won't tell Uncle Edward? I just walk away, and ignore the screams every night, and pretend we know nothing, and that's it – that's all?'

Isaac nodded. 'I solemnly swear. I won't breathe a word about seeing you at the top of that tower.'

'Fine, we'll walk away.'

'Abby?' hissed William, but I ignored him, all my concentration focused on the ring on my finger, on coiling my defences and controlling my breathing, controlling *myself*.

'You've made a good choice, Miss Crowe,' said Isaac, holding out his hand. 'So I'll be taking that Wardstone now.'

'That what?'

'The amber stone. The one that Miss LeNoir gave you so that you could break into the tower. The one that triggered her Curse. Doctor Crowe will need it to be able to undo the damage – and it's not like you need it anymore, not if you mean what you've said.'

And how he'd managed to catch me! The amber stone burned against my leg, even through its grey cloth. What was it that the gardener had written? *A costly light.* It had cost her everything to give it to us, to give us the power to free Damon. It was the only power to defend against the shades–

And it was killing her.

Even if I hadn't needed to convince Isaac that I was telling the truth, knowing that the stone was the only hope that Beatrice had, I would've given it to him. It still would've been unfair, it still would've been the worst decision I'd ever had to make, but it was really no decision at all. Beatrice was *dying*. We'd find another way to free Damon – we had to. I fished the stone out of my sock as Isaac stood waiting, and I met his eyes with my own glare as I dropped it into his outstretched hand. 'There,' I said.

He closed his fingers over the stone, and stepped away from the door. 'I do hope you keep your promise, Miss Crowe. Because I fully intend to keep mine.'

'Of course you do,' I said, as I grabbed William's arm and pushed past him, out through the main room of the cabin, and back into the Blackwood. I could only hope that we hadn't just made a terrible mistake – that *I* hadn't. 'We have to find another way into the tower,' I said to William once we'd left Isaac and the cabin behind. 'We have to.'

'You did make the right decision,' he said.

I paused a moment, shivering. 'Did I?' It didn't feel like it.

'We couldn't leave her like that–'

'Yes, but what if he's lying?'

'Then we deal with that, too. It's not like things could get much worse.'

I nodded. He was probably right. We hurried back through the wood toward the house and slipped in through the greenhouse, racing up the spiral steps to the hall lined all with windows. Through the second floor corridors and into the East Wing, we needed to get back to our rooms, to sit down and regroup and figure out our next move.

Unfortunately, William, as it turned out, was wrong. Worse was waiting for us – much worse. She stood and turned to face us as we stepped into our sitting room.

'You two,' said Mother, her face a mask of anger, 'are in *deep trouble*.'

Crime and Punishment

I paused just inside the doorway, debating if it was worth running, but the next moment, the option had disappeared, as Uncle Edward stepped up behind us, ushering us further into the room and closing the door behind him as he followed. The door snapped shut, and all four of us stood, Mother tense and fuming, Uncle Edward as calm and terrifying as ever, and me and my brother, trapped between a rock and a hard place, waiting for the avalanche.

Uncle Edward let Mother have the honours:

'What do you have to say for yourselves?' she said, her voice harsher than I'd ever heard it. She rounded the couch to approach us. 'What could you possibly have hoped to achieve by this?'

William and I exchanged a look. The answer really depended on exactly which 'this' Mother meant – and I couldn't help but hope that there were still at least one or two 'this's that Mother and Uncle Edward hadn't found out about yet. 'What did we do?' I ventured.

'Let's make a list, shall we?' said Uncle Edward, his voice so low and calm that I began wishing he'd just let Mother get back to yelling at us. At least that was a threat we knew how to handle. He stepped away from his post at the door, coming to a stop in front of us, close enough that he towered over us, and there was nowhere left to back away. 'From the very first day you two stepped into this house,' he began, 'you have shown a blatant disregard for authority. The few simple rules that have been laid down in front of you – for your *own protection*, no less – you have repeatedly broken and flaunted. Neglecting curfew, eavesdropping, breaking and entering, trespassing, *theft* – all of this was already bad enough. But now *arson*–'

'You set a hall on *fire*, Abigail!' Mother broke in.

I couldn't help but breathe a sigh of relief that Emily's pyromania was the only reason we were in trouble. 'Well, you put it out, didn't you?' I said. 'Besides, what makes you think it was *me*?'

Mother gave me a weary look. 'If Mrs. Thompson had not survived said fire, we would be having a very different conversation right now.'

'But I didn't–'

'It was me, Mum,' said William. He stepped forward. 'Abigail didn't set the fire, it was an accident, and it was my fault.'

Mother pressed her lips together. 'Why would Mrs. Thompson say otherwise?'

'Because she hates me, Mum,' I said.

'Really, Abigail,' said Mother. 'I've very nearly had *enough*–'

But Uncle Edward held up a hand to cut her off. 'Whatever Mrs. Thompson might or might not have done does not *matter*. Your actions are inexcusable, and what is done has been done. The only question now is that of appropriate punishment.'

His threat hung in the air, full of countless silent possibilities, none of them pleasant. We knew what he was capable of. I clenched my jaw against the memory of Damon's blood-curdling screams, and clasped my hands together to steady them, running my defences over and over, filling myself with them against the panic. I couldn't show weakness – not now, not here. And no matter what happened, I refused to let myself cry – not in front of him.

'Empty your pockets,' he said finally, and then, looking straight at me, 'And your socks.'

William and I exchanged a look, but there was nothing to be done for it. He pulled out his last box of matches and the smoke bombs that Isaac had returned to him at the Wintersnacht party, and I pulled out the clockwork key, though I had to say a silent thanks that the amber stone was no longer there. Uncle Edward looked over the items in question and pocketed them, his eyes lingering on the clockwork key for an unpleasantly long moment.

'Is that all?' he asked.

I nodded.

'Very well. What shall we do with you then?' he asked.

I met my uncle's cold grey eyes, and then, calmly, deliberately, I looked past him, to Mother, still standing just behind the couch.

'I want to talk to you without *him* here,' I said.

Mother raised an eyebrow, but Uncle Edward chuckled, half turning to her to make a show of asking permission. 'Shall I give you a minute?'

'Please do,' she answered.

And with a nod, he hobbled out of the room, leaving Mother to face us alone. For a long moment after the door had snapped closed, none of us spoke, and I wondered if we were actually any better off than we'd been with Uncle Edward. I waited for her to say something – *anything* – but all she did was stand there, frowning, as if she'd already given up on us. It was more than unbearable, and at last, I couldn't take it any longer:

'What's he going to do to us, Mum?'

'Abigail,' said Mother with the heaviest of heavy sighs. 'I honestly don't know where or how you got some of these ideas into your head, but this is not some gothic novel full of deceit and betrayal and your uncle is not a murderous villain–'

'He *is* a magician though,' I countered. 'You must have realized at least that, by now. And that's bad enough without the rest of it.'

She closed her eyes, and lifted her face, as if asking for patience from some higher power. 'And what would you have me do about that, Abigail? Subject him to Inquisition?'

'It's worse than that, Mum–' began William, but Mother silenced him with a frown. I had to choke down my anger. After all of it, after everything we'd done and everything we'd been through, Mother wouldn't even give us a chance to tell her what we'd found out. It would've been one thing if she didn't believe us – believing was one thing, and you couldn't always help that. But she wasn't even refusing to believe. She was refusing to so much as *listen*.

'Look, Abigail. William. *Dears*,' she said. 'Nothing good is going to come from poking any further into any of this. There is nothing that needs to be fixed here, no one who needs *rescuing*. I just need you to *trust* me. I need you to trust that we–'

'You *know*,' I said, the words escaping as the realization dawned on me. 'You know what he's hiding in the tower.' I watched her eyes for some sign of fear, of confusion, of curiosity even – for any sign that there was still hope–

But there was none. She simply pressed her lips into a thin, grim line and shook her head.

'You are wandering into dangerous territory, Abigail. If you could do anything for me, if you could just for once in your life, *listen*–'

'You can't be serious!' I said. 'I'm not going to just stand by while you let this go on. There was a reason Dad hated him. He's dangerous. He's evil. He must be stopped. He already used magic on *us*...' My voice faded into silence. I'd run out of words.

Mother let the silence simmer before responding. 'Your uncle and I thought that it would be best if you two were confined to your rooms for the rest of the day,' she said at last, 'while we figure out how best to deal with–'

'You *can't* lock us up!'

'We most certainly can,' said Mother. 'Especially since you seem to be intent on causing damage.'

'But that's not fair! He's the one using illegal magic! He's the one–'

'Then you know as well as I do that he could do much worse than lock you up for the night!' snapped Mother.

I couldn't do anything but stare, my entire body trembling with the injustice of it. When had she turned against us? And what had we done to deserve it? 'Dad would never have let this happen,' I said at last.

At that, she looked away, one hand coming up to clasp the locket at her neck. 'Yes, well, he isn't here anymore is he?' she said. She shook her head. 'I have everything under control. That is all you need to know.'

I didn't recognize the Mother standing in front of me. My Mother had always been stiffly formal: stern but never completely cold. And even if she'd always been more concerned with making a proper impression than having fun, at the very least, she'd been mostly harmless.

But this Mother... *this* Mother was a different woman entirely. She'd known *everything* – and she'd never let on, not even for a moment. *This* Mother was willing to lock us up to stop us from being a nuisance, and even now, I could see her calculating, measuring. Had she really been this way all along? How could I not have seen it?

'We will figure this out tomorrow,' said Mother at last. 'For now, it would be best if you had some time to think about what you've done. Try to get some rest.'

And before I could muster the will to protest, she'd already crossed the parlour and slipped out into the hall, locking the sitting room door behind her. William and I were left in our empty room as the fire burned down. I sank onto the couch. 'She knew,' I said. 'I can't believe it, but she *knew*–'

'Maybe... maybe that means we should let it be,' said William. 'Maybe she's right, and we just have to trust them–'

'Or maybe Uncle Edward put her under a Curse, like he did Beatrice,' I said. It made more sense than I wanted it to. 'Why else would she be acting this way? How else would he have ever gotten her to agree to mar–' I couldn't even bring myself to finish the sentence.

William started fidgeting with his shirt buttons. 'I – I don't think he cursed Mum,' he said.

'How could you say that?'

'I just... I don't think he would've needed to,' said William. It was an awful thing to say, and I glared at him for saying it, until he shrugged and slipped away from the couch, retreating into his own bedroom to leave me to myself.

The fireplace burned down to its embers as I sat turning everything around and over itself again and again in my head. Mother had known Uncle Edward was a magician. She knew that our cousin was locked in the tower, and it would be just our luck that she'd probably already told Uncle Edward that we'd found out as much. So much for my deal with Isaac Carver. And despite all that, despite everything, she expected us to trust her – to trust Uncle Edward.

Not that it mattered much. Without the amber stone or the clockwork key, there was no way for us to do anything at all. Perhaps it would've been best to just accept what was happening. It wasn't like we could change it. As the last of the coals in the fireplace went cold, and the full dark of night settled outside, I gave in to the cold and made my way to my room, changing into my nightclothes before slipping into bed – though even in the warmth of my covers, I couldn't help shivering.

Sleep wouldn't come.

I lay with my eyes open to my darkened room, running my defences against the creeping sense of helplessness.

The First Defence is always with you, but this ring will help you remember it.

The Second Defence is self-control, and you must master your breath to maintain it.

The Third Defence is your sanctuary. It is your heart and centre. Know how to find it and you will never be deceived for long.

And with that magic coiling through me, I found myself once again in my garden, the scent of cherry blossoms and touch-me-nots surrounding me, the garden blooming in the corners of my room, the twilit sky fading in through the ceiling. I lay staring at the stars in my mind, trying to sort through those troubling thoughts once more.

In the end it came down to this: Uncle Edward was a liar and a murderer, and he'd killed our dad in cold blood. He'd done worse too, keeping his own son locked away in the highest tower of Ravenscourt. And yet Mother insisted we trust him. So did Isaac. And even Uncle Edward still insisted that he'd done nothing wrong.

When had everything become so confused? And what was I supposed to do now?

And why, why, *why* couldn't Dad be here to help? He was the one who had always been able to make things make sense, to explain everything that seemed to defy explanation, to help me see what had to be done next.

Once, when I was five, I'd come back from catechism class with my fingers red and welted from the Dame Inquisitor's switch. Dad had caught me afterward, crying in my room – the violent, hiccup-y type of crying that was impossible to keep quiet.

'Tears, Abby?' he'd asked. And he knelt next to me to find out what happened.

So I told him about how five minutes into the lesson, the Dame Inquisitor had given me ten switches on the knuckles and sent me to stand in the corner, all because of a single, innocent question:

'But what makes magic bad?'

'And did she ever give you a proper answer?' asked Dad.

I shook my head.

'Sounds like Dame Inquisitor needs to brush up on her Inquisitory Code,' muttered Dad under his breath. He kissed my knuckles to make them better and put ice on them, and only when they'd finally gone all numb and tingly did he try to help me figure it out.

'So what do you think the answer is, then?' he said. 'What makes magic bad?'

I stared at him. 'I don't know,' I admitted. 'That's why I asked.'

He laughed. 'True enough. But let's look at what we do know. Magic affects the spirit. And what is the spirit?'

'It's you,' I said. 'The thinking, feeling part of you that decides what to do.'

'Correct. So when you use magic on someone, you affect the part of a person that's most wholly them: you can make them think things that aren't true, or feel things that hurt. You can make them do things they would never even consider doing otherwise. So now, can you tell me what makes magic bad?'

'It… it's bad because you don't let a person have their own thoughts and feelings,' I said finally. 'It lets you make other people's decisions for them. It takes away their choices.'

'Just so,' said Father, and his smile warmed the entire room. 'It can be used that way – and too often, that's exactly why people decide to learn it. But there are many other ways of taking away people's choices, Abby. Don't forget that. That's why you always need to be aware of your own thoughts and feelings, because, in the end, you will be the only one who can decide whether they're true or not.'

I opened my eyes to the darkness of my room in Ravenscourt. Mother insisted that she had everything under control. And perhaps Mother had her reasons for trusting Uncle Edward. I was even willing to admit that it might be possible that we were wrong about the whole thing, and that everything that was happening now was necessary and right and that it would all turn out best if we just stayed out of it, like the adults wanted us to.

But I also knew that I wasn't going to stay out of it.

Maybe that would be a mistake. But the only thing that I was completely sure of was that this situation wasn't right. I didn't know the excuses that Mother and Uncle Edward had made for themselves to justify their actions. I didn't understand why Mother had brought us to Ravenscourt in the first place. I didn't know a lot of things, but I knew what we had to do:

We were going to get Damon *out*.

I stalked out of the room to find William sitting on the couch, waiting for me. 'So, what's the plan?' he said.

'We're getting out, and we're going to rescue Damon.'

He nodded. 'Took you long enough.'

We checked the door once more, just in case, but it remained firmly shut, the lock impossible to pick. The windows were just as hopeless – we could open them a little to let the air in, but the bars on the other side made certain we couldn't get out that way. I searched the grey walls, the worn furniture, my eyes running over the brown, wilted houseplants that lay drooping on the fireplace mantle. I bent down to pick up one of William's candles from the edge of the fireplace when the sound of the wind made me look up.

The fireplace was big enough to fit two or three full-grown men, and looking up, the rest of the chimney stretched up two or three stories beyond. But the thing that stopped me, the thing that I noticed, was the small, square patch of star studded sky that twinkled down on me from far above.

'That's it! William, we're getting out of here!'

William joined me at the entrance to the fireplace. 'You can't mean–'

'The chimney will get us onto the roof – it's perfect! Here, I'll give you a boost up.'

'And what about you?'

'It might take a bit more for me to get up, but I'm bigger than you, so it'll be easier once I'm in. Come on.'

I knelt with my fingers knitted over my knee so that William could clamber up into the lower part of the chimney, pulling himself into the crooked space below the flue. Once his feet disappeared from inside the smoke chamber, I scrambled to pull myself after him. And then it was up – straight up through the flue, so arrow-shaft straight that it was almost impossible to move at all, except by bracing your feet against one side and your back against the other, shuffling up nearly twenty feet, with the soot and the char and the dirt all crumbling down around you, and everything close and dark. But at last, William called that he was at the top, and I saw him pull himself over the lip of the chimney to land noisily on the roof, and after that, he reached down and pulled me out after, my night dress stained with all the lovely things that a chimney tends to collect from years of letting out smoke. We paused to catch our breaths.

The tower loomed beyond – far across the width of the house – due south, the light from its window blazing like a warning beacon. And between it and us lay a treacherous valley of angled roofs and vaults and gables: a landscape broken by bits of the house that rose here and there, and balustrades, and even a couple gargoyles perched in all the oddest places. We picked our way across, William giving out more than one yelp of fear as he slipped on the shingles, our feet going frozen as we realized we'd forgotten our shoes.

But for the sake of Damon, we pressed on, ignoring the damp and the cold seeping in through our stockings, until, at last, we neared the tower. We ducked below the window, chilled to the bone, listening carefully for any sign of anyone in the tower room.

Silence.

Taking long, deep breaths and trying to ignore my chattering teeth and the bracing cold, I lifted my head above the window ledge, sneaking a peek into the room before ducking back down again.

Empty.

I nodded at William to say, *all clear*, before standing up and hauling myself over the ledge.

The tower room managed to be just warm enough for us to stop shivering as we stepped into it. The light of the chandelier and the flickering lamps cast everything in a warm, yellow glow. Damon was pacing behind the bars of his cage, and he looked up in surprise as we entered.

'You were caught,' he said. 'That wasn't very clever of you.'

'We're getting you out,' I answered. And without waiting for a response, I turned to the place in the wall where the control panel was hidden. William found the lever, the wall cracked open. The numbered dials were still set to two and five. 'Do you know anything about how this works?'

'What does it look like?'

'Two numbered gears. It's set to two and five right now – or twenty-five.'

'Try zero zero.'

I spun the dials until the two zeros were together in the centre of the panel. As the gears turned, the humming of the electrified bars rose to a frenzy, before going suddenly silent. I took a breath and flipped the switch.

At once, the bars of the cage sank into the floor, and warily, Damon stepped onto the other side of the room. His eyes darted to and fro, as if seeing everything for the first time. He stretched – joints cracking as he raised his arms – and he threw back is head and laughed – in relief, in delight, in some other overwhelming feeling that I couldn't possibly identify. Turning to us, he smiled. It lit up his hollow face.

'You two– you're amazing. I–' he trailed off, his face going suddenly grim. A soft cough sounded behind us. I turned, only to find myself face to face with Uncle Edward.

'LOCKED DOORS ARE LOCKED FOR A REASON'

He wasn't alone. Behind him, the Butler cracked his knuckles, and Isaac Carver stared grimly at me. All of us waited for someone else to make the first move, none of us daring to do much more than stand and stare and hope someone else would back down before we did.

'Well, Father,' said Damon at last. 'How lovely of you to join us.' He pushed forward until he was standing not three feet away from Uncle Edward, his hands clasped behind his back as he faced his father. 'I suppose you'll be asking me to get back into the cage now?'

'I would rather we not have to resort to violence,' answered Uncle Edward. The Butler cracked his knuckles more menacingly, and Damon shook his head.

'Then step aside,' he said, 'and let me go.'

'I am afraid I can't do that,' said Uncle Edward. Another minute passed in tense silence. Damon refused to back down, and Uncle Edward shook his head. 'Galen,' he said.

The boy stepped back as the Butler lurched toward him, reaching forward to grab him by the arm. But Damon lifted his hand – slowly, almost lazily. He looked the Butler in the eye.

The next moment, the room had exploded into chaos.

William and I were thrown backward, as the Butler smashed against the other wall with a sickening crack and slumped limply onto the floor. Wind howled through the room as the window shattered, books and chairs and broken glass spinning through the air, even as I clawed at the walls, trying to pull myself upright, trying find something to cling to in that awful chaos, gripping William close as his hand found mine.

Only Damon and his father remained unharmed. The room seemed to tilt around them, their still, tense figures the eye of a raging storm. I teetered on the edge of collapse – something wet and sticky ran down my cheek. I raised a hand to press my fingers to my forehead. They came away stained with blood. But at least I had William with me. At least he was safe. My legs crumpled–

But before I could hit the floor, Isaac Carver was there, holding me steady. He gripped my shoulders, and his face wavered in front of me. He was saying something, but the words were all fuzzy. I couldn't grab hold of them, couldn't put them together. I tried to focus on Isaac's face, tried to meet his eyes, but everything was spinning. I looked to Damon, who stood facing Uncle Edward in the middle of the floor. His cold blue eyes were strangely alight, and he laughed as he dropped his hand.

'By the way, Father,' he said. 'Did I mention that I happened to neglect taking my medicines this morning?'

'Miss Crowe!' Isaac gripped my shoulders, but I couldn't look him in the eye. That word was bouncing in my head, reverberating. *Medicines*... My eyes raked over the room, sifting through the scattered debris: the broken furniture and sharp glittering glass and the torn books. The Carol house hadn't looked much different, that night after William's fit. It had seemed impossible then, because the idea that my brother could set an entire house shaking was far outside the powers of magic. It still didn't seem possible now. And yet we were surrounded by the reality of it, the sheer impossible reality of it. I pulled William close, even as Isaac shook my shoulders once more.

'Please, Abigail– I have to get you two out of here–'

But there was no escape. Not from this. Not now that I knew what Damon was capable of – what *William* might be capable of.

I held up a hand, trying to ward the boy away from William. 'Stay back!' I said.

The floor began to tremble, Damon once again summoning his magic–

But no, *this* wasn't magic. This was something *else*, something *worse* – more than a Command or Curse or Illusion, more than Defences or Wards, more than control. This was raw, impossible power that could outright shift and mould, power that could *destroy*. I raised a hand to shield my face against it.

Isaac let go. I peered past my hand, to see him turning, reaching into his coat as Damon stepped forward, all his anger, all his rage bearing down on Uncle Edward, the rest of us forgotten. Isaac lunged forward.

Light flashed off the point of a needle. I closed my eyes.

The room fell still.

I wanted to be sick. In the middle of the floor, Damon sank to his knees, Isaac gripping him tightly by the arms. Pain flickered in my wrist, and I looked down to find William's fingernails digging into my skin. And still Uncle Edward made no move.

One minute became two, then three, then five. Time might have frozen, for all I could tell, except that my beating heart still pounded away the seconds. It was as if Uncle Edward held the moment in his hands, stretching it out, considering it. The threat of his decision hummed in the air, making my chest tight as I breathed it in.

'We will have to keep him fully sedated for the time being,' said Uncle Edward finally.

At that, Damon started to struggle once more, but his movements were sluggish, weak. There'd be no escaping now, not for him, not for any of us – and maybe that was for the best. Maybe Damon's power was meant to be contained. Maybe Uncle Edward had been right–

But no.

I looked at him. He towered over his son, his grey eyes cold and merciless as ever, the rest of his face blank of emotion. This was the man who had killed my father, the man who had kept Beatrice under a Curse that could've killed her, that might *still* kill her, if Isaac hadn't kept his promises. If Uncle Edward felt no shame in murder, in Curses, in locking up his own son, if he could justify that and feel nothing, then what might he do to us?

What might he do to *William*?

I looked down as William tugged on my arm, pointing with his eyes to the chandelier hanging from the ceiling, almost directly above Isaac's head. He didn't have to say a word for me to understand. I followed the chain of the chandelier down to where it hooked into the wall, not two feet to my left. And as Uncle Edward prepared another syringe, I took a deep breath, stepped sideways, and loosened the chandelier from its hook.

It rattled as it fell, and Isaac had just enough time to pull himself out of the way, dragging Damon with him as Uncle Edward stumbled backward against the wall. The chandelier hit the floor with a smash of twisted metal, and Damon immediately took advantage of Isaac's distraction to grip his fingers to the older boy's throat.

'*Sleep*,' he Commanded groggily. Isaac sank to the ground, unconscious. Uncle Edward pushed himself up from the ground, as Damon raised his hand–

But the explosion didn't come. Damon let out a yell of rage and despair, as Uncle Edward lurched forward, holding his cane like a baton. In a moment it would all be over, everything we'd done would be for nothing.

I leaped forward, and kicked Uncle Edward squarely in the shin.

He crumpled immediately, stumbling forward, a marionette cut from his strings. The next instant, Damon had thrown him against the back wall and pulled me into the main room. William was already at the controls. He flipped the switch and the iron bars rose up, trapping Uncle Edward in his own horrendous device.

The three of us stared, our breaths ragged, while Uncle Edward winced in pain. Neither William nor I dared a single word.

'Well, now isn't this poetic?' said Damon, breaking the silence. He was the first to approach the cage, and though his entire body was trembling, his voice was steady. 'Did you ever imagine, Father, that you would be in such a position?'

Uncle Edward didn't reply, but closed his eyes and tilted his head back, his mouth twisted in pain. Damon's smile wavered, and his eyes narrowed to slits.

'Answer me,' he hissed.

I reached for his arm, pulling him to face me. 'Damon, we should go–'

But he shook me off. 'Not yet. I've some business to take care of.' He came to the controls of the cage, letting his scarred fingers drift over the dials. 'Ten years you kept me locked up in that thing,' he said to Uncle Edward. 'Fortunately for you, I don't have another ten years to waste. We'll get this over with quickly.' He spun the gears, the electrical buzz of the bars rising to a frenzy that filled the room with tingling ozone.

He was going to kill Uncle Edward.

'Damon! You *can't–*' I reached out, to pull him away from those controls, but he grabbed my arm and pushed me forcibly back. I found myself caught between him and the wall, his eyes full of something worse than anger.

'*Don't tell me what I can't do!*' he said. 'Do you know what he did to me? He should be thankful I'm not doing worse.'

The air began to pop, the hairs on my legs and arms and all along my neck standing on end, goose bumps trembling down my spine, the scent of electricity tainting the air.

'But it isn't right. That doesn't make this *right*,' I said. 'If you hurt him, if you– if you kill him…'

'SO WHAT IF I DO?' yelled Damon, his raging face so close to mine that I could count his teeth.

'Then you're no better than he is!' I struck back.

'Maybe I don't *want* to be better,' said Damon, his blue eyes daring me to press further. My arms were going numb under his cold fingers, but I refused to turn away from him, or to let him off the hook.

'Then maybe you deserve what you got,' I said.

Damon's eyes narrowed, his entire face twisted with rage and betrayal, and the air crackled with energy. He let go of my arm, and lifted his hand. I closed my eyes and turned my face away from the blow that I knew was coming–

But it didn't come. Instead there was the tick of the dials turning, and the buzz of the electrified bars quieted to a low whisper. The air grew still, the energy released in a mournful sigh.

'I'm not like you,' spat Damon at his father.

I opened my eyes to see Uncle Edward sag against the wall, breathing heavily. Pain wracked his face, but he still refused to say anything. Damon wrinkled his nose, as if dismissing something he'd found on the bottom of his shoe, and turned to me.

'What are we going to do about him, then?' he said.

'Just leave him,' I answered.

'He might escape. He built the damn thing, after all.'

I looked from him, to Uncle Edward, and back. Damon was studying me, as if waiting for me to make the wrong move. 'I'll stay then. William can get you off the grounds, and I can make sure he doesn't get out.'

'You promise you won't let him out? No matter what he says?'

I nodded.

'Promise,' said Damon, his voice edged with danger.

'I promise,' I said, though I couldn't meet his eyes as I said it. For a moment, there was deathly silence.

'Fine,' said Damon with a nod at last. 'I'll send someone for you once everything is sorted. Sit tight.' And with that, he turned toward the window, stepping over the Butler's sprawled form as he did. 'Come, William!'

William hesitated, looking to me. I could do nothing but give him a short, sharp nod, though I was sure it came out less than reassuring. William threw one last glance at our uncle, before clambering out the window, and onto the roof.

The sounds of the boys' bare feet on the snow-covered roof grew steadily softer, and within a few minutes, they'd faded completely into silence. I was left alone with my uncle and the unconscious bodies of the Butler and Isaac Carver, the room growing cold. I clutched my nightdress close.

'Abigail.'

My uncle's voice was weaker, but it still held its usual authority, and before I'd even realized it, I was looking at him once more. He was a sorry sight: his greying hair had fallen into his face, and his eyes were sunken, his cheeks drawn – he looked more like Damon than I'd realized.

'Abigail,' he said again, 'you must listen to me–'

'After everything you've done? I should think not!' And I forced myself to turn away.

'What have I done?' he persisted. 'Tell me.'

'You– you trapped and tortured an innocent boy – your own son, no less! You kept Beatrice under a Curse that could kill her. You killed my father, even though he was no longer a threat to you. You're disgusting – a monster! And whatever you did to Mother to make her agree to– to–' Words failed me. I was facing him, not a foot away from the iron bars of his cage, and despite my best attempts at control, I'd been yelling.

Uncle Edward bowed his head. 'I cannot say that your negative opinion of me is not partially my fault. That said, I would like to make a few things clear. I certainly did not murder your father. As you may be able to tell by now, the situation is a bit more complicated than a simple revenger's tragedy.'

'Father betrayed you.'

'Your father made a mistake which, I will admit, caused me a great deal of anguish. But what is important now is for you to understand what is at stake. Abigail, Damon is… very sick.'

He paused, as if waiting for me to fill the gap. With what, I wasn't sure. I waited for him to continue.

'There is an illness which runs on my mother's side of the family – an illness unique to the Raban line, which is one of the noble houses of the Fey Court. For centuries, the Raban were exiled by the Fey, forced to the edges of the world, in order to spare the Court their curse. Usually, the illness lies dormant, but given the right circumstances…' He paused, shook his head, continued. 'Damon's mother, Ariel, was a distant cousin on my mother's side. I should have seen the probable consequences of our affair, but we were young and thoughtless. When your father found out about our involvement, he feared what the child would become. He told our mother, thinking that she would be able to help us, advise us – that she would be able to find a path through this mess.

'She did, and it was Ariel who paid the price: despite our mother's attempt to kill the child, Damon survived. He even seemed healthy enough, but within a few years, the symptoms of the illness began to show. He had to be put under surveillance. At first, we tried to be as lenient as possible, but eventually, he had to be locked up – both for his own safety and the safety of those around him. And so it was done. And for ten years, I have tried to find a cure–'

I shook my head. 'And you think that justifies all this?'

'Justifies it?' echoed Uncle Edward. 'That depends on what you mean by *justify*. If you are wondering whether I feel it is a good reason – then indeed, I do see it as justified: it was not only prudent, but necessary that this be done. If you mean, rather, whether or not it was *right*, well, that answer, I am afraid, must be left to those with better definitions of morality.'

'He's dangerous?'

'More so than you can imagine, Abigail.'

'And his illness… it's what William has. Isn't it?'

He fell silent. I waited, trembling with fear for his answer, and finally it came: one silent, heavy nod. Horror clutched at my stomach. 'Then how am I supposed to know that you won't do *this* to William?' I asked finally.

'You have my word–'

'And what is that worth?' I exclaimed. 'You've done nothing but lie to us and keep secrets, and now I'm just supposed to trust you–?'

'All I need you to do is to trust me more than Damon. All I need you to do is trust me enough for us to protect your brother. And I need you to make that decision as soon as possible, because every moment we spend here is another moment where I'm not sure what Damon will do.'

I took a deep, shuddering breath. If Uncle Edward was lying, which wasn't at all outside the realm of possibility, then releasing him would be dooming an innocent boy to more years imprisonment and torture. But if not – and this was the catch – then could I really just do nothing, and let Damon go free: sick and perhaps deadly dangerous? And worst of all, if Uncle Edward was telling the truth...

Had I just sent William into danger?

Turning to the controls, I opened the cage.

Uncle Edward leapt up, grabbing his cane. Straightening his jacket, he stepped out of the cage, kneeling down next to the butler and pressing his fingers to the man's lolling head. He pursed his lips, then tsked. 'Sometimes, Galen, your talents are more a hindrance than a help,' he muttered under his breath.

Isaac was next, and this time, when Uncle Edward set his fingers to the boy's temples, I could feel the pulse of magic that passed through them, just before the boy sat up, blinking groggily. 'Where–?'

'The High Road,' said Uncle Edward. 'You will be in charge of the girl. Get her a coat.'

We descended the tower stair, Isaac ushering me through the laboratory and offering me a coat and a pair of overlarge boots from one of the closets before we headed out a side door of the West Wing. And then it was out into the Blackwood, Uncle Edward leading the way through the snow that lay thick on the forest paths.

We walked for what must have been close to an eternity. Uncle Edward remained ahead of us, not even leaning on his cane as his feet fell heavily on the snow, leading us down the path that Beatrice had shown us the day she told the story of Lily Crowe – the path that led to the circle of trees with the aspen arch in the middle, the one called the High Road. I couldn't imagine why they called it a road – as far as I'd seen, there'd been no paths leading out of the clearing, and the aspens were more doorway than signpost, though where you might end up when you stepped through them, I couldn't begin to guess.

Despite the warm coat and the shoes that Isaac had gotten for me, I shivered in my stockings. How had Damon and William managed to make it so far? And both of them only in their night things!

Suddenly, Uncle Edward stopped, raising a hand for quiet. Isaac and I both froze, listening for whatever he'd heard. But there was only silence – an eerie silence broken by nothing but our own ragged breaths. Whatever Uncle Edward was listening for, I couldn't hear it.

He looked over his shoulder to meet Isaac's eyes. 'Stop them,' he mouthed. And then Isaac was off – rushing forward through the trees, racing to stop Damon and my brother.

'Come,' said my uncle, his voice barely a whisper. He offered his hand, but I refused it, walking past him, into the aspen clearing as it opened in front of us. The snow-covered ground glittered in front of me, scattering bits of moonlight, and the air hummed. Isaac faced Damon on the other side of the clearing, the older boy blocking Damon's path through the intertwined trees. Their magic hummed through the air, the power of it almost unbearable – but where was William?

I scanned the clearing, finally spotting him lying face down between the two boys. Cold tears pricked at the edges of my eyes, and I would've rushed forward if my uncle's hand hadn't shot out to stop me doing anything rash. I looked up, but Uncle Edward's face was grim.

'Damon,' he said softly. 'Damon, what are you doing?'

'Tell your pet to stand down,' said Damon without looking away from Isaac for a moment. 'Tell him to stand down, *now*.'

Uncle Edward's voice was tense. 'Damon, we need to help William. Do you think he'll survive much longer with the way you–'

'I've done nothing!' yelled Damon, turning toward his father. It was all Isaac needed. He moved forward, diving toward William and scooping the boy into his arms. But before he could carry my brother back to safety, Damon spun, and with a yell of rage, he shouted a Command, one hand thrust toward Isaac–

'STOP!'

Isaac stumbled to the ground, William slipping from his arms to land limp in the snow. Again I lurched forward, and again my uncle held me back.

'William–'

'Damon, that is enough!'

'I'll tell you when it's enough!' said Damon, his concentration never breaking. He strode up to Isaac and gave him a vicious kick, which sent the older boy sprawling back, hands clutched to his nose. Damon knelt down next to William.

Uncle Edward stepped forward–

'Not an inch closer!' snapped Damon. He looked at us over his shoulder, his scarred hand on William's forehead. 'One more step, and I swear, I'll–'

'NO!' the word ripped out of me, leaving my throat raw. Uncle Edward's hand was still on my shoulder, but I was shaking – with cold, with fear, with horror.

'Damon,' said Uncle Edward, 'This has nothing to do with the boy, let him go.'

'You really expect me to do that?' said Damon. He laughed, his lurid eyes wide, and looked back down at William, lying pale and still in the snow. 'From what you've told me, he might come in useful…'

'He's no use to you dead!' said Uncle Edward, and his voice shook. 'Just let us help him. Let me help *you*–'

'I don't want your help! I want you *dead*.'

'If you want your revenge, take it!' said Uncle Edward. He tossed his cane away and leaned his full weight on my shoulder. I looked up to see pain written across his face. 'Take it,' he said in defeat. 'I won't stop you. Just… don't harm William.'

Damon seemed to be considering the offer. But whether he took it or not, we were going to be in trouble. William's face had started to blue, and Isaac had been knocked out cold. Uncle Edward looked desperate. I had no doubt that if Uncle Edward forced Damon to face him again, face him one-on-one, with no more interference from me, no more tricks, he'd manage to overpower his son yet again. But no, the man was willing to surrender – he would give up his control, his *life*, in order to save William, even if it meant Damon would have his revenge, even if it meant sacrificing himself.

But if Damon did what he meant to, then what? I saw the moment that Damon realized the same thing. He smiled and stepped forward, picking up his father's discarded cane, raising it as a weapon.

I was the only one left who could change any of this now. I squeezed my father's ring between my fingers and took deep breaths, my defences settling over my shoulders.

I charged.

Before I could give myself away, I darted forward, racing past Damon toward my brother. But Damon was quicker. Like lightning, he lashed out before I could get past him. He spun, bringing his weapon low and sweeping my legs out of the way. I crashed into the snow, tumbling onto my back, and before I could push myself up, pain burst to life in every limb – a hot, searing burst of magic that ate at my skin and fragmented my bones, the threads of it winding through every single muscle, tearing through every cell–

My throat went raw from screaming.

And then, suddenly – as suddenly as the snuffing of a candle – it stopped. I sensed Damon still moving somewhere, and I knew he'd be facing Uncle Edward. Threads of magic thrummed through the trees, and I pulled myself over the snow to my brother, taking off my coat to wrap him in it. The cold air squeezed the breath from my lungs, but I held William close, watching for signs of life.

The ground began to tremble. I looked over my shoulder to see Damon standing with his arms outstretched, eyes closed in concentration, the world beginning to shift around him. Beyond, the space between the aspen trees had started to shimmer – like the surface of some ethereal mirror. Cold wind whirled through the clearing. The sky had gone dark, and heavy flakes of snow began to drift down. They caught on my eyelashes, and each one that landed on my skin pierced me with a needle of ice. I closed my eyes as the entire world shook.

It was so cold.

A puff of warm air brushed against my cheek. I opened my eyes to see a weak wisp of steam escaping my brother's mouth. I pulled him closer. It was odd how similar warmth and cold really were. My hands had gone stiff, the air biting, but I could almost imagine it burning – fire rather than ice. It was a warm thought. Warm enough to wrap yourself in, a thought that could take you to sleep.

The world went still.

There was Uncle Edward, looking down at me, and there were his hands, clasping my shoulders. There was his voice, pleading with me:

'Stay with me, Abigail. Stay awake.'

And then, there was nothing more.

A Thing Worse Than Magic

It was the clock that reached me first, ticking in the place beyond darkness. I drifted through the emptiness, the dark weighing down on me like a heavy cloak as I looked for some sign of the clock itself, searching for the source of it in this place with no floors or walls. There was nothing here, nothing but the whispers, and maybe, somewhere, somehow, a clock.

The ticking grew louder, and I realized that it wasn't so far away now. A little to my left, perhaps? The thing weighing me down wasn't darkness – it was a blanket. Rough sheets pressed against my skin. I opened my eyes.

I was in a strange room, somewhere in Ravenscourt House, if the cobwebs in the corners and the faded wallpaper were any sign. I pushed myself up, blinking in the white light that streamed through the room's barred window. I wasn't alone. As soon as I sat up, Isaac was kneeling next to me with a glass of water.

'Good afternoon, Miss Crowe.'

'Isaac? Where's William?'

'Safe and sound upstairs. He recovered a bit more quickly than you did,' said Isaac. He pressed the glass of water in to my hands. 'Drink it all.'

I gulped it down until the glass was empty, and still I could've drunk more. 'What happened?' I asked, handing the glass back.

'Hypothermia, among other things,' said Isaac. 'You passed out, and Damon escaped. Luckily, there was no permanent damage. Doctor Crowe asked me to keep an eye on you while he talked to your mother.'

I let that sink in. Isaac stood and busied himself with neatening the room, rearranging the curtains and straightening the picture frames, giving me a moment to catch my breath. Slowly, bits and pieces of what had happened came back to me – the standoff in the forest; Damon's strange magic and the biting cold; before that, the fight in the tower. Useless and stupid, all of it. 'Sorry I dropped a chandelier on you,' I said to Isaac.

He paused in the middle of straightening a portrait of Atreus Crowe. 'Yes, well, so long as you don't try to kill me again, I think I can forgive you for it.'

'I… really messed up, didn't I?'

Isaac bowed his head and knelt next to me once more. 'Honestly,' he said, 'something was bound to happen sooner or later. Secrets like that can't stay buried forever.'

'I was just trying to find out what happened to Dad,' I said.

The ticking of the clock rose up to fill the space between us as we sat considering each other. 'I… I think that's a question we'd all like the answer to,' he said, lowering his eyes. 'Though, as far as we can tell, it looks like a member of the Court might have finally managed to get rid of a Crowe.'

'You mean–'

Harried footsteps sounded in the hall, and a weak shout cut through the room, just before the door banged open. Mother appeared in the doorway, her eyes settling immediately on me.

'You are in *deep trouble*, young lady!' she said.

I looked to Isaac for help, but he'd somehow ended up on the opposite side of the room, as far away from Mother as possible.

She, for her part, didn't spare him a glance. 'After *everything*,' she said at me, her words carrying her further into the room, 'after everything we've done – everything *I've* done – to keep you safe, you still decide that you know better, and run off trying to save the day. Are you *out of your mind*?'

'No,' I said. 'But we were starting to think you were.'

Mother's lips thinned as she exhaled a heavy, long-suffering sigh through her nostrils. 'Abigail, you can't keep assuming that–'

But Uncle Edward had finally made it to the room, and before Mother could launch into her full tirade, he placed a hand on her shoulder, attempting to guide her back out the door. 'Maris, perhaps we could save the scolding for when she is more fully recovered?'

Mother rounded on him, giving him a glare that would've sent anyone else running. 'You, sir, are also in trouble,' she declared. And with that, she swept out of the room, the door slamming behind her.

All three of us – Uncle Edward, Isaac, and me – stared at the closed door for a full minute after she was gone, half expecting her to burst back through it. But finally, Uncle Edward sighed and hobbled toward the window, dismissing Isaac with a nod. 'Thank you, Carver.'

Isaac gave him a salute before slipping out the door and closing it with a click. I was left to face Uncle Edward on my own.

'How are you feeling?' he asked, leaning against the window.

'Not awful,' I answered, and I was surprised to find I meant it. 'Not particularly wonderful either, though.'

Uncle Edward tilted his head in acknowledgment. 'I was assuming there would be some things you wanted to talk about.'

He was right of course. There were so many things still unanswered, so many questions that we needed to figure out, and yet now that I honestly thought about everything that had happened in the past two months, I realized that I had no idea how to ask any of it. I didn't know what to say. Again the clock's incessant ticking rose to fill the silence, but Uncle Edward made no move to start. So finally, I said the only thing I could think of:

'It all started with a story about the death of Lily Crowe.'

Uncle Edward nodded, and with a sigh, he turned to the window, but said nothing.

'Beatrice told us,' I said, the words coming easier. 'We– we thought that Dad's death must have had something to do with hers, since neither of them had been rested. And when we found out about Ariel – well, we thought you'd tried to kill him, as revenge for losing her and Damon. And then we heard about the Lady Rosalind, and we thought… we thought you must still have Dad's spirit. And so we tried to find him. But we found Damon instead…'

'Too curious for your own good,' said Uncle Edward softly, though there was no malice in it.

'It just seemed to make sense,' I said softly. 'About Dad, I mean. Because I remembered you fighting…'

He bowed his head. 'Yes, your father and I fought. And unfortunately, we were far less kind to each other than we should have been.' He took a deep breath. 'After Ariel's death, I was distraught. Your father's betrayal stung, but he was my brother, and he was as horrified at what had happened as I was, if not more so, due to his own mistakes. I decided that something needed to be done, but it was our mother who was to blame – and I was uncertain of what further steps she would take if she ever found out about Damon's survival. So, I decided to poison her.'

'Of course, our father being who he was, he saw the need to retaliate, but Lewis was quick to cover for me – and as Father had always favoured him, his punishment was light: he was exiled.'

'I… did not try to stop him. Perhaps at that point, I did blame your father for what had happened to Ariel, to some extent. And I suppose that Lewis, himself, saw his act as some sort of atonement. But understand this: whatever unkindness there was between your father and me, we were, first and foremost, brothers. I still regret the distance that grew between us – between your father and myself – over the years he was away,' he said. He breathed a heavy sigh. 'And I am afraid I shall always regret it now.'

His eyes drifted, focusing on something very, very far away. In the wintry light of the window, he looked more tired than sinister, and I wondered why I'd never managed to notice it before. There was no doubt in my mind that, even now, he could've wiped my memory or silenced me forever with a word, but here he was, talking with me openly and honestly. Perhaps Isaac had been right when he said that restraint was as important as ability.

Finally, I was convinced. 'You didn't kill him then.'

'No, I did not.' His eyes met mine, and even now I could see the pain as he said it. 'Believe it or not, Abigail, I tried to be as honest as possible with you – it is my own fault that I could not be as open as I should have. Suffice to say that your father and I have many enemies–'

'You mean the Court.'

Uncle Edward nodded. 'I mean the Fey Court. You met the Lady Rosalind on Wintersnacht – you know as well as I do that they have… a vested interest in these matters.'

'Dad was worried about William, then, wasn't he? That's why you two fought.'

'He was,' said Uncle Edward. 'And so was I. Damon had degenerated so quickly – almost from the moment he was born, he began to succumb to the corruption. Eventually his fits became powerful enough to break everything around him, to bend the laws of this world – to kill. It was a thing worse than magic. I wanted to warn your father. I thought him a fool for not taking precautions. And then…'

'And then the Court killed Dad and took his spirit because they knew about William. They knew that he…' The words died in my throat. It was bad enough that William was sick, that he'd been sick since he was five years old. The thought that it put him in danger of the monsters from bedtime stories was too horrible to say out loud.

'That is what we have been led to believe, correct.'

'Then we have to stop them!' I said. 'If they're after William, we have to–'

'You will leave the handling of those things to us adults,' said Uncle Edward firmly. 'The reason your mother brought you here in the first place was to keep you – *both* of you – out of their reach. There has never been anything binding her here other than concern for your safety.' And he didn't need to say anything for me to understand that he meant all my suspicions were unfounded, that like everything else I'd accused him of, he was innocent. He hadn't put Mother under a Curse, hadn't forced her into any of her decisions. 'And whether or not you believe me,' he continued, 'I can assure you that Ravenscourt is the safest place for you – it is ancient, and its protections are not easily breached.'

'But the Lady Rosalind–'

'Was here at my invitation. Needless to say, no member of the Court will be extended any sort of hospitality, however limited, again.' He took a deep breath and turned back to the window. 'For now, here, you are safe, and that matters more than chasing after murderers or…' he trailed off, his eyes searching the grounds beyond the window, as if trying to find something there that he had lost. The confrontation with Damon had drained him.

'Could he have been cured?' I asked.

He sighed. 'Perhaps. Isaac and I had been developing a medicine to dampen the effects, but it is difficult to say – even if we had cured the symptoms, the disease itself may have already taken too hard a toll on his being – his… spirit, if you will.'

'And William?' I said. 'You don't think he could…' My voice failed. I didn't want to think of my brother in that state.

'He won't,' said Uncle Edward. 'Your father and I might have disagreed on a great many things, but I believe it is safe to say William came out the better for it. Perhaps Lewis was correct in thinking that blood is not the only factor. There has always been too much darkness, too many secrets in this house. With his current treatment… I should say that William has a long and happy life ahead of him, thanks in no small part to your care. So long as you two stay close…' He trailed off, and his eyes drifted back to the window. 'In any case, you ought to be quite back to normal by now. I'm sure your brother will be eager to see you.' And he offered his hand.

With his help, I managed to make it upstairs, to our secondfloor rooms, where William was waiting. As soon as we stepped into the sitting room, he tackled me with a hug.

'You're alright!' he said.

'I'll be fine. But it seems we have a great deal to discuss.'

The months following the incident passed like a pleasant dream, which is to say that they were quick, quiet, and utterly forgettable. Mrs. Thompson decided to take a short leave of absence, citing the effect of children on her mental health, and so we were given full reign over the house and grounds. Uncle Edward even allowed me to have the clockwork key back, since it had, after all, been a Wintersnacht gift, and he no longer had to worry about us unlocking the wrong doors. And so, while the staff prepped and pressed for the approaching wedding, William and I explored the house and ranged throughout the entire Blackwood, though we still had to be back before dark, when the grounds continued to turn rather unpleasant.

Some weeks after everything had begun to settle, we ventured into the greenhouse to find Beatrice tending to several clinging growths of Kingsgrail vines, their large, golden flowers heavy with the scent of coconut and sunlight. She was wrestling the plants onto their trellises, looking none the worse for nearly having died from a Curse.

'Ah! Miss Abigail. Young William,' she said brightly without turning around. 'I was wondering when you'd show up. Been busy, I take it?'

'Not really,' said William. 'We've just been... catching up with family. You know how the holidays tend to be.'

Beatrice laughed at that.

'Are you alright?' I asked. 'I mean, with the... with your–'

'My Curse, you mean?' Beatrice finished pinning up the vines and turned to us, her golden eyes bright. 'I'm quite fine, Miss Abigail, quite fine all things considered. Curses are not particularly forgiving things, but Edward's never let a little thing like unbreakable spells stop him from finding a cure. So, now that I'm free to say what I will, which family secrets would you like to hear first?'

'What about the one with the boy who was locked in the tower?' I said. 'You still haven't really finished that one.'

She tilted her head. 'I think you handled that one admirably. Between the who, what, where, when, and how, I think you've covered all the bases. What else is there to know about it?'

'You missed the *why*,' I said. 'Because I still don't understand: why did you want him released?'

'The same reason you did, at one point,' she answered, her voice gentle. 'Because it was the right thing to do.'

But I shook my head. 'How can you be so sure of that? Didn't you know what he was? What he could do?'

And once again, her eyes lit up, this time with mischief.

'Oh, but Miss Abigail,' she said. 'How could I not?'

We left it at that. And though we often saw Beatrice in passing as we wandered the woods, it was never quite the same with her again. The months grew cold and lonely, and even Mother seemed to be avoiding us, though of course, she had the excuse of needing to prepare herself for her upcoming wedding.

And then, one morning in March, I woke up and saw spring outside the windows. William suggested that we take a trip to the glacier lake at the edge of the property, and as we made our way across the manor gardens, we found Emily sitting at the entrance to the rose hedge maze. She waved without smiling, and I stopped in my tracks.

'I'll let you two talk,' said William, ducking into the maze as Emily stood from her bench. She took me by the arm and began a leisurely stroll around the gardens. We could've been two high-born ladies wandering Hyde Park.

'So, Isaac hunted me down as soon as Doctor Crowe realized where you had gotten some of your information,' said Emily with a roll of her eyes. 'Though I guess it all works out in the end. We accomplished what we set out to do.'

'I'm not so sure that's a good thing anymore.'

Emily shrugged. 'I guess we'll have to wait and see.'

We stood quietly under the shadow of a bush trimmed into the shape of a giant rabbit and watched the clouds scuttling overhead. Emily bent down and plucked a flower from the grass, holding it out for me to take.

'Ravenscourt's first flower of the season,' she said.

I took it.

As for the wedding, I absolutely refused to attend the ceremony, no matter how much Mother threatened and bribed me. That morning, I remained sulking in my room long after William gave up trying to convince me to come, and it was only after the ceremony was finished and the sounds of the garden reception began to drift up through my window that I even managed to crawl out of bed. I dressed and made my way to the sitting room, to sulk on the couch instead.

Sulking was always better with some variety.

A knock sounded at the door, and I grumbled at the intruder to state their business, but whoever it was simply knocked louder. The knocking grew insistent, until finally, I couldn't take it any longer, and I stomped over to the door to wrench it open.

It was Uncle Edward.

'Oh,' I said, judging him from behind my fringe. 'Hi.'

'Walk with me,' he said.

We made our way through the empty halls, neither of us speaking, but simply tolerating each other and itching at the silence. It was only when we reached the door leading to the reception in the gardens that he finally broke the silence.

'Your Mother wanted me to talk to you,' he began. 'She is intent that you not be upset by the recent... change.'

'Now why ever would I be upset, dear uncle?'

'I will thank you not to use sarcasm when addressing me,' he answered firmly, but without menace. 'I guess, Abigail, that I just want to assure you. Things will be different from now on. I only hope that you can see that the differences are not all bad. Some things will be better. Some things will always be worse. I was not lying when I said that our world is a sadder place without Lewis.'

There was no way for me to argue with that. So I frowned at him and said nothing, while he opened the door, letting the sunlight into the dusty hall. He took my hand and pulled me out into the garden, leading the way along the edge of the party, until we came to the rose hedge maze, and he settled onto the bench at the entrance. I sat down next to him, watching the small group of guests on the lawn as they laughed and exchanged toasts and gossip. Laurie and Samantha, both fully recovered, sat with Isaac and Emily, all of them leaning in close as they commented on the scene. Among the pink and pastel of the gathered townspeople, Mother stood out like a raven among doves – her wedding gown had been netted in black lace, only appropriate for a bride in mourning, of course.

But Uncle Edward was speaking again. 'Abigail,' he said, 'I will never be able to replace your father, and I know that. I am not trying to. I simply hope that eventually, with time, we will be able to give each other the trust and respect that we both deserve. Until then, I will simply settle for our interactions being *civil*.'

I studied my boots. I couldn't say I'd ever felt particularly fond of my uncle, but with everything that had happened since coming here, to Ravenscourt, I was tempted to admit that he might have his good points – or, at the very least, one or two of them. I wasn't sure if I trusted him though, and I definitely wasn't going to trust him any time soon. Still, even if he wasn't a complete scoundrel, he was, more than anything, a force to be reckoned with. And I'd have to put up with living in his house somehow.

'A truce, is it, then?'

He nodded. 'Truce.'

I looked at him sideways as he pretended not to notice. 'Very well,' I said. 'I promise to be civil and proper if you promise not to be evil.'

The corner of his mouth gave just the slightest twitch. 'I promise,' he said. 'Now, do let us enjoy this lovely reception – I'm sure your friends are eager to see you back.'

And with a smart bow, he took his leave, wandering back to the wedding party. He paused at the edge of the crowd, and Mother turned to find him, drifting forward to take his hand, and to pull him into the crowd.

'Well, there's a happily ever after if I ever saw one,' said someone at my elbow. Beatrice stood at the entrance of the maze, dressed in a fine gown of pale green silk.

'If you say so,' I said. 'Personally, I don't think it's a very happy ending at all.'

'One person's tragedy is another man's comedy – or wedding, as the case may be. But of course, I'm sure you'll cause more than enough trouble if the need arises. Speaking of which...' She pulled her amber stone from some pocket and held it out to me, waiting for me to take it.

I looked down, but refused to touch it. 'That's not mine.'

'I rather think you'll have more use for it in the future than I will, Miss Abigail. Consider it a parting gift.' And she pressed it into my hand, closing my fingers around the charm. It pulsed warm against my palm. 'It was very nice to have met you, Miss Crowe. I hope we shall have the chance to meet again.'

'What do you mean?' I said. 'Won't you be here, at Ravenscourt?'

But the gardener shook her head, smiling silently. With a wink and a wave, she walked off, winding her way toward the edge of the Blackwood, leaving nothing behind but the sound of laughter.

Dying Arts Press is a collaborative publishing collective that makes bookish things for readers ages twelve to fifteen. We work closely together on all our publications to make them the best they can be before finding their way to you.

If you write stories, make art, or are otherwise interested in creating books for tweens, we would love to be able to work with you. Feel free to send us samples of your words, art, or passion projects by email via: editor@dyingartspress.com.

Otherwise, we'd love to connect with you through DyingArtsPress.com, or on instagram, facebook, and twitter @dyingartspress. We look forward to hearing from you!

Lightning Source UK Ltd.
Milton Keynes UK
UKHW011831040319
338453UK00005B/9/P